THE (OF SAMUEL JOHNSON, LL.D. AND JAMES BOSWELL, Esq.

CONTAINING

A STUDY OF OCCULT AND SUPERNATURAL PHENOMENA

VOLUME I

THE FALL OF THE HOUSE OF THOMAS WEIR

ANDREW NEIL MacLEOD MMXXI

Burning Chair Limited, Trading As Burning Chair Publishing
61 Bridge Street, Kington HR5 3DJ

www.burningchairpublishing.com

By Andrew Neil Macleod
Edited by Simon Finnie and Peter Oxley
Cover by Burning Chair Publishing

First published by Burning Chair Publishing, 2021

ISBN: 978-1-912946-19-8

Ghoul (n.) from the Persian *gul*: A demonic entity that robs graves and devours the corpses.
Ghoulish (adj.) Having a morbid or unhealthy interest in death.

From *A Dictionary of Demonology, Doctor Samuel Johnson, 1775*

A raven came to court me
Through the wind and driving rain.
His big black beak went *tap tap tap*
Upon my windowpane.
He fixed me with a beady eye
As cold and black as sin:
A ragged hole in daylight
Where the night comes keekin' in.

Old Nursery Rhyme

In Loving Memory

My Grandparents Calum and Margie

Always, Your 'Wee Pal'

Alexander Boyle didn't believe in ghosts. As nightwatchman for the most haunted cemetery in Edinburgh, which is to say the most haunted cemetery in the world, it was one indulgence he couldn't afford.

He reached for his hip flask and raised it to his lips, watching the sun cast off its faded raiment from behind the Flodden Wall. Tombstone shadows crept across the yard like fingers in a black velvet glove. Boyle consulted his pocket watch and wound it, knowing that when the shadows touched the east wall it would be time to lock the gates for the evening.

A pragmatic man, Alexander Boyle prided himself on his common sense. There were no such things as bogles, kelpies, selkies, banshees, hobgoblins or any of that kind of foolishness, and the only ghost worth a tinker's curse was a Holy one.

After locking the cemetery gates Boyle took a turn of the grounds; past the cold and silent gravestones with their crumbling inscriptions, past the frowning, soot-black mausoleums and their leering *memento mori,* peering into every shaded nook or cranny for fornicators or drunkards to chase off with his stick. Once in a while he might interrupt a pair of graverobbers going about their gruesome business but, for the most part, Greyfriars Cemetery was as quiet as... Well, as quiet as the grave.

The MacKenzie Crypt stood between the church and the south wall in a shaded area known as *the Heights*. It had a fearsome reputation. By the time Boyle arrived it was almost dark, and his heart struck a note of fear in his breast. He would fortify himself with another wee dram from his flask. No harm in that. There was no way of avoiding this gloomy part of the cemetery, but at least the whisky made it tolerable.

The mausoleum itself was no different from any other, yet something about its domed octagonal tower had always made Boyle a little uneasy. Perhaps it was the gnarled, claw-like trees framing the entrance, or the fact that songbirds shunned the area altogether. Perhaps it was the reputation of its tenant, the cruel and tyrannical Lord Advocate George MacKenzie of Rosenhaugh, or the way the crypt itself seemed to taunt him: its half-domed alcoves two peering eyes, its grated entrance a mouth waiting to gobble him up.

Some time ago, on his first day as nightwatchman, Boyle had succumbed to an irresistible urge—call it an imp of perversity— to unlock the door to the crypt and step inside. It was an act that to this day he was at a loss to explain: a gesture of defiance perhaps, a temporary madness even. Whichever way he looked at it, Alexander Boyle would rue the day he ever set foot in the black crypt of 'Bluidy' George MacKenzie.

The five family caskets had lain undisturbed for years. Boyle approached the nearest coffin and blew the dust away. Then just as he was about to lift the lid, the rotten beams under his feet gave way.

The ensuing years had done little to diminish the horror of that moment. The hidden underground chamber had been sealed so effectively that the one-hundred-year-old plague victims were only partially decomposed. As Boyle struggled to release himself the cadavers jerked to life. Arms rose to claw at him. Grotesque faces reared up in a kiss of death. Boyle writhed in terror, drowning in a sea of rank, mortified flesh. He was almost lost when, by chance, he found the footholds some careful worker had left all those years ago. Boyle scrambled up the side of the pit then collapsed to the floor in an exhausted heap until, overcome with horror and revulsion at his surroundings, he picked himself up and bolted for the exit. The door clanged shut behind him as he scurried across the yard to the sanctuary of his gatehouse. Once inside he drew the snib, blew out the candle and lay shivering on the bed in his still-reeking clothes, sobbing and laughing with hysterical relief.

He drank himself to sleep that night... and the night after that.

Now, twenty years later, he approached the Heights with a kind of grim fascination, and a respect born of experience. As the mausoleum loomed before him, he was suddenly struck by the impression that he was not alone. A shadow crouching in one of the domed alcoves confirmed Boyle's worst fears. He cleared his throat to speak.

'Who's there?' he said in a voice that sounded braver than he felt. 'Step down at once, by God, or I will see ye hanged for trespassing!'

The scrawny waif who clambered down from his hiding place was no older than ten, his eyes wide with terror. Boyle could have laughed with relief. 'What in the name of all that's holy are you doing there, boy?'

It all came out in one breath. 'Please sir it was a dare sir my pals said if I spent the night in the cemetery they'd gie me a penny sir.'

'A *penny!*' Boyle almost hugged the lad. 'Here's sixpence. Now off you go and don't come back, or the next time I'll lock you in that crypt with only George MacKenzie for company!'

The street urchin didn't need to be told twice. He caught the sixpence, scrambled over the wall and disappeared down the cobbled street, never to return.

Boyle shook his head and chuckled to himself. He and his friends used to play something similar when he was a lad, daring each other to knock three times on the mausoleum door.

Bluidy MacKenzie, come oot if ye daur, lift the sneck and draw the bar!

He muttered the words of the old nursery rhyme to himself, then shook his head and laughed at his own credulity.

A chill wind shook the leaves overhead; Boyle felt a shiver course through his entire frame. He was just about to return to the safety of his gatehouse when he spied a padlock swinging loose from its latch on the mausoleum door. Strange. Nobody had access to the master keys but himself. He stood on tiptoes and peered in through the grille. The coffins were unmolested.

Everything appeared as normal, unless.... that clean spot in the dust of the nearest coffin lid. Was it in the shape of a hand?

The hairs pricked up on the back of Boyle's neck: a sure sign of something 'crossing over' from the other side, if the old wives' tales were to be believed. He turned to peer into the shadows. Sure enough, a hunched figure in rags was stealing up the path towards the Heights.

His first thought was of another child playing a prank. 'You there,' he cried, clenching his fists by his sides. The intruder came shambling towards him, hobbling on lumpen, bandage-swathed legs. Something about the way it moved, something *inhuman*, curdled the blood in Boyle's veins.

When the intruder was only an arm's distance away it stopped.

'Raise your hood,' said Boyle, struggling to master the fear in his own voice.

The stranger obliged him… and even as the scream found its way to his throat, the part of Alexander Boyle that scorned the existence of ghosts—and laughed in the face of bogles, kelpies, selkies, banshees and hobgoblins—was gone forever.

Chapter 1

The Ghoul of Greyfriars

Edinburgh, July 14th, 1773

*L*ate in the evening I received a note from Doctor Johnson that he was arrived at Boyd's Inn at the head of the Canongate. With a glad heart I left my home on James Court and went to him directly. He embraced me with great warmth, and I exulted in the thought that I now had this true-born son of England here with me in Edinburgh.

What can be said that has not been said already about the man? Of his Christian piety, good sense and natural generosity, much has been written. Also his impetuous, irritable temper and his love of order and logic which, when united with a fertile imagination, gives him an extraordinary advantage in argument.

His antipathy towards the Scots, though there is much good humour in it, has been well documented, though I hope to persuade him to revise this poor opinion on our long-awaited odyssey, which will take us the length and breadth of Scotland in search of her mysteries.

Perhaps less well known, for reasons touching on matters of national security, is Doctor Johnson's genius in the fields of occult and supernatural sciences, and his struggles against those malignant powers of darkness that routinely threaten to engulf mankind.

I held my friend at arm's length, and gazed affectionately upon those features which had for so long been denied to me through the vagaries of time and distance. Though in person he is a giant of a man, whose brooding countenance recalls those statues of antiquity on Easter Island, Doctor Johnson can be extremely personable when the mood takes him, and he soon charms even the most unyielding of foes into a forgetfulness of his external appearance.

'My God, sir,' he boomed, looking me up and down. 'You've hardly changed a day.'

I returned the compliment, though in truth he appeared somewhat pale and haggard, and he depended on his oak-staff a little more generously than before.

His voice is loud, and in the autumn of his life (he is sixty-four to my thirty-three) he has become a little hard of hearing. His sight has always been somewhat weak; yet, so much does the mind govern, and even supply the deficiency of organs, that his perceptions are uncommonly quick and accurate.

As for his dress, he wears a full suit of plain brown clothes, a bushy grey wig, a plain shirt, black worsted stockings and silver buckles on his shoes. For this tour he has opted for leather boots and a heavy great-coat with voluminous pockets, in which it is his curious habit to store scraps of orange peel.

I picked up his valise, which was surprisingly small and light, and we stepped out onto the busy thoroughfare, narrowly avoiding the wheels of a horse-drawn carriage as it clattered past.

Edinburgh is a town of curious contrasts: the only place in Europe where a Dowager Countess may happily live above a cobbler, while a gin-addled prostitute plies her trade from the basement of the same building; a hub of Enlightenment, where a man may stand on a street corner and shake hands with twenty men of genius in a day, or be drenched by a bucket of piss-water thrown carelessly from a tenement window above.

I have only recently moved my small family from a ground-floor apartment on James Court, up three flights of stairs to the former apartment of that celebrated genius Mr David Hume (who has since taken up residence in Edinburgh's fashionable New Town). Our new apartment is spacious, with a

The Fall of the House of Thomas Weir

study, a drawing-room and two guest-rooms, allowing us to receive guests in a style that our formerly cramped surroundings rendered impracticable.

Mrs B opened the door, and little Veronica flew straight into Doctor Johnson's arms with such unreserved devotion that it nearly moved the old man to tears, giving lie to rumours of his stern and unapproachable demeanour.

Exhausted from his travels, Doctor Johnson retired early and did not rise until noon the following day. After his ablutions he put on his battered slippers and made his way down to tea, where he was eagerly assailed by a host of well-wishers, including my dear friends Doctor Webster, Doctor Blair, and the Reverend Baxter: a personal favourite of Mrs B's.

Lady Colville put in an appearance at midday with some artist friends of hers, most notably the poet Robert Ferguson and young Henry Raeburn the landscape painter, all vying with one another to secure the good opinion of our esteemed guest. The Doctor himself was in fine fettle and deported himself admirably, giving pleasure to all with his mirthful countenance and kind words.

From *The Casebook of Johnson and Boswell*

As Mrs Boswell poured the tea, one of the young men of the company produced a morning paper and read aloud the headline with boyish glee: '*GHOULISH GOINGS-ON AT GREYFRIARS!*'

'I see the worthy editor does not shirk from the use of alliteration to create an effect,' observed Doctor Johnson.

The other artists crowded round, while the young man with the paper read the rest of the article in his high, excitable voice. 'Night watchman Alexander Boyle (53) was discovered slumped against the wall of Greyfriars Kirk in the early hours of Sunday morning, claiming to have witnessed a dreadful APPARITION entering Greyfriars' notorious MacKenzie Crypt. Witnesses report that his (Boyle's) hair had turned from grey to white overnight.'

The article went on to describe in lurid detail the events of the night in question. Doctor Johnson sat with his fingers pressed together to form a steeple under his chin, his stern features impassive, though wholly attentive.

'*Post Scriptum,*' the young man added. 'The editor notes that the celebrated Doctor Johnson is currently residing with our very own James Boswell, in anticipation of their much-vaunted tour of the Scottish Highlands. We at the *Caledonian Mercury* hope the Doctor finds our city to his liking, and does not feel too homesick for the trappings and diversions of the *second* city of Britain. As a gesture of our goodwill, we wish to issue the author of *The Rambler* with a challenge: Should he be able to provide a satisfactory explanation for The Ghoul of Greyfriars, we at the *Caledonian Mercury* pledge to provide our noble guest with an annual pension befitting his exalted status.'

'Why those impudent devils!' spluttered Johnson, though his eyes shone in a way that told Boswell he was secretly flattered to find himself the subject of so much speculation. 'What does "befitting his exalted status" mean?'

'You will take up the challenge, of course?' said Lady Colville teasingly.

'I fear I must disappoint you on that point, Lady Colville. For the one way to prove that a corpse has returned to life as a ghoul or a vampire would be to exhume the body, and as a committed Christian I am unprepared to commit *violation of sepulchre* on the word of a drunken nightwatchman. Besides, my annual pension from the Crown is quite sufficient for my modest needs.'

With a tangible sense of anti-climax, the young artists lit their pipes and resumed their conversations, while the ladies retired to a quiet corner to escape the fug of pipe smoke that hung like a vaporous fog in the middle of the room. Mrs Boswell tinkled a little silver bell, and the Boswells' Bohemian manservant, Joseph Ritter, came striding in to open a window.

'Mrs Boswell,' began Lady Colville, casting an admiring glance at her surroundings. 'I love what you've done with the place.'

'Why, thank you, Lady Colville.'

'And yet I fear you've had your work cut out for you. Mr Hume may be a great many things, but a paragon of domestic solicitude he is not.'

Lady Elizabeth Colville— *'Lady Betty'* to friends—had an earthy sense of humour, and unlike her contemporaries a hearty disdain for airs and graces. Her infectious cackle, licentious in its abandon, filled the room with joy, prompting those within earshot to smile despite themselves. Mrs Boswell, who felt almost dowdy by comparison, warmed to her instantly, though she was aware that her own husband's eye strayed towards this famous beauty and doyen of Edinburgh's tea-rooms a little too often for her liking.

The two women were conversing quite naturally when a curious incident occurred that, while it seemed such a trifling thing at the time, would come to have a profound and lasting effect on Mrs Boswell. While she was talking, Lady Colville reached out and seized her companion roughly by the wrist.

'What is it? What are you staring at so?' said Mrs Boswell, struggling to remove her hand, which was still grasping her teacup, from Lady Colville's vice-like grip.

The rest of the company turned towards the two women, startled by the abruptness of Lady Colville's transformation.

The older woman then spoke in a voice scarcely recognisable as her own. *'You thought you lost your mother's hat pin in your last apartment, but it is here, under the loose floorboard beneath your feet!'*

Mrs Boswell stared at Lady Colville for some moments in amazement, then bent down and, lifting the floorboard where there was a small gap, retrieved something which, on opening her hand, was revealed to be a little golden salamander with rubies for eyes.

'Bravo!' cried Doctor Blair.

'Remarkable,' said Boswell.

'Pshaw!' the Reverend Baxter exclaimed. 'A mere parlour trick. Cooked up, no doubt, by those two mischievous minxes for our entertainment.'

'Come on, confess!' cried one of the younger men, clearly delighted by this latest turn of events.

'I assure you, sirs,' said Mrs Boswell, still staring at the hat pin, expecting it to evaporate into thin air at any moment. 'I had no foreknowledge...'

'Fascinating,' said Johnson, leaning forward in his chair, his brow furrowed in a way that told Boswell he was absorbed in some mental conundrum.

Lady Colville blushed. 'It's nothing, really. Just a knack I seem to have inherited,' she explained. 'My grandmother would find missing things all the time: people too, sometimes. She had the Gypsy blood, they say, and could stop clocks just by looking at them. My grandfather used to say she was a changeling.'

'Come, Lady Colville, no need to be so modest!' said Robert Ferguson, the handsome young poet who had been casting admiring glances at his muse all afternoon. 'It really was a remarkable piece of showmanship.'

'Lady Colville,' said Johnson. 'You must allow me to make a study of this unique talent; under the strictest scientific conditions, of course.'

'You mean you don't believe me, Doctor Johnson?'

'On the contrary, my dear lady. The subject of second sight is of great interest to me. Indeed, it is one of the reasons I made this pilgrimage in the first place. There have been numerous reports of the phenomena in Scotland. It's in the blood, you might say. I merely wish to pick your brains for my journal. Oh, I will be very discreet, I assure you, and you will be guaranteed anonymity. Besides, who is going to read some stuffy old scientific paper?'

'I can just see it now,' said the impudent young artist with the newspaper, raising his hands in the air and fanning them out. '*The Mysterious Lady X! Marvel at her powers of perception as she retrieves lost hatpins!* The circus would make a fortune.'

'That's enough, Charles,' said Lady Colville, slapping his hand with her glove.

Mrs Boswell, delighted to be reunited with her lost hat pin, regarded her guest with something akin to awe. 'Lady Colville,' she said, her eyes shining with admiration. 'I don't know how to thank you.'

'To see you happy is reward enough for me, Mrs Boswell,' replied Lady Colville, taking her new friend's hands in hers.

'Call me Maggie, I insist.'

'Then you must call me Lady Betty.'

'But are you sure you are quite yourself?' cried Mrs Boswell. 'You do seem rather pale.'

Lady Colville admitted to fatigue from her mental exertions and, after paying tribute to her hostess, she was escorted to the door along with the rest of her entourage.

'One more thing,' said Robert Ferguson, before joining the rest of the group in the carriages waiting outside. 'I shall be dining tonight in the Isle of Man Arms, where I would be delighted to induct you and Mr Boswell as honorary members of my club.'

'My dear Mr Ferguson,' Johnson protested. 'I am far too long in the tooth to be seen carousing and cavorting with the young rakes of Edinburgh on some Caledonian bacchanal.'

'I assure you, sir,' said Ferguson warmly, 'that as an honorary member you may forgo the customary yard of ale expected of other... well, less *illustrious* inductees.'

'Then we would be delighted, of course. And what is the name of your club?'

'We call ourselves the Knights of the Cape,' said Ferguson, and with a flash of a smile he was gone.

Chapter 2

The House of Thomas Weir

Edinburgh Old Town, July 15th, 1773

The Old Town sits high on a sloping ridge, an island of volcanic rock surrounded by fields, boggy marshes and ancient hills, and extends one mile from the lofty Castle all the way down to Holyrood Palace, the official residence of the King when he deigns to visit. The tenements that run the length of this Royal Mile are overcrowded, and as the ancient city walls prevent them from expanding laterally, climb to a dizzying height, with foundations burrowing deep into the bedrock to accommodate an already burgeoning population. The wealthiest residents inhabit the topmost floors, escaping the ubiquitous stench of rotten fruit, fish-heads and human waste which rises insidiously from the gutters.

Further down on street level one is met with a cheerful hive of vice and industry, where sunless wynds and vennels crisscross the High Street like so many veins and capillaries. Descending further still, one enters a forsaken region of underground streets and tunnels, where plague victims were bricked up long ago and left to rot. None but the most foolhardy or vice-ridden dare

The Fall of the House of Thomas Weir

to enter that reeking cesspit of crime and corruption, and many an unwary traveller who ventures in does not return, or if he does, does not emerge unchanged by the experience.

From *The Casebook of Johnson and Boswell*

After the last guest had taken his leave, Johnson and Boswell enjoyed a late lunch before setting out to explore some of the more lugubrious parts of the city. Doctor Johnson was in a sportive frame of mind, eager to judge for himself whether Edinburgh deserved its reputation as the most haunted capital in the world.

'I must say,' he said, taking his friend's arm as they stepped out onto the busy High Street. 'One almost becomes used to the smell. Indeed, I could almost grow to like the place, given the right set of circumstances.'

'And what sort of circumstances would those be?'

'Oh I don't know,' replied Johnson. 'If I were a rat, perhaps?'

'Now there's a thought,' said Boswell, laughing. 'But I see you more as a curmudgeonly badger.' He didn't dare mention *Ursa Major*, the name some of Johnson's more jocose colleagues called him behind his back.

The two men crossed Land Market onto West Bow, where a bewildering array of timber-fronted tenements all jostled for position down its steeply winding gradient. One bleak house stood apart from the rest, a rotten tooth in an otherwise healthy—though crooked—mouth, with blackened bricks, crumbling masonry and sickly looking weeds projecting from the fissures.

'What is that tall, gloomy house on the corner with the pentagonal tower and crow-stepped gable,' said Johnson, pointing with his stick, 'that passers-by cross the street to avoid?'

'They are right to avoid it. It was once the home of Major Thomas Weir, the *"Warlock of West Bow"*, whose apparition may still be seen at night, flitting like a black and silent shadow about the street.'

'My dear Boswell, I may be considered a walking encyclopaedia in dear old London, but must confess your local myths and legends have somewhat passed my notice, and you shall have to enlighten me.'

'Major Thomas Weir was a well-known figure around town, a confirmed bachelor who lived in that house with his sister Grizel. Every morning he could be seen stepping out in his long black cloak, swinging a curious ebony cane which had a human skull carved on its handle.'

'A pantomime villain, by the sounds of it.'

'You might think so, but he was once a pillar of the community, a rigid Presbyterian whose pious ways earned him the name of *"Angelic Thomas"*. People would flock from miles around just to hear his sermons. But old Thomas was a vile hypocrite, polluted by crimes of the most despicable nature, and blasphemies too terrible to repeat.'

'*Beware of false prophets who come to you in sheep's clothing, but inwardly are ravening wolves,*' murmured Johnson. 'So what became of the old rogue?'

'When he reached his seventieth year, sick in body and mind and unable to endure any longer the shame and guilt of his secret life, he stood up in the middle of church, and before a shocked and scandalized congregation confessed to the most sickening crimes, involving not only himself and his sister, but some of the most prominent members of society.'

'I do remember something of the sort, now you come to mention it,' said Johnson. 'It was an interesting case. He claimed to be in league with the devil, did he not? But because of his good reputation the authorities were unwilling to convict. Claimed he had lost his mind. It was the sister that damned him, confessing to her share in the brother's misdeeds.'

'Adding some sins of her own for good measure,' said Boswell. 'But old Thomas had friends in high places, friends whose positions would be compromised had the pair's scandalous relations come to light. The authorities couldn't risk sending Weir to the Tolbooth. The scandal would have been too great. They sent the pair of them instead to a heavily guarded leper colony on the north side of town by Caltoun Hill. But before the case could come to trial the hospital burned to the ground.'

Johnson gazed up at the solitary attic window and suppressed a shudder. One of the panes had been knocked in by some adolescent marksman and, just for a moment, Johnson fancied he saw old Grizel herself on her rocking chair, her goblin's face appearing, then disappearing, then appearing again from behind the tattered lace. 'Let us move on,' said Johnson, telling himself it was just an illusion caused by the play of light and shadow. 'It is unseemly to speak of such things in the shadow of that accursed place.'

The steeply sloping West Bow descended onto Grassmarket, a broad thoroughfare surrounded by cheerfully coloured tenement flats in the lowest part of the Old Town. Here farmers, drovers and other types connected to the horse- and cattle-trade met to do business, talk shop or find lodgings for the night.

At the south-east corner of the rectangular enclosure stood a massive block of sandstone, having in its centre a square hole which served as a socket for the gallows tree when in use. The sight of the gallows block still gave Boswell a chill. The apparatus was always assembled at dawn, and when he was a child he would think the huge black gallows had sprung wholesale from the earth during the night.

Every afternoon at precisely five o'clock, George Pratt the town crier took his place upon the gallows-block to address the crowd gathered below. Resplendent in his ceremonial robes of state, street urchins would follow him everywhere he went to a chorus of '*quack quack quack*,' like a gaggle of little ducklings waddling behind a richly feathered, preening drake. On this occasion, Pratt took to his podium with a more-than-usual sense of dignity, while the crowd, sensing he had something of importance to convey, drew close.

'*Oyez oyez!*' cried Pratt to the accompaniment of his clanging bell. '*Greyfriars Ghoul sighted at various locations in and around Old Town... He is described as a faceless cadaver in a coarsely woven monk's habit, with an unseemly smell of corruption about his person. Ladies are advised not to travel unaccompanied at night, and to keep well away from darkened closes, particularly the immediate areas surrounding Greyfriars Kirk, including the Grassmarket, Canongate and Cowgate.*' Then in a lighter tone of voice he added, '*Calf thinks he's a sheepdog! Read all about merry antics on local farm as calf is reared by a border collie...*'

His job done, George Pratt descended the gallows block by means of a wooden ladder, nailed his flysheet to a nearby door, and turned with great majesty onto the Cowgate to repeat the ritual elsewhere.

'Very interesting,' said Johnson in an aside to Boswell. 'Perhaps there is more to this nightwatchman's story than at first meets the eye.'

The two men crossed the Grassmarket onto Candlemaker's Row, where the stench of burning tallow was almost unendurable, even by Edinburgh standards.

It was late afternoon by the time they reached the cemetery gates. A crow hopped down from an overhanging tree and onto the gate to greet them, announcing their arrival with a harsh, grating *cronk*.

'Well Doctor, here is the infamous Greyfriars Kirk, the scene of last night's little drama. Shall we take a turn of the grounds?'

Johnson peered through the wrought iron bars at a gloomy set of stairs beyond. Despite his promise to Lady Colville, he never could resist a challenge. 'I'm sure a quick look around won't harm us.'

Boswell rang the bell, summoning nightwatchman Alexander Boyle from his gatehouse.

'More reporters come to laugh at me?' said the wraith, startling the two men with his unkempt hair, deathly pallor and madly staring eyes.

'No sir,' said Johnson, raising his hat. 'My name is Doctor

The Fall of the House of Thomas Weir

Johnson and this is my associate, James Boswell. We merely wish to establish—'

'They call me insane, you know. All of *them*,' Boyle cried with a wild sweep of his arm, indicating unseen faces in every shadow. 'But they too will stand before the seat of judgement at the end of days; *for their flesh shall rot while they are still on their feet; their eyes shall rot in their sockets, and their tongues shall rot in their mouth*—'

'Calm yourself, man. We're not here to judge, merely to establish the truth of the matter. Would you let us in? I promise we will only take a moment of your time.'

The nightwatchman's eyes narrowed as he scrutinised the visitors, then his shoulders seemed to sag, and with a weary sigh he turned a key in the lock and swung open the gates.

Boyle led the visitors up to the Heights, the scene of his unearthly encounter. Though Greyfriars's Kirk was situated within shouting distance of Grassmarket, the area that sheltered the MacKenzie Crypt was protected by a high wall, into which a row of lichen-covered tombstones had been set, blocking the sun and lending an air of desolation to the scene, particularly at twilight.

'Over there,' cried the nightwatchman, grasping Johnson's arm and pointing frantically to the path down from the Heights. 'That is where I saw him. I can see him still!'

The fading light cast strange shadows across the yard, throwing the silhouettes of stone angels into stark contrast against a pale and colourless sky.

'Can you describe your vision, Mr Boyle?' said Johnson.

Boyle described, in his own inimitable way, a shuffling creature in rags whose face had 'all rotted away'.

'Is there anything else you can remember?'

Boyle frowned. 'He had a sack slung over his shoulder, full of lost souls struggling to get out, I shouldn'a wonder!'

Their interview concluded, Boyle ushered the two men back to the entrance.

'Well that answers one question,' said Boswell as the cemetery gates clanged shut behind them. 'The man is clearly drunk. And quite mad.'

Johnson nodded grimly but held his peace.

As the two friends circled back onto High Street, the Bells of St. Giles struck seven o'clock, and they hurried to make their appointment with Robert Ferguson.

Chapter 3

The Knights of the Cape

Isle of Man Arms,
July 15th, 1773

he Cape Club is but one of many social clubs that became popular around the turn of the century, and still flourish to this day. There is the Spendthrift Club, whose members are forbidden from spending less than four-pence halfpenny a night; the Boar Club, whose members are encouraged to express, in their choice of venue and discourse, the habits of pigs and boars; the Dirty Club, where no member is allowed to appear in clean linen; the Alphabet Club (the hardest drinking of the whole bunch), whose members only get to meet on days containing the letter A; and numerous other thinly veiled pretexts for men to meet and drink together in convivial surroundings.

Compared to the notorious Hell Fire Clubs of Dublin and London, the exploits of Edinburgh's Knights of the Cape seem positively benign; each new member is 'knighted' and given a name according to some personal anecdote or characteristic, hence Robert Ferguson is Sir Precenter, *the landscape painter Alexander Runciman is* Sir Brimstone, *Gavin Wilson the shoemaker is* Sir Macaroni, *Deacon Brodie the cabinet maker is* Sir Lluyd *and so on and so forth, with each of its twenty-five members boasting similarly eccentric soubriquets.*

On the whole, this disparate group of fellows have stayed true to their motto Concordia Fratrum Decus, *which is unique, given that unlike the largely aristocratic members of the Poker Club or Crochallan Fencibles, the Cape Club's members are chosen from all walks of life, and though the club boasts artists and gentlemen of leisure among its ranks, the great majority are tradesmen: shoemakers, tailors, glovemakers, smiths, saddlers, marble-cutters, barbers, brewers and the like.*

From *The Casebook of Johnson and Boswell*

'Good evening, gentlemen,' said Robert Ferguson, bowing with mock ceremony. He was standing outside the Isle of Man Arms, where he had been waiting patiently for the past half hour. 'I am your knightly sponsor for the evening. Please, come this way.' Ferguson led Johnson and Boswell inside and escorted them through a small doorway at the rear of the inn, where a wine cellar had been requisitioned as the Knights of the Capes' official headquarters.

The Sovereign of the Cape, in civilian life an unassuming newspaper editor whose true name was irrelevant, was enthroned at the end of a long, low-vaulted chamber, with a tin crown on his head, a cape around his shoulders, and in each hand a poker representing the kingly sword and sceptre. Ferguson led Boswell and Johnson forward, while other members moved back against the walls, murmuring and nudging one another with barely restrained glee.

'Who is willing to sponsor these men?' cried the Sovereign.

'I,' said Robert Ferguson, stepping forward into the circle of light. 'Sir Precenter.'

'Then let them come forth, Sir Precenter,' said the Sovereign, 'and make good account of themselves.'

This was the signal for each candidate to relate some anecdote or youthful scrape for the amusement of the crowd. Happily for Boswell, he had experienced enough romantic dalliances and alcohol-inspired high-jinks to keep him supplied with free drinks for the rest of his natural-born life. He did not disappoint. When it was Johnson's turn, the whole company leaned forward with great interest. Here was a man who attended church every Sunday, was unfailingly kind to children and animals, never smoked, rarely drank more than half a glass of porter with his supper, and had memorised the entire Common Book of Prayer by the time he was three years old. The audience were desperate to know what youthful transgression, drunken escapade or foolish indiscretion this man, practically a saint, was about to relate.

Before his captive audience, Johnson related an anecdote from his youth in which he entered the wrong bedroom in a drunken stupor and climbed into bed half-naked beside his wife's younger sister. When the mother-in-law rushed in to correct the son-in-law's error, rather than jumping out of bed and owning his mistake, Johnson looked from the frenzied old woman at the door to the innocent young maiden by his side, and promptly fell asleep. The whole company roared their approval and, when passed his yard of ale, Johnson drained the stuff in a matter of seconds.

'I dub thee Sir Loin,' cried the Sovereign amidst the general merriment, 'and thine aide-de-camp Sir Rake!'

The whole company surged forward as one to greet the new members and pump their hands enthusiastically. After the initial excitement had died down, Johnson and Boswell availed themselves of a quiet table in the corner where they could watch the evening's events unfold at their leisure.

'Who are those two playing cards?' whispered Johnson, rolling his eyes at two members playing a high-stakes game of piquet at a neighbouring table. One player, a tidy little man with narrow shoulders and shifty eyes, was evidently losing; while the other, a foreign-looking gentleman in richly embroidered clothes, clearly had the upper hand. Rather than concede defeat, the smaller man kept shovelling more and more money onto the table in the hope that his luck might change.

'The smaller man is Deacon William Brodie, master cabinet-maker and locksmith. I understand that he enjoys a rather wholesome reputation when not gambling in the club, which is, I might add, generally frowned upon. The other man is Lord Sinclair, King's Treasurer in Scotland, though we have never been formally introduced.'

'And that fellow who keeps nodding off in the corner?'

'That is the landscape artist Alexander Runciman, who just got back from a tour of Rome.'

'And the tall, gaunt fellow sitting next to him?'

'Ah, now there's a noteworthy character. Sir Joshua Hunter. I understand he has recently been offered the role of private physician to the King, though whether or not he will take up the position is another matter.'

'Doctor Hunter?' Johnson remarked. 'They say he is quite brilliant, though there were some questions raised concerning the number of dead bodies passing through his doors.'

'All in the name of progress,' replied Boswell breezily. 'And besides, he was cleared of any wrongdoing by the Court of Sessions.'

After Johnson had learned to recognise each member by sight, talk turned to their planned tour of the Scottish Highlands, including possible locations for the fabled Stone of Destiny. Though Johnson was enjoying his prolonged stay in Edinburgh, he began to tire of the cramped, unhygienic conditions and longed for adventure.

It was pouring with rain by the time the two men stepped outside. It rushed down the sloping street, a purifying rain that dragged with it the detritus of the city. Here and there a bedraggled figure rushed past to find temporary shelter, while Johnson and Boswell ploughed a cheerful furrow upstream, arms linked in tipsy solidarity. Johnson was grateful for his new leather boots and waxed coat as the occasional half-drowned rat, chunk of human excrement or butcher shop carcass drifted past, feeling eighteen again as he sloshed through the flooded streets with his boon companion by his side.

When they finally reached home, they removed their wet outer garments and sat before the fire in silent communion, mugs of hot broth—courtesy of Mrs B—cupped in their hands to ease their aching joints.

So enjoyable had the day been that Boswell and Johnson agreed to resume investigations the following morning, provided that the alcohol had not diminished their faculties too much.

Before turning in, Boswell told Johnson how surprised he was to find that his friend had been such a rake in his youth.

'Oh that?' said Johnson, suppressing a yawn. 'All made up, I assure you.'

'But—'

'What else was I going to say to amuse such a sordid group of fellows? That I once stole an apple from the farmer's orchard?'

Boswell was still laughing as he climbed into bed beside his wife and blew out the candle.

Chapter 4

A Murder of Crows

Arthur's Seat,
July 16th, 1773

dinburgh is built (like Athens) on seven hills; the largest being Arthur's Seat, an extinct volcano on the outermost fringes of town.

What a wonderful solitude reigns there! Many a happy hour have I spent wandering those familiar peaks, worn smooth by the passage of time, lost in contemplation amidst its ancient ruins, and not a single soul to interrupt my meditations the whole day long.

From *The Casebook of Johnson and Boswell*

Mrs Boswell filled a basket with bread, cheese, wine and various other sundries, then wrapped a scarf around her husband's neck to protect him from the blustering heights of Salisbury Crags. After kissing his little family goodbye, Boswell selected a stout walking stick and joined his friend on the cobbled street outside.

It was a short walk from Canongate to the base of Arthur's Seat, cutting down a side street onto South Back of the Canongate, then circumventing the foothills to the north of the Crags.

From certain angles the dual hills are said to resemble a lion couchant, the easiest ascent being from the east, a grassy slope rising gracefully above the village of Duddingston, ascending by degrees to the lion's haunch. The hill dips slightly where the hollow of the back would be, before rising steeply to Salisbury Crags, the lion's head.

When they reached the summit the two men chose a spot near the edge of Salisbury Crags and gazed in wonder at the city spread out before them. From their vantage point they could see the whole panorama of the New Town, rising from its scaffolding to a fanfare of distant clanging hammers. 'Oh, brave new world!' exclaimed Johnson, removing his hat and placing it to his breast, 'that has such wondrous things in't!'

Connected to the Old Town by means of the new North Bridge, which spanned the valley on three elegant arches, the New Town, unlike the sprawling maze of the Old Town, was designed with order in mind, set out with geometrical precision by a coming together of the greatest architects, stonemasons and master-craftsmen the nation had to offer. The white sandstone buildings sparkled in the morning sun, providing a stately backdrop for the great and the good, who crowded the elegant squares and gardens like so many ants to Boswell and Johnson from their lofty vantage point.

Down in the valley the ancient Nor Loch was in the process of being drained, with a series of pumps in their bulky wooden frames deployed along its banks. The murky waters took on a reddish hue in the morning sun.

Boswell unfurled a blanket, letting it billow in the breeze before laying it down flat. Johnson opened the basket and looked inside, smacking his lips at the various goodies on offer.

The morning wore on, and a fine mist crept up over the edge of the crag to obscure the view, thickening by degrees, until the sun was no more than a smudge of white in the sky. The last few stragglers had already turned to make their way back down the hill, and before long Johnson and Boswell were the only two people left on that bare, forlorn stretch of ground.

Boswell opened the claret and took two tumblers from the basket, pouring a little wine into each. Johnson proposed a toast to Mrs Boswell and they eagerly drank down their glasses.

After Boswell's second glass he needed to relieve himself, and chose a spot a little further along the ledge to do so at his leisure. By the time he had buttoned up his breeches the mist was so dense he could barely see his hand in front of his face. He looked around for some landmark. If he was near the edge, one false move could mean certain death.

It began as a buzzing in his ear. Boswell swatted his hand around his head in a shooing gesture, frantically looking around to find the source of the disturbance. Strangely, he could not be sure if the sound was coming from within his own head or somewhere out there in the fog. The noise increased, and with it Boswell's feeling of unease.

He peered into the murk and caught sight of something moving a little further along the crag. Wreaths of mist shifted and cleared in the breeze, revealing a small child in a pale-grey cloak. Boswell cried out a warning. At the sound of his voice the child turned to reveal a pale face under a grey hood. His daughter's face.

Boswell's heart leapt to his throat. 'Veronica! *Stop!*'

With a tinkling laugh, his only child ran off into the mist.

Boswell gave chase, this time not caring to look where he was running.

*

Boswell was gone a full ten minutes before Johnson started to worry. He consulted his pocket watch then squinted his eyes at the impenetrable wall of mist. Perhaps his friend was only constipated. No point in disturbing him, or risk getting lost. He would stay put while nature took its course.

After finishing the last oatcake, Johnson eyed Mrs Boswell's fruitcake appraisingly. Such a thoughtful, considerate woman. He picked out a raisin and popped it in his mouth. Seconds later, the whole slice disappeared. He waited exactly five minutes and gave a sigh. A rich slice of fruit loaf was the last thing anyone with an upset stomach would want. He picked up the knife and thoughtfully cut Boswell's portion in two, transferring the larger half to his mouth. After another five minutes he made the second half disappear as well.

Feeling guilty, and with the stirrings of a vile stomach ache, Johnson picked himself up and peered into the mist, calling out for his friend. The only reply was his own voice, echoing across the valley to diminishing returns.

It began discreetly at first, the faintest quiver in the atmosphere. Then, almost imperceptibly, it became a low hum, a frequency just below the range of Johnson's conscious hearing.

As the vibration increased, so did Johnson's stomach ache, accompanied by an acute sensation of being watched. He remembered reading somewhere that compasses failed on Arthur's Seat, a curious geological phenomenon peculiar to the place, and wondered if the sensation now troubling his constitution was an effect of this strange magnetism. The hum was now clearly perceptible, though it was impossible to tell whether he could hear it, or feel it in the marrow of his bones. He was aware of a pulling sensation, a sense of violation, as if the vibration were a living thing, a disembodied life force attempting to sap his vital spirits. He looked around trying to find the source of the disturbance, only to be met with white void all around. He felt his legs weaken and, leaning forward with his hands on his knees, he ejected his breakfast across the turf.

The harsh, metallic cry of a crow brought him to his senses.

Moments later, a second call came from the opposite direction, answered by the first, a little closer this time. It sounded sinister in the gloom, and Johnson had the disturbing impression of being stalked through the mist by some monstrous, prehistoric bird. Suddenly a whole croaking chorus erupted around him, like the clamour that accompanies the farmer's plough.

From out of nowhere, a crow swooped down and pecked at Johnson's wig. This was rapidly succeeded by another crow, and then another, going straight for the same spot on Johnson's head. The hardness of their beaks struck his scalp like hammer-blows, one after the other in rapid succession, a ghastly tattoo raining down on his skull.

He started to run.

*

Boswell cast around in every direction, searching for his child. In desperation he cried out her name. There was a throbbing, pounding in his head now, like the churning of machinery. He clamped his hands to his ears and begged it to stop. A peal of laughter cut through the vibration, coming from somewhere behind him. He turned to face the pale image of his daughter, her ethereal form seeming to float on a cloud of mist. He raised his hands in a placatory gesture. 'Please... don't run,' he pleaded.

As Boswell advanced his foot struck something, a rock or a root, and he fell flat on his face. When he looked up the child had disappeared. He reached out to retrieve his hat, only to find the ground came to an abrupt end a few feet in front of him. Boswell was lying at the very edge of the abyss!

*

The blood from Johnson's head wounds seeped into his eyes, and still the crows kept coming. Their raucous cries were deafening. He was running carelessly when his knee gave way. He collapsed to the ground and, reaching out his hands to support his body, felt the familiar contours of his oak staff. He had come full circle. He grasped the reassuring heft of its girth and used it to clamber back to his feet.

With a threatening croak, another crow swooped down to strike at his eyes. He only had one chance. With his feet planted firmly on the ground, Johnson swung his oak stick like a club. The connecting blow sent the crow spinning like a grotesque shuttlecock, striking the ground in a flurry of black feathers. Johnson raised the staff again and brought it whistling down on the bird's skull, bashing in its brains. Emboldened, he struck the next one that attacked, and then another, until a pile of crows lay dead at his feet.

Observing the fates of their brethren, the rest of the flock dispersed, their rasping cries shrinking into the mist. The whole unpleasant incident had taken no longer than perhaps fifteen minutes. Johnson lay on his back, his chest rising and falling with exhaustion.

'Doctor Johnson! Thank God!'

Johnson raised his head an inch and mustered a smile. Boswell dropped to his knees, gasping at the blood.

'Don't cluck like a mother hen, Boswell. It looks much worse than it feels.'

'It looks bad enough, Doctor.' Boswell removed a hip flask of whisky from his inside coat pocket. 'Brace yourself: this might sting a bit.'

'I imagine the loss will sting you more, sir,' replied Johnson drily.

Tut-tutting, Boswell removed his friend's shaggy grey wig and sprinkled the liquor over his scalp, washing away the dried blood. 'You'll smell like a Glasgow drunk,' he said, 'but the alcohol should sterilise the wounds.' Boswell ripped the sleeve from his shirt and wrapped it securely around Johnson's head, tying it under his chin before returning his wig and hat. 'That should do for now, Doctor. Take my arm and we'll head down to the nearest village.'

One hour later, Johnson and Boswell were comfortably ensconced in the Sheep Head Inn of Duddingston, a picturesque little village to the east of the Crags. The owner of the inn, a bent old man with a scowling, toothless face, placed two bowls of broth before them.

'What the dickens happened up there?' was the first thing Boswell wanted to know.

'We were exposed to a psychic attack of considerable intensity,' Johnson replied, liberally salting his soup before tasting it.

'By whom?'

'Someone or something that doesn't like us.'

'But what was it?'

'I don't know. I have never met with such a demonstration of power. A Black Magic practitioner of some sort. A Magus, possibly a Hierophant, one of the Order's highest initiates. Whoever or whatever it was, we are treading on dangerous ground, Boswell.'

'You speak of an Order like it was the Freemasons.'

'There are many covert groups who strive for mastery of the black arts,' said Johnson, waving his spoon in the air. 'The Illuminati; the Order of Draco; the Sons of Belial; the Brotherhood of the Snake; the Knights Templar; the Rosicrucians; the Church of Saturn, all of whom I have had the misfortune of running afoul of at one point or another in my career... Yes, even the Freemasons. It all adds up to the same thing in the end.'

'What? The stuffy old Freemasons?' said Boswell incredulously. 'You seem to forget that I am a Mason myself, Doctor. As are you, for that matter. I am sure we would have noticed any witches or warlocks knocking around the Lodge. Broomsticks are a confounded nuisance in the reading room, you know.'

'Don't be so naive, Boswell. Do you think the Masons are all about shaking hands, slapping backs, and the old "hail-fellow-well-met" routine?'

'I am sure there is more to all those confounded rites and rituals than a preamble to a jolly good drinking session. But black magic and witchcraft?'

The Fall of the House of Thomas Weir

Johnson broke off a piece of bread and dunked it in his soup. 'The Order is not evil in and of itself, Boswell. Your average member just wants to get along in life—find a job, get a promotion maybe—without sparing a thought for what goes on over his head. But just think a bit: a global organisation using secrecy as a currency. It's the perfect cover for any number of covert groups who strive for influence on a grand scale. I've seen it happen before. A coven uses the host organisation as a cover, say a reading society or a gentleman's club, then gradually introduces its own agenda. It starts like a canker, the parasitical agent slowly spreading its malignant influence from the top down. Before you know it, those poor wretches in the lowliest station are the unwitting foot soldiers for the coven. The parasite will use the host to do as much damage to the social order as possible, then when it has finished it discards them, and moves onto the next group of victims.'

'And you believe the Freemasons have fallen victim to one such coven?'

'Intelligence I have gathered over the past six years leads me to believe that the Order of Freemasons has been infiltrated at their highest levels.'

'You surprise me, Doctor. So how do you propose to go on?'

'Very carefully, I should say.'

'Do you think this has anything to do with the undead creature that nightwatchman claims to have seen?'

'If a Necromancer is involved, I would not discount it. Whatever we are dealing with, it has mastery over the elements and the birds of the air. It can also induce visions, perhaps even shapeshift if the evidence of your eyes is to be trusted. One thing's for certain: we had best tread carefully from now on. Something doesn't want us poking our noses around its city.'

*

After the terrors of Arthur's Seat, the two men enjoyed a leisurely stroll back to town, ambling among the pleasantly wooded foothills to the north of the Crags. When they came to the fork at the foot of Canongate, they chose the right-hand path, forsaking the busy thoroughfare for the more pastoral charms of Northback, a farm road in the shadow of Caltoun Hill. They passed the College Church and its magnificent landscaped gardens, then the path descended onto the banks of the Nor Loch. The Loch's dirty waters were tinged with red—blood-red to the more superstitious observer—but according to the morning papers the phenomenon was caused by a mysterious algae which had appeared recently from out of nowhere. Local farmers moved their cattle from the fields immediately surrounding the area, claiming the pestilential odours were to blame for the recent outbreak of cholera among their livestock, a disease which had spread to the outer fringes of the city, infecting the old and weak from the poorest districts.

From higher up on North Bridge, Johnson and Boswell had a better view of the Loch. As they watched the steam-pumps reduce what was once a substantial body of water to a boggy marsh, a corpse broke the surface, its swollen belly a miserable grey island surrounded by clumps of gorse and furze. The workmen whose task it was to drain the water retrieved the corpse by means of a hook attached to a long stick. As they dragged the body towards the bank it broke apart, leaving only a head with the spine trailing behind it. Soon other corpses appeared; first one, then another, until within the hour the ground was awash with decomposed bodies, their empty eye sockets gazing listlessly into a slate-grey sky.

Boswell turned away and hid his face in his sleeve. 'Good God,' he cried. 'Are we to be visited by the ten plagues of Egypt now?'

Some of the workmen crossed themselves, while others scrambled up the steep banks of the Loch to firmer ground. As if to confirm Boswell's portentous words, a mass of frogs followed suit, slithering up the edges of the bank and hopping onto Princes Street, where they were crushed in their hundreds by the oncoming rush of traffic.

Chapter 5

The Mad Earl of Drumlanrig

The following excerpts are taken from a series of letters between key members of an organisation known as Ordo Draconis *or* The Order of Draco. *These letters contain indisputable proofs of a conspiracy. They disclose the principles, the object, and the means of the Order; the essential parts of their code, the diligent correspondence of the adepts, particularly that of their chief, and a statement of their progress and future hopes.*

Those who may harbour any doubt as to the authenticity of this collection, have only to apply to the office where the secret archives are kept at Munich, and where orders are left to show the originals.

James Boswell, 1773

Electorate of Bavaria,
2ⁿᵈ July, 1746
Brother Rastaban,
My associates and I have been following the train of your thought most assiduously—particularly your letter in the Times dated June twelfth, which rails against the corruption of the clergy, and your pamphlet entitled Star of the North, *which argues in no uncertain terms why monarchies should and must be abolished.*

May I assure you, sir, there are many of us here in the Electorate of Bavaria who share your noble sentiments; kindred spirits who would welcome you to our fold, providing a safe haven from the storms of public disapprobation.

Should you choose to honour our fledgling society with your membership, you will find our modest aims are surely in alignment with your own; namely to make of the human race, without any distinction of nation, condition, or profession, one good and happy family.

I Remain, Your Humble Servant &c.

Brother Thuban

Alpha Draconis

Boswell and Johnson returned from their ramble on Arthur's Seat flushed from their experiences. A brush with death has a galvanising effect on the human spirit, and the two men were singing and laughing like drunkards as they climbed the stairs to Boswell's apartment. Veronica was having a tea party for her dollies on the kitchen floor as they entered. Boswell dropped to his knees and wrapped his arms around his daughter, clutching her to his breast to establish that she was real. Mrs Boswell, standing over a pot at the stove, rolled her eyes in world-weary resignation at her husband's foolish display of affection, but smiled despite herself.

'Good day, Mr Johnson,' she said, turning to her guest with perfect equanimity. 'I trust you two have had a pleasant day?'

'Tolerably so, madam,' said Johnson, taking a seat at the kitchen table.

'There is a letter for you,' she said, taking the sealed letter from her pinafore and placing it before Johnson on the table. With great curiosity Johnson broke the seal and read the contents aloud. It was an urgent summons from William Douglas, 4th Duke of Queensberry. Having no literary pretensions or love for the arts, neither Johnson nor Boswell had the faintest idea why the Duke would desire their company, and so with the greatest curiosity they grabbed their hats and coats and headed for the door.

The Fall of the House of Thomas Weir

'And just where do you think you are going?' cried Mrs Boswell, with such authority that even Johnson froze with his hand on the door handle.

'We have been summoned, Maggie dear,' Boswell explained. 'The Duke of Queensberry has need of our particular skills.'

'I care not a jot if it is the King of Sweden,' said Mrs Boswell. 'You will sit at the table and eat the dinner I have been slaving over all day!'

The two men returned with cowed expressions and took their places, while Mrs Boswell heaped angry dollops of mince and tatties onto their plates.

Johnson said grace, or rather mumbled a few words into his chest, then the two friends set to with astonishing alacrity. They couldn't have eaten fast enough; the sparks practically flew from the silverware. After they had cleaned their plates Boswell looked expectantly at his wife, while Johnson tapped his foot so violently he almost overturned the table. They appeared to Mrs Boswell in that moment as nothing more than absurdly overgrown schoolboys eager to rejoin their friends in the street, and it was all she could do to keep her laughter in check.

'Oh for heaven's sake!' she cried, exasperated. 'Go! Just go!'

With a pat on the head for his daughter and a loving kiss for his wife, Boswell took his friend's arm and they almost flew out the door.

*

Queensberry House was an imposing whitewashed mansion on the edge of town. It was beginning to rain as the two men stepped down from their buggy and crossed the central courtyard, glancing nervously at the grimly darkened windows. They were received at the door by an elderly butler in full Highland dress. 'Are you the Justice of the Peace?' he asked, squinting at them through a gap in the door.

'No, man,' said Boswell. 'I am James Boswell, Advocate of Law,

35

and this is my good friend Doctor Johnson, whose name speaks for itself. I believe your master is expecting us?'

The butler poked his head out and glanced furtively from left to right, then ushered them into the hallway. As he took their wet coats, the visitors were startled by a series of muffled thumps coming from upstairs.

'Hurry, please,' said the butler, 'or there will be a murder before the night is through.'

The two men climbed the opulent staircase and entered a room decked with fine furnishings and costly drapes, only to be met with a shocking scene of violence.

In the middle of the room, a young man of perhaps eighteen was tied to a chair. His nose was bloodied and there was an angry swelling at his cheeks. A big man towered over the boy, his shirtsleeves rolled to the elbows, while a young maid cowered at the bully's heels, pleading with him to stop.

Though clearly a nobleman, without his wig there was something of the pugilist about the Duke of Queensberry. Coarse-featured, nose broken in several places with grey hair cropped close to the skull, the impression he gave was of a man with a great propensity for violence. 'Ah, gentlemen, there you are,' he said, as if they had just interrupted him playing a mildly fatiguing sport. 'Doctor Johnson, perhaps you can get this boy to talk. They say you are the cleverest man in all of England.'

'Please sirs,' cried the boy through swollen lips. 'Tell him I didn't do it! Save me!'

'I must insist you lower your fists at once, Your Grace,' said Johnson, shocked by such casual brutality. 'Please, let us go alone to a room where we can talk privately. This really won't do, I assure you!'

'Very well,' said the Duke of Queensberry, wrestling his boot from the serving girl's frantic clutches. 'Come into my study.'

Doctor Johnson gestured for the butler to bring some water for the boy, then he and Boswell followed the Duke into a small, simply furnished room at the opposite end of the corridor, that smelled of stale pipe smoke.

'Last night my wife and I went to the opera. Not my cup of tea, I grant you, but still… have to keep the little lady happy, eh?' said Queensberry, once the three men were alone. 'Anyway, while we were away some impudent swine broke into my house and robbed me blind. The better half is inconsolable. Won't leave her room.'

'I see,' said Johnson. 'And what leads you to believe the boy is the culprit?'

'The only body in this wing of the house last night was the serving maid. She's been fooling around with that stable flunky for God knows how long. He throws stones up at her window every night then climbs up the drain to have his way with her, the pasty-faced little pervert. I've turned a blind eye to it in the past—I ain't a saint myself, God knows—but it's obvious to anyone but a damned fool she let him in last night, and the little ruffian came in and ransacked the place. It's as clear as the nose on your face.'

'It may seem that way, Your Grace, but let us proceed with caution,' suggested Johnson. 'Tell me what was stolen.'

'Precious family heirlooms. Diamonds, rubies, emeralds, that sort of thing.'

'But why contact us? Why not call for the magistrate?' said Boswell.

The Duke of Queensberry shuffled his feet and gazed awkwardly at the floor. 'Some of my staff claim there is more to this than meets the eye—some sort of funny business going on, if you know what I mean—all nonsense of course, but I don't want them blabbing to the authorities about ghosts and whatnot. I'd be a laughing stock! Besides,' he added, lowering his voice, 'there were some documents taken as well. Sensitive stuff I'd rather was dealt with discreetly, if we understand one another.'

'I see,' said Johnson, stroking his chin to hide a certain *frisson* of excitement at the prospect of a supernatural investigation. 'And now, Your Grace, if you could kindly bring me the boy, and anyone else who was in this wing of the house on the night in question. One at a time, please. And *gently*.'

Queensberry stalked off, returning moments later with the terrified boy grasped firmly by the scruff of the neck. He threw the boy at Johnson's feet, then stood by the door and folded his big arms.

'Alone, if you please, Your Grace.'

With a sigh which reminded Boswell of a petulant schoolboy, Queensberry stalked off to console his wife, while Johnson turned to address the boy. 'Well, lad, stand up. Don't look so scared; I ain't going to hurt you. I believe the young lady out there is your sweetheart?'

'Yes, sir. But I didn't touch her! I only go to her room now and then to talk, and that's all.'

'To talk, eh?'

'Yes, sir. To talk.'

'Young man. What you do or do not do with that lady is no concern of mine. But I must insist you tell me—truthfully, mind— where you were last night?'

'I wasn't here, sir. Honest I wasn't.'

'Then where the deuces were you?'

'I was with my brother, sir. We were drinking in the Jolly Judge.'

'All night?'

'From six o'clock until closing, sir.'

'And you were drinking all that time?'

'Yes, sir. I was very drunk, truth be told.'

'And where did you find the money to get drunk, sir?'

'It was my brother stood me rounds. He's a butcher. Makes quite a tidy sum on Fleshmarket Row.'

'Hmm. And if I ask the patrons of the Jolly Judge, they will vouchsafe for you?'

'On my oath, sir.'

Johnson stared hard at the boy, then abruptly shook his oak stick in his face. 'D'ye see this big stick? If I find out you are lying, boy, then I swear I will beat you about the head with it.'

'Yes sir. I mean no sir. Sorry sir.'

'Off you go for now and clean yourself up. Send in the young lady on your way out.'

Moments later, in came the serving girl.

Johnson smiled kindly and indicated a chair.

'Now don't look so frightened, Miss...?'

'Mary Swann, sir,' said the girl, taking a seat and straightening her dress and hair with a nervous hand.

'Now Mary, I have the whole story from your beau, so no lying to me, d'ye hear?'

'No, sir. And he's not my beau, sir,' she said tartly. 'I care for him, is all.'

'Madam, how you choose to conduct your private life is no concern of mine, though I might remind you of Psalm 18:26: *With the pure thou wilt shew thyself pure; and with the forward thou wilt shew thyself forward...* Now which is it to be?'

'The pure, sir. I'm a good girl, sir.'

'As you say. But I must warn you, Mary, that this is a very serious matter. Do you understand that?'

'I do, Your Grace.'

Doctor Johnson glanced at Boswell and caught his smile. 'A simple "*sir*" will do, Mary. Now tell me, in your own words mind, what happened last night while the Duke and Duchess were away.'

'I was dusting the cabinet when I heard a noise coming from downstairs.'

'This cabinet here?'

'Yes, sir.'

'Go on. What sort of noise?'

'It was the cellar door opening, sir.'

'And how do you know it was the cellar door?'

'I know the sound, because I keep telling Crookshanks—'

'Crookshanks?'

'That's the butler, sir. I keep telling Crookshanks it's needing oiled, but he never does it. It sent a shiver down my spine, what with the house being empty and all.'

'And where was Crookshanks last night? And the rest of the staff?'

'They were all drinking in the servants' quarters, sir. It's in the other wing of the house quite a ways from here.'

'And there's no way they could have heard anything?'

'I don't think so. It's too far away.'

'I see. Please continue.'

'I... I heard footsteps coming up the stairway, sort of shuffling and uneven, like a man with a limp...'

'And then?'

'Then the footsteps started coming down the corridor towards me...' Mary threw her head in her hands and started to tremble. 'I can't, sir! It was too horrible. I was terrified!'

Johnson stood over Mary and placed a plump hand on her shoulder. 'There, there. You are doing very well. Now tell me what came through that door.'

Mary ran a hand through her long dark hair, rolled her eyes, and tried to compose herself. 'It was wearing a black hooded cape, so I couldn't see the face. But it saw me. It came towards me, and it reached out its hand...'

'And?'

Mary started trembling again, and spoke in a voice stricken with emotion. 'It was all black and scaly. Like charcoal. And the smell, sir. Like rotting flesh. I... I can't remember what happened after that. I fainted. And when I woke, that's when everything was gone.' Mary put her head in her hands again and burst into tears.

'That's all, Mary. You did very well.' Johnson reached into his pocket and passed her his handkerchief. After she had blown her nose, Johnson dismissed her as gently as his gruff manner would allow. 'And please send in Crookshanks,' he added, as Mary closed her fingers around the door handle. 'You won't have to look far. He's right outside with his ear pressed to the door.'

When the girl opened the door, Crookshanks straightened with comic dignity.

'Come in, sir, please,' said Johnson.

The butler entered.

'I suppose you have heard all about our mysterious intruder?'

The Fall of the House of Thomas Weir

'Yes, sir.'

'And what are they saying about it downstairs?'

'That it was the *ghost*, sir.'

'The *ghost*? And what ghost would that be?'

'James Douglas... sir.'

Boswell bolted upright in his chair. 'Surely you don't mean... the Mad Earl of Drumlanrig?'

'Am I missing something here?' said Johnson, looking askance at his friend.

'*The Cannibalistic Idiot,*' said Boswell. 'A tale of such horror it defies credibility, had it not the distinction of being entirely true.'

'Let's have it then,' Johnson sighed. 'I could use a good laugh.'

'It is no laughing matter, sir. The tale concerns James Douglas, Earl of Drumlanrig, who was the current Duke of Queensberry's uncle,' said Boswell. 'The Mad Earl was the first son of James Douglas to survive infancy. Douglas was the second Duke of Queensberry, whom you may recall was the driving force behind the 1707 signing of the Union between Scotland and England.'

'Thank you for the history lesson,' said Johnson drily. 'I seem to remember he made a tidy sum of money from the deal.'

'Some say it came with a curse. The Earl of Drumlanrig, his first son and heir, was a violently insane imbecile, kept under strict lock and key in the cellar of this house. On the night the treaty was signed, there was a terrible storm. While the rest of the household were busy celebrating the union of our two great nations, the Mad Earl broke free, killed a lad who worked in the kitchen with his bare hands and stuffed the body in the oven. When they found the Earl, he was dining on the roasted flesh of his victim. Some say the son's insanity was a curse on the Duke for profiting from the treaty, and selling out his own people.'

'It was judgement from God right enough,' said Crookshanks in hushed tones. 'For his odious share in the Union.'

'Of course the Mad Earl was removed from the succession, stripped of his titles and never seen again. He was succeeded by his younger brother Charles, the current Duke's father.'

'Fascinating stuff,' said Johnson. 'But we are forgetting one thing. How many ghosts do you know that rob their own household?'

'Indeed,' said Boswell, 'I have yet to hear of a ghost with the power to affect material substance, unless of course it be a poltergeist.'

'*Tsk tsk*, Boswell. I'm afraid you are putting the cart before the horse again. I have often said that when you have eliminated the natural, whatever remains, *however improbable,* must be the *super*natural; but first let us exhaust the former before we proceed to the latter. Tell me,' said Johnson, turning to Crookshanks, 'is this the Duke of Queensberry's private study?'

'It is that, sir.'

'And that is the cabinet where the Duke kept his private papers? The ones which were stolen?'

'Yes, sir.'

'Then it would follow, that among certain other incriminating documents, were those pertaining to the 1707 Act of Union, detailing funds received by James Douglas, 2nd Duke of Queensberry, for his share in it?'

'Sir, I would not presume—'

'But it would seem like a reasonable assumption, would it not?'

'If you say so, sir.'

'Ah, but I do say so, sir. Now tell me, what was the condition of this room when you found it?'

'Condition, sir?'

'I mean what state was it in?'

'It was just as you see now.'

'What? No overturned furniture, no broken locks, nothing scattered on the floor?'

'No, sir. Other than the stolen items, the room was unmolested.'

'Rather as if someone knew what they were looking for?'

'I... I suppose so, sir.'

'And who keeps the key for this cabinet?'

'Only His Grace, sir.'

The Fall of the House of Thomas Weir

'There were no spare sets made?'

'No, not as far as I know.'

Johnson turned to examine the cabinet, running his fingers over its smooth surfaces, then bent down on one knee to look underneath, grunting with the strain.

After Johnson had made a careful examination of the study, Crookshanks showed the men the other rooms that had been ransacked, then escorted them down to the kitchen, where the infamous oven used to cook the kitchen boy was still in use. Johnson insisted on questioning each member of staff individually in Crookshanks' private quarters.

Afterwards, he called the Duke of Queensberry back to the study.

'Well?' said Queensberry.

'Your Grace, not one member of your household has the audacity or resourcefulness to steal so much as a spoon from this house, let alone a fortune in valuables and government documents.'

'Then who the blazes did it? Come on, Doctor. I can see by your face you have an idea in that noggin of yours. Let's have it.'

Doctor Johnson swallowed his irritation. 'Your Grace, I may have one idea, I may have a great many ideas, but until my theories have been put to the test, they are simply just that. Ideas.'

'Fair enough,' said Queensberry. 'So what do you propose?'

'I propose to see the cellar, sir.'

As none of the staff were willing, the Duke of Queensberry took them there himself. He used his master key to open the creaking door and led Johnson and Boswell down some stone steps into a well-stocked wine cellar. A second door at the far end of the cellar led to a gloomy vault that would serve to dampen even the liveliest of spirits.

'So this is where mad Uncle James was kept,' said Boswell, pausing to examine deep gouges in the walls, the peeling paintwork, and gibberish daubed with what appeared to be dried excrement. In the corner of the room, a set of rusty manacles had been attached to the wall, with a heap of gnawed bones nearby.

'No one has been in here since the days of my uncle,' muttered Queensberry by way of explanation for his bad housekeeping.

The three men followed the sound of splattering water through a series of similarly derelict rooms until they came to the last chamber. On the far wall, an unlocked iron grille some ten feet from the floor looked onto a gloomy side street. The rain, falling heavily now, was seeping in, and they could see the boots of the occasional passer-by hurrying past. On the ground beneath the grille was an overturned stool.

'So much for your *ghost,* gentlemen,' said Johnson. 'Clearly the perpetrator gained access by means of that grille, and escaped the same way.'

'But what of the maid's description?' said Boswell, struggling to hide his disappointment.

'A simple disguise would take care of that,' Johnson replied. 'While an odour of rotting flesh may be achieved simply by secreting spoiled meat around one's person. A similar effect was produced ten years ago in London. I must say I'm surprised at you, Boswell. Do you forget the case already? It was in all the papers at the time, and you yourself wrote a rather flattering account of my part in it.'

'Of course!' cried Boswell. 'Scratching Fanny of Cock Lane!'

Queensberry began to grow impatient. 'Cocks and Fannies!' he blurted. 'What about my valuables?'

'Let me assure you, Your Grace,' said Johnson smoothly. 'The real thief will be captured, and your belongings returned to you, all within the next forty-eight hours.'

Queensberry remained leery, though he was grudgingly impressed by the calm confidence in Johnson's voice.

'Do your best, sir,' he said as he walked his visitors to the door. 'The security of the nation—and my wife's happiness—depend upon you.'

'I shall bear the burden with honour, Your Grace,' said Johnson with a bow; and not a little irony, which only Boswell, his friend of ten years, could detect.

The Fall of the House of Thomas Weir

As they crossed the courtyard towards their carriage, Johnson swung his stick over his shoulder and breezily announced, 'Well, Boswell. I think we will pay the Knights of the Cape a visit tonight, if you are willing.'

'Certainly, Doctor. But I never thought—'

'You recently moved upstairs from the ground floor apartment, did you not?'

'Yes,' replied Boswell.

'And you still have keys for your former apartment?'

'I believe so, yes.'

'Excellent. I may need to borrow your old lodgings for a few days.'

'Sir! We are more than happy to have you stay in our guest rooms.'

'I will also need to borrow some furniture, and that ghastly Rubens copy you keep in your study.'

'Certainly,' said Boswell. 'But whatever for?'

'Authenticity,' Johnson replied, with a look of profound self-satisfaction.

'And what of Lady Colville? Perhaps, with her unique abilities, she could assist with—'

'Ah, ye of little faith,' said Johnson, shaking his head sadly at Boswell. 'You are overlooking the unique abilities of Doctor Samuel Johnson, Lexicographer!'

Chapter 6

Three Sleekit Craws

Holborn, London,
August 3rd 1747

rother Thuban,
The greatest strength of our Order lies in its concealment; let it never appear in any place in its own name, but always covered by another name or occupation. None is fitter than the three lower degrees of Free Masonry; the public is accustomed to it, expects little from it, and therefore takes little notice of it. Next to this, an organisation in the form of a reading society or gentleman's drinking club may be similarly employed. By recruiting converts from among the working and artisan classes and placing them in positions of responsibility and power we may, by sure and steady influence, turn the public mind which way we will.

Your Humble Servant &c.
Brother Rastaban
Beta Draconis

The Fall of the House of Thomas Weir

'Be careful with that Queen Anne!' cried Mrs Boswell from the landing, wringing her hands with anxiety as the two men heaved some of her best furniture down to the ground floor apartment.

Despite Doctor Johnson's best intentions, he could be a most vexatious man. First of all, he was stealing her husband to go off on some foolish excursion for God knows how long and, allowing for certain concessions that had to be made for a man of his genius, his personal habits left a lot to be desired. Mrs Boswell counted them off with her fingers: he snored loudly, he kept strange hours, he dressed like a vagrant with holes in his stockings, and always a stain of some sort on his collar; and as for his eating habits—where to begin?—chewing with his mouth open, belching, drinking tea from the saucer, not to mention the nervous tics; the incessant humming, the drumming of fingers and shaking of legs, as if constantly waiting for something to happen.

It would be small wonder if Veronica did not pick up some of his bad habits. She had already taken to sitting propped up on her highchair next to the Doctor, taking her tea from her saucer just like him. And now this! Despite her ambivalence, Mrs Boswell took it as a personal affront that Doctor Johnson no longer wished to stay in the guest room. If he got so much as a scratch on her new furniture, she would be sending him the bill. Make no mistake about that!

*

Once the last piece of furniture had been moved into the small two-room apartment on the ground floor, Johnson looked around and nodded, pleased with himself. 'It's perfect, wouldn't you say?'

'If you say so, Doctor,' said Boswell, brimming with curiosity but knowing better than to ask.

'And now,' said Johnson, 'if you would be so kind as to go

upstairs and ask Mrs Boswell to take your daughter and leave town first thing in the morning. Perhaps she can stay with your father, Lord Auchenleck. I am sure he would be delighted to see his little granddaughter. Things might get a little heated round here over the next few days.'

Boswell rolled his eyes towards the ceiling, where his long-suffering wife was no doubt cursing her husband for ever having invited Doctor Johnson into their lives, and heaved a sigh.

*

The members of the Cape Club were delighted and more than a little surprised to receive Boswell and Johnson for the second consecutive night. Doctor Johnson seemed in fine spirits, quick to laugh, hospitable and full of largesse. He ordered a second magnum of champagne for the company, followed by a third, until Boswell was obliged to intervene. 'Doctor Johnson, have you entirely lost your mind?' he said, pulling his friend aside. 'That first bottle alone is worth half your pension for the entire month!'

'Don't worry, Boswell,' he whispered back. 'If my plan succeeds, it will be worth every blasted penny, and we can send the Duke of Queensberry the bill.'

Johnson recognised many of the same faces from the previous night. There was old Runciman asleep in the corner, and Doctor Hunter brooding over his brandy. The younger men were guzzling fresh oysters and washing them down with the champagne Johnson had provided, raising their glasses every so often in a toast to their benefactor. Deacon Brodie was playing piquet at the same table with his aristocratic gentleman from the previous night, although this time the locksmith's luck seemed to be looking up, judging from the money piled on his side of the table.

After losing several more hands, Lord Sinclair stood with a look of disgust, then collected his coat and made his way to the exit. Brodie merely chuckled to himself and began piling his winnings into his pocket, before ordering himself another drink.

The Fall of the House of Thomas Weir

The waiter who brought the tray refused Brodie's coin.

'Whassa' matter,' said Brodie, beginning to feel the effects of the alcohol. 'My coin not good enough for you?'

'Perfectly good, sir,' replied the waiter. 'But the gentleman in the corner has already settled your bill.'

Brodie squinted his eyes towards the corner by the fire, where the two newest members were comfortably ensconced. Johnson nodded in acknowledgment and raised his glass.

'Good evening sirs,' said the Deacon, standing to take a bow. 'My name around here is Sir Lluyd. What are we celebrating?'

'It is a bittersweet occasion, I confess,' said Johnson. 'Allow me to introduce myself. I am Sir Loin, and my companion here Sir Rake. Join us, please.'

Brodie's eyes flicked suspiciously from Boswell to Johnson then, throwing caution to the wind, he pulled up a chair and sat across from the two men. 'I'm obliged to you, sirs. And what would be the occasion?'

'An aunt of mine died.'

'My condolences, sir.'

'It is of no consequence. Truth be told, she was a blasted nuisance of a woman. But I suppose I should be grateful to the old battle axe. She left a sizable inheritance.'

At the mention of the word "inheritance" Brodie's ears pricked up, though he immediately disguised his reaction by producing a jewel-studded snuff horn from his pocket and taking a pinch. 'In which case,' he said, sneezing delicately into a silk handkerchief. 'My congratulations, sir.'

'Allow me to propose a toast,' said Johnson, raising his glass. 'To dear old Aunt Gertrude, and pastures new.'

'Pastures new,' said Boswell, beginning to catch on.

Brodie looked thoughtful as he sipped his drink. 'Am I to understand you are leaving us?'

'Tomorrow we ride for Aberdeen. My doctor tells me the bracing sea air will be beneficial for my health.'

'Then you should be careful. There are many bandits on those back roads.'

'That's all right. We won't be carrying anything of value with us.'

'I see. But permit me to ask, what about your inheritance? Have you made arrangements for any valuables you might leave... unattended?'

'Well I never thought of that. Why didn't I think of that, Sir Rake?'

Boswell looked at Johnson and shrugged his shoulders.

'It is my business to think of such things,' said Brodie, sobering in an instant. 'You see, I am a locksmith and cabinet maker by trade. The best in the business, as it happens. I might just have the very thing, for the right price. Allow me to give you my card. Why don't you drop by my warehouse tomorrow morning?'

Johnson turned the card over in his hand, taking careful note of the address. 'You know, I think I just might,' he said as he drained his glass. 'And now, Sir Lluyd, we must leave at once. We have some packing to do.'

*

Unlike her husband, an incurable hoarder, Margaret Boswell was ruthless. Boswell kept anything from old coupons and ticket stubs to chess sets with missing pieces, broken bits of crockery and burnt-out candles. Mrs Boswell was quite the opposite, the problem being she often forgot to replace the discarded item, and then the harmony of the household would be broken by Boswell shouting from the top of the stairs for his razor, or looking for a matching stocking, or trying to find something to dry his face with.

Today, she and Veronica would be visiting St Agatha's, the new orphanage for girls on Canongate. Truth be told, she was glad for an opportunity to get out of the house. She had long expressed a desire to perform some charitable act, and now that her husband and his great nuisance of a friend needed the rooms for a few days, she would make her long overdue visit to the orphanage; her great friend the Reverend Baxter had hinted several times they were in need of donations. She and Veronica would bring presents for the girls, then hire a carriage to take them to Ayrshire to surprise Boswell's father Lord Auchinleck. If she were honest with herself, she found the latter prospect rather daunting—the musty old rooms, the austere halls, the joyless dinner table, and the dour old man himself—and yet her father-in-law was as soft as pudding when it came to Veronica. The old man positively doted on the child.

With great purpose, Mrs Boswell moved from room to room, ransacking larders and emptying closets. After stuffing a bag full of blankets she moved on to Veronica's room and began folding baby clothes onto the bed. The little girl sat cross-legged beside her, clutching her dolly and eyeing her mother warily.

'Mama,' she said, 'those are all my clothes!'

'Nonsense, girl. These clothes are much too small for you now. And besides, what did we agree about helping those less fortunate than ourselves?'

'Yes, Mama.'

Once Mrs Boswell had emptied the contents of the wardrobe, she looked thoughtfully at the dolly.

'No Mama, not Fiona!'

'Now, dear. You're much too old for dollies now, are you not?'

'I'm only four-and-a-half!'

'Exactly. Just think of the happiness it will bring some poor little orphan.'

The little girl clutched Fiona even tighter and buried her face in the crook of its neck.

Mrs Boswell changed tack with a crafty glance at her daughter. 'If you give me Fiona... We'll go to Mrs Cochrane's for some candied apples on the way to Grandpa Alexander's.'

Her daughter's little brow furrowed as she weighed up the benefits of each offer, before finally surrendering her beloved doll in favour of the candied apples. She had a sweet tooth like her father, reflected Mrs Boswell.

'Now get your coat on; it's spitting outside.'

With her daughter's hand grasped firmly in her own, Mrs Boswell walked briskly down High Street in the rain, weaving her way past early morning traders opening their barrows, and oyster-girls and flower-girls hailing each other shrilly across the street.

At Merkat Cross a small crowd had gathered to hear George Pratt, the town crier. The clanging of his bell resounded through Old Town as he made his announcements.

'Greyfriars' Ghoul Strikes Again!... Spate of high-profile burglaries rocks town... Ghostly carriage seen clattering down West Bow at midnight... Mysterious comings and goings at Nor Loch... Laidlaw's Gentleman's Outfitters half-price wig sale ends soon!'

His job done, the town crier nailed a flysheet to a post in the middle of the square and moved on.

As Mrs Boswell threaded her way through the crowd, several gentlemen tipped their hats and said her name. For a moment she thought they were addressing someone else.

As Miss Margaret Montgomerie, she had spent her formative years in the quiet country village of Stewarton. She had been all of sixteen when she fell for her first cousin, James Boswell. She had accompanied her future husband to Dublin on his mission to court a young lady named Mary Ann Boyd, a wealthier and more distant relation than wee Maggie Montgomerie. Along the way, the two found much in common, including a shared sense of humour, which her mother always told her was a vital ingredient to any marriage. James was warm and engaging, a childlike soul who made her laugh until tears came to her eyes and her stomach hurt. Somewhere on the road to Dublin they had left the carriage to picnic in a cornfield that waved enticingly in the summer breeze, lulling her scruples into submission. He had held her tightly then, and kissed her thrillingly.

It had not been her intention to make him fall in love with her. Well... maybe just a little. He was young, handsome, virile, witty, brilliant... Why *should* she let some Irish colleen have him, when he could have a good Scots woman to come home to, someone to mend his stockings and keep his bed warm at night?

He had a roving eye, that much was true, but what man was without flaw? After the marriage she would tame his wilder impulses, curb his excesses.

How many women have told themselves the same thing through the ages, before coming to earth with a resounding thump! The truth is that Boswell couldn't help himself. Inconsistency was in his blood. It was part of what made him who he was. And yet she loved him despite all, and would put up with his dalliances like so many generations of women had before her with their own men. At least he had the delicacy to feel ashamed of his indiscretions, if the tearful midnight confessions and vows of future fidelity were to be believed, though sometimes she wished he would just do his business and keep quiet about it, like the French.

To add to the balance in his favour, he had given her a beautiful daughter, the apple of her eye, and for that Mrs Boswell could forgive much.

As if sensing the warm current of affection, Veronica tightened her grip on her mother's hand and looked up at her with wide-eyed innocence. She was fortunate to have all the love and security her parents could provide. Countless weren't so lucky.

Though the Orphanage of St Agatha was run on donations from the Kirk, the girls who peered through the bars were hollow-eyed, ragged things with dirty faces and spindly limbs, and it smote Mrs Boswell's heart to see them so deprived, when she and her daughter enjoyed all the luxuries that her husband's salary as an advocate of law provided.

With her daughter firmly in hand, Mrs Boswell approached the tall, grey building with bars on its windows, and rapped three times on the door before explaining the purpose of her visit. The Sister who answered seemed nervous and reluctant to admit them but, lacking any genuine reason to deny them entry, she had no choice but to step aside.

Mother and daughter entered a vast hallway with balconies

on each level looking onto a tiled reception area. The place was spotless. Sterile. Everywhere cleaning ladies were busy dusting, polishing, sweeping. The acrid smell of disinfectant filled the air, reminding Mrs Boswell keenly of her schooldays. On the other side of the reception desk a staircase led to a landing which divided into the east and west wings. A marble bust, possibly some benefactor with a social conscience, sat on a plinth at the foot of the stairs; but otherwise the area was devoid of ornamentation.

'We are expecting an important visitor,' the young Sister explained.

'I see,' said Mrs Boswell. 'And who would that be?'

'The president of the orphanage,' said the nun breathlessly.

'Is that his sculpture over there?'

'Yes, ma'am.'

'How very nice for you. I can see myself from here.' Mrs Boswell took Veronica's hand and made her way towards the staircase.

'Madam!' cried the nun, running to catch up with the visitors. 'Madam, you mustn't—'

As Mrs Boswell ascended the stairs her way was blocked by a tall and stocky woman with stern features beneath a stiffly starched wimple.

'Who is this? Really, this is most irregular, Sister Grace,' said the imposing figure, addressing the young receptionist over Mrs Boswell's shoulder. 'Did you take this woman's name?'

'No, Mother Superior. I tried to, ma'am.'

*

Mother Superior had been expecting the President all morning. Her hands were raw from scrubbing the girls' backs with soap and a wire brush, changing the bathwater when it turned black, pricking rows of little fingers, instructing the girls to rub the blood on their cheeks to get some colour onto their pale faces. They wouldn't get chosen, she told them, if they seemed feeble or sickly. Of course, the girls had been drilled to perfection on how to behave when the President arrived. They were to curtsy, speak only when spoken to, and under no circumstances to make eye contact with their superiors.

Mother Superior stood with her arms folded, an imperious expression fixed onto her face, as if disapproval were her default mode. Twenty pale little faces appeared through the balcony railings behind her, peering down hopefully at the visitors, grasping the railings like the prisoners they were.

Theirs was a life of drudgery, except for that one special day each year when the President came. He seemed like a god to those girls, bringing the promise and wonder of the world outside. They would line up before him as he inspected the ranks, tilting a chin here, squeezing an arm there, sometimes pulling down a lower lip to inspect the gums like a farmer at a cattle auction, all the while asking Mother Superior all sorts of questions regarding birthdates, diet, which girls had started bleeding; the youngest didn't know what this meant, but they didn't like the sound of it. The older girls, already initiated into the mysteries of menstruation, didn't know why such personal matters should be any of his business but, if answering his silly questions helped them to get chosen, who were they to argue?

After retreating to a quiet corner with his colleagues, the President would announce the winner. The girls would cheer, and for once Mother Superior didn't seem to mind. She wasn't a bad sort, really. The President seemed to bring out the schoolgirl in her, and she flushed with pleasure whenever he graced her with so much as a look or a compliment.

Swept away by the hand of providence and planted into a new life, the lucky winner didn't have time to collect what few belongings she had. The new home would have everything her heart desired: silks, dolls, a room of her own, and an endless supply of sweet things to eat. But most importantly of all, she would have a rich father and a loving mother, with lots of new brothers and sisters to look out for her.

Once she had buttoned up her little coat, each winner received a final pinch on the cheek from Mother Superior before being swept into the loving embrace of a Real Family, and a hopeless sense of melancholy would descend on the orphanage once more.

*

'Please don't blame the girl,' said Maggie, taking an immediate and instinctive dislike to the Mother Superior. 'I'm afraid I can be quite persuasive—even forceful—when the mood takes me. I am Mrs Margaret Boswell. The Reverend Baxter of St. Giles said the orphanage was in need of donations, and I rather hoped I might spend some time with the girls.'

Mother Superior looked more put out than ever. 'Yes... Well... I am sure Sister Grace already explained we have a very important visitor coming today. Give me your donation, and I'll be happy to—'

'That won't be necessary, Sister Daphne. Mrs Boswell is most welcome.' The voice was rich, educated, with just the hint of a foreign accent. Maggie Boswell turned to face a tall, distinguished-looking gentleman standing in the doorway. He was accompanied by two other gentlemen, all three giving the impression of great importance and significance in the world. The man who had spoken approached Mrs Boswell, took her hand and raised it to his lips like a proper Frenchman. 'Permit me to introduce myself,' he purred. 'My name is Sir William. Your husband is well, I trust?'

'Yes, thank you,' said Mrs Boswell, resisting the urge to curtsy. 'He is spending time with an old friend.'

'Ah yes,' said the gentleman. 'The great Samuel Johnson. Do you know, it took him only seven years to compile his Dictionary of the English Language? Quite the achievement!'

'Especially when you consider,' retorted Mrs Boswell, 'it took a team of forty scholars fifty-five years to complete the French *Dictionnaire*.'

'Indeed,' replied Sir William, ignoring the slight. 'How fortunate for Doctor Johnson, to have the pleasure of your charming company.'

Mrs Boswell could see how Sir William's surface charm might soon wear thin on cynical ears. 'You do me too much honour, sir.'

Noticing Veronica for the first time, he bent down on one knee to examine Boswell's daughter. 'And who is this delightful creature?'

'Answer the gentleman,' Mrs Boswell whispered, gently nudging her daughter forward.

'V'ronka.'

'Veronica? What a pretty name.' Sir William reached out a hand to caress the girl's hair. 'And such lovely hair you have. Like summer corn.'

'Ank-you.'

'And you have come with presents for all the little orphans?'

Veronica nodded.

'Well, these two gentlemen and I have some important business to attend to. Perhaps you and your mother could visit the girls while we are doing that?'

Veronica nodded again.

'Then it's settled,' said Sir William, getting to his feet and addressing the Mother Superior. 'We will make some preliminary assessments in the dormitory, then take the girls one at a time for examination. Perhaps one of the sisters would be so kind as to show Mrs Boswell around?'

'I'll do it,' said Sister Grace, before Mother Superior had a chance to object.

After securing Mrs Boswell's promise to join him in Sister Daphne's office afterwards for tea, Sir William rubbed his hands together and turned to confer with his colleagues, who with their frowning faces, long noses, black frock coats and spindly legs reminded Mrs Boswell inexplicably of three sleekit craws.

Chapter 7

Secrets in the Attic

As they climbed the stairs, Mrs Boswell took the opportunity to find out a little more about Saint Agatha's, probing gently for useful information.

'Sir William envisions our orphanage here as an ethical alternative to the almshouses,' explained Sister Grace. 'Where the girls would be exposed to all sorts of criminal and deviant behaviour. We rescue our foundlings from a life of crime and prostitution, by providing them with the skills needed to make their way in the world.'

'And what skills would those be?' asked Mrs Boswell, as she and Veronica followed their guide to the third floor, then down the corridor.

'Oh, housewifery, mainly: the culinary arts, deportment, music, needlepoint—'

'And what about their learning, Sister Grace? Surely you don't mean to raise a gaggle of illiterates?'

'Why yes,' Sister Grace replied, 'we have a French Governess who visits once a week.'

'Hmm. And what about Sister Daphne? Does she play a formative role in the children's upbringing?'

Sister Grace paused before answering, and seemed to choose

her words carefully. 'Sister Daphne is responsible for the girls' moral and spiritual welfare.'

'And the girls are happy here?'

Sister Grace paused with her hand on the doorhandle. 'I... I...'

Mrs Boswell reached out and gently took Sister Grace's hand. 'Sister Grace,' she said candidly. 'I want you to know if you have any concerns about these girls' welfare, or for your own well-being, then you can talk to me. I am good friends with the Reverend Baxter, and my husband is an advocate of law. And I am no slouch myself, where I find an injustice.' Mrs Boswell turned the sister's hand in hers and held her gaze searchingly. 'I would so like you to trust me.'

Sister Grace tried to smile, and seemed on the point of saying something, then rather than responding she threw the door open and ushered Mrs Boswell and her daughter into the girls' dormitory, before gliding nervously back down the corridor.

*

Halfway down High Street was a narrow close between two tall tenement houses, and a rusty sign that swung above the arched entrance in the form of a key. Boswell and Johnson entered a shaded courtyard at the far end of the close and followed stone steps down to a vaulted chamber, where the smell of freshly cut timber and varnish filled the air.

Deacon Brodie was the leader, or "deacon", of a guild of skilled tradesmen, a position which also gave him a seat on the city council and plenty of prestige. He was lovingly varnishing a small casket at his workbench when the little bell attached to the door tinkled to announce the arrival of customers.

Brodie got to his feet at once. 'Gentlemen!' he said with an ingratiating smile, smoothing down his wig and extending a hand in welcome. His grip was surprisingly soft and clammy for someone whose hands were his livelihood.

'Good day to you, Deacon Brodie,' said Johnson. 'Or should I say *Sir Lluyd*?' he added with a wink.

Boswell and Johnson took a turn of the warehouse, admiring the quality of craftsmanship on display. Brodie hovered nearby, rubbing his hands obsequiously while Johnson stopped to examine a sturdy-looking cabinet, well-made with short, squat legs and a walnut finish.

'A wise choice, sir,' said Deacon Brodie. 'You will be hard pushed to find another piece its equal in all Europe.' He produced a little silver key from his sleeve and, in one fluid movement, unlocked the front panel. 'The frame is reinforced. As you can see, we have secret drawers hidden here and here, ideal for keeping valuables... or letters of a compromising nature, perhaps?' Brodie's insinuating manner was beginning to grate on Johnson's nerves.

Brodie slid open a drawer to the bottom of the cabinet that glided effortlessly on well-oiled runners. 'These drawers have a false bottom, perfect for concealing secret documents.'

'This is exactly what I am looking for,' said Johnson. 'I'll take it.'

'But I also have—'

'No,' said Johnson. 'This one's perfect.'

'Of course, sir. When do you want it for?'

'Today, if possible. We are leaving for Aberdeen this afternoon.'

'Splendid. I'll get my boys to load it onto a cart at once. And your address is...?'

'I have taken up ground floor lodgings at James Court.'

'Ah,' said Brodie, waggling his eyebrows up and down. 'Very nice.'

The cabinet was duly loaded onto a cart attached to a rather aged Clydesdale horse, who showed little interest in promptitude, or any sense of urgency at all, for that matter. Brodie's men tugged and cajoled the brute along the crowded High Street, while Johnson, Boswell and Deacon Brodie sauntered alongside, chatting amiably about nothing in particular.

When they arrived at the address, Brodie's workmen carefully lifted the cabinet and followed Johnson, Boswell and Deacon Brodie through the front door.

The Fall of the House of Thomas Weir

'Put it here please,' said Johnson, indicating an empty space in the corner.

'That will be all for now, lads,' said Brodie, once the cabinet had been slid into place. 'Wait for me in the cart.'

'Will you take a promissory note, Deacon Brodie?' said Johnson.

'That will be fine.'

'And what was the price again...?' Johnson made a point of seeming unconcerned.

'Five pounds.'

Boswell was outraged. 'Now see here, Brodie. That's not the agreed—'

Johnson raised a hand. 'Now, Mr Boswell. One cannot put a price on quality. Isn't that right, Deacon Brodie?'

'That's right, sir.'

Johnson opened his bureau drawer and rifled through a pile of documents. With one eye on his mark, Brodie took a turn of the room, pausing to examine an oil painting above the mantelpiece depicting three buxom maidens, naked as cherubs, dancing in a forest glade.

'I see you are an art lover?' said Johnson, noticing Brodie's interest.

'I'm no expert,' Brodie confessed, 'but I know a good painting when I see one.'

'Then I must commend your good taste,' said Johnson. 'That is an original Rubens.'

'And how much would you get for a thing like that?'

'I'm afraid it is not for sale, Mr Brodie. There is no price too high for such an exquisite expression of feminine beauty. But what I *can* tell you is that it was insured in London for three hundred pounds.'

Brodie's Adam's apple moved up and down his throat. '*Three hundred.... pounds?*'

'English pounds, mind! But it is a mere trifle, compared to the rest of the valuables I have in my possession. Which is why,' Johnson added, handing Brodie the newly signed note and tapping the side of his nose, 'I am very grateful to you for this very fine and ingenious piece of craftsmanship.' Johnson wandered over to caress the new cabinet with a plump hand.

'Now it is *your* taste which must be commended, Doctor Johnson.'

'Indeed, Deacon Brodie. You are an artist in wood, much in the same way that Michelangelo was an artist in marble, or Rubens a master in oil.'

A flicker of suspicion checked Brodie's expression, until vanity got the better of him and he flushed with pleasure. 'I almost forgot,' he added, taking the little key from his pocket and placing it on the mantelpiece.

Their business concluded, Brodie walked to the door and grasped the handle. 'One more thing,' he said, almost as an afterthought. 'How old is this lock?'

'I don't know. As old as the building, I suppose. Why?'

'Hmmm, I see. Anyway, I must be off. The devil makes work for idle hands, you know!'

'Woah, just hold on there!' said Johnson. 'What do you mean: "*hmmm*", you rogue?'

Brodie looked as if he were deciding whether to remain silent or not, finally deciding it better just to come out with it. 'This is a very old style of lock. A thief could easily just kick it down. Look at the rust! A house is only as strong as its weakest lock, I always say. I'll tell you what. I could add a new lock of my own—free of charge, mind!—I keep my tools of the trade in the carriage. It will only take a few minutes...'

'That is uncommonly kind of you, Sir Lluyd. Isn't it Sir Rake?'

'Yes, Sir Loin. Uncommonly kind.'

Once Brodie had fitted the new lock and taken his leave, Boswell rocked with laughter. 'Three hundred pounds indeed! That was a nice little touch.'

'I worried for a moment I had overstepped the mark. Everybody knows the original *Three Graces* hangs in the Royal Palace of Madrid, and is about twice the size. But despite Brodie's talent as a craftsman, he is a Philistine after all.'

'I can see why you don't like him. He is a singularly shifty fellow. But what led you to suspect him of the Queensberry affair?'

'Rudimentary, my dear Boswell. Even the most discreet craftsmen cannot resist leaving their mark somewhere on their work, and I found Brodie's initials carved on the underside of the cabinet in the Duke's study. Once I had eliminated the household staff as suspects, who else would have an intimate knowledge of the house, including access to the master keys?'

'It all seems rather simple, now you've explained it,' said Boswell. 'But you are taking quite a gamble, are you not? I presume that Brodie waited several months before letting himself into Queensberry House, to avoid immediate suspicion.'

'It is a gamble, yes. But this Brodie strikes me as a rather desperate character. No doubt he will gamble all his winnings at the card table tonight, and if this Lord Sinclair be the sharpster I take him for, Brodie will lose everything. It is my prediction that we can expect a visit from our friend the Deacon tonight; tomorrow, at the latest. I have placed a very juicy worm on the end of my hook, and I'll be damned if our *Debonaire Cod* doesn't mean to swallow it hook, line and sinker.'

Debonaire Cod was an anagram of "Deacon Brodie", a sally of wit of which Doctor Johnson was excessively proud.

'Well, Doctor,' said Boswell. 'My faith in you has never been proven misguided in the past. You understand human nature better than any man I know. How do you intend to proceed?'

'We will make a great show of departing this afternoon and ride for the city walls, returning under the cover of darkness. I will enter the apartment via the rear door and lay in waiting, while you establish yourself outside the Isle of Man Arms and follow our friend wherever he goes.'

'Simplicity itself,' replied Boswell, beaming with satisfaction. 'What could possibly go wrong?'

*

'A moment of your time, ma'am?'

Maggie Boswell and her daughter were sitting on a dormitory bed, surrounded by a gaggle of excited girls, each with a piece of homemade shortbread in her hand, listening and watching with wide-eyed wonder as Mrs Boswell read to them from a beautifully illustrated book of fairy tales. Sister Grace, silhouetted in the doorway, was nervously fidgeting with the rosary around her waist.

'Of course, Sister.' said Mrs Boswell. 'What is it?'

'Alone please, if you don't mind.'

'Very well,' said Mrs Boswell, closing the book and getting to her feet. The girls let out a groan of disappointment. 'Veronica,' Mrs Boswell called over her shoulder. 'You stay here. I'll only be gone a minute.'

Sister Grace, who had evidently resolved to trust Mrs Boswell, led her up a narrow flight of stairs and into the eaves of the building.

Mrs Boswell looked around with undisguised curiosity. She found attic rooms quite the most interesting part of any house. They reminded her of jumble sales. Here amidst the detritus of folks' lives might be found a rare antique, a beloved doll whose owner had long since passed away or a threadbare wedding dress; perhaps a collection of love letters, a last will and testament or envelope full of cash; even a hidden child or two, if the romance novels were to be believed, the illegitimate heir to a stolen fortune, a cripple or a mental defective, a deformed monster...

If ghosts existed, then surely they would congregate here, amidst the cobwebs, covered antiques, dolls and rocking chairs of the attic.

Motes of dust, briefly illuminated in the light streaming through the window, drifted into obscurity like snowflakes on water. The room smelled vaguely of the same nostalgic mustiness typical of all attics, with piles of junk shored up against the eaves. Sister Grace locked the door behind her and rummaged through a box of yellowed papers to retrieve a stack of letters. She spoke in a nervous whisper as she passed the pile to Mrs Boswell. 'These are letters we've received over the years from the girls who left us.'

Mrs Boswell selected one at random and began to read. It was signed three years ago by a girl called Abigail, full of praise for her new home, gushing with details about day trips to the beach, silk dresses, a bedroom all to herself with her own dressing table, and a rich man she called "Papa".

'It sounds almost too good to be true,' said Mrs Boswell, passing the letters back to Sister Grace.

'That's just it,' said Sister Grace. 'Now look at this one.'

Mrs Boswell scanned the second letter. 'It's similar in tone to the first,' she said. 'Identical, almost. And the handwriting is the same.'

'This letter is signed by Susan, a little girl who left us last autumn. Only I *know* Susan's handwriting, and that isn't hers.'

'Well maybe she got someone else to write it for her?'

'Susan loved reading and writing. It's not like her to ask for help with anything. It doesn't even sound like her. She was a quiet girl who would hide away in some corner with a book. She wasn't interested in new clothes or ponies, like the girl in the letter.'

Mrs Boswell flicked through letters dating all the way back to 1764. Each one was written in the same distinctive, slanting hand. 'What are you suggesting, Sister Grace?'

'I hardly know what to think,' admitted the nervous young woman. 'All I know is this letter is not from Susan.'

Chapter 8

The Prisoner in the Vaults

Electorate of Bavaria, 1764

Brother Eltanin,

All preparations have been made... nothing has been left to chance... we can anticipate the Ritual to take place on Midsummer's Eve, in a secure location where there will be no bothersome interferences. My only reservations now lie with Brother Rastaban, whose heart, I suspect, is no longer invested in our exalted project. He still has a hankering for the Christian God, and his squeamish intractability in this matter may hamper our efforts, if not sabotage them from the very outset.

You will travel to England immediately to sound out our friend, and if you feel he is not up to the task at hand, to bring about his expulsion from our order. I leave it to your discretion to dispose of him as you may, and select a more suitable candidate from among the ranks.

I eagerly await your response,

Brother Thuban

Alpha Draconis

The Fall of the House of Thomas Weir

The President of the orphanage was sitting across from Maggie Boswell with a pile of letters on the desk between them.

'Mrs Boswell. What you have just said sounds incredible. And you say that these letters are forgeries? You do realise that you are making a serious allegation?'

'I did not say they were forgeries, Sir William. But Sister Grace—'

'Sister Grace, let me remind you, has barely been with us a year.'

'I see. And her predecessor?'

'Sister Janet brought the girls to their new homes, and never once made any suggestion of forged letters.'

'But surely it would do no harm to check these addresses?'

'Sister Daphne personally visits each girl to check on her progress. Surely, if there were something untoward going on, she would have taken it to me, as President of the orphanage.'

'Sir William. Far be it from me to carry tales about any member of your staff. But Sister Grace seems terrified of her superior.'

Sir William nodded sympathetically. 'She can be rather... intimidating, wouldn't you say?' He was sitting back with his fingertips resting together to form a steeple, when suddenly he sat up in his chair. 'Mrs Boswell. Thank you for bringing this to my attention.'

'And you are going to do something about it?'

'I see no harm in personally visiting some of the host families, if only to put your mind at rest.'

'Thank you, Sir William. And now I really must go. Veronica will be wondering where I am.'

'Ah yes, Veronica... But stay a while, please, Mrs Boswell. It isn't often I receive visitors. Won't you have a drink?' Sir William reached for the cabinet behind his desk.

'Oh no, Sir William, I really mustn't—'

'Oh, come, Mrs Boswell. One glass of sherry won't kill you?'

She gave in for politeness' sake. Sir William poured two glasses from a crystal decanter and slid one across the table.

As Mrs Boswell sipped her drink, Sir William leaned forward, a strangely expectant smile touching the corners of his mouth. The liquor was strong with a bittersweet aftertaste. The early evening sun streamed in through the window, obscuring his face in shadow, but for one woozy moment Mrs Boswell could have sworn...

The vision passed, and Sir William—Lord Sinclair—was himself once more. With a shrug, she drained her glass.

*

Johnson peered through the gap in the curtains, then snapped them shut. He had to be careful. The apartment was supposed to be unoccupied, and the slightest movement might betray his presence to anyone watching from outside. The trap was set; all he had to do was wait. Like a bear grown fat in captivity he paced back and forth, obsessively counting his steps from the mantelpiece to the window and back again.

Just one of many superstitious habits he had contracted early in life: if his left foot did not reach the window within an allotted number of steps he would walk back to his original position and start again on the other foot. His dear departed Tetty had been a stabilising influence, but ever since his wife's passing Johnson's obsessive tics and habits had returned with a vengeance.

Hang it all, he thought as he peeked again through the curtain, then checked his pistols for the umpteenth time. *This will never do.* He chose a book at random from the bookcase, a dull history of the Reformation, then sank down on the settee to peruse its contents. He must have nodded off, for it was nearly midnight when he woke to the sound of a key being turned in the lock. Jumping to his feet, Johnson grabbed his weapon and concealed himself behind the drapes.

The intruder wore a hooded cassock of sackcloth; a parody of those monks who mortify their flesh as penance. Johnson tried to steady his breath, clutching the pistol to his breast as his lips moved in silent prayer. As the figure passed the window Johnson could detect the sickly-sweet odour of decay. Now was the time. He stepped out from his hiding place and raised the weapon. The intruder turned; when its eyes met Johnson's, the pistol fell clattering to the floor.

*

Boswell reached for a flask in his pocket and took another sip of whisky. He had chosen a flight of stairs on a side street just across from the inn, where he could observe the patrons come and go while remaining himself hidden in the shadows. He would be in for a long night. The rain was coming down in sheets, and the damp close provided little in the way of shelter. Boswell drained the last dregs of whisky, and heaved a sigh.

From his hiding-place, he caught snatches of random conversation from passers-by...*drunk as a lord he was, fell into the Nor Loch...didn't find his body for three days...all swollen...stole everything, so they did, from the forks to the candlesticks... never seen such a thing... like a walking corpse it was...said it was the Mad Earl come back for revenge...as dead as a doornail...rats had been at her...something else...a dog, maybe...*

At around midnight Brodie emerged, staggering and cursing his way up the close. Boswell stalked his quarry from a safe distance, following him onto Fleshmarket Row, losing him and finding him again as they bobbed and weaved their way among the lost souls of the smoke-filled Edinburgh night.

Brodie turned the corner onto Bridge Street and disappeared into a notoriously disreputable inn. '*Hullo,*' murmured Boswell, pressing his back against the wall in a vain attempt to conceal himself. 'What business does our "outstanding pillar of society" have with a place like this?'

One hour later, Brodie re-emerged, arm in arm with a second gentleman, singing and laughing as they passed a bottle between them. The second man was well-fed and elegantly dressed in an embroidered waistcoat, silk hose and silver buckles on his shoes, a moon face beneath an extravagantly powdered wig that nodded back and forth as he walked, threatening to topple at any moment. Boswell followed the two men as they navigated the maze of the Fleshmarket, negotiating their way past drunkards, vagabonds, pimps and streetwalkers until they came to a quiet district in the lowest part of Old Town on the banks of the Nor Loch. Brodie stopped before a dark close. His companion seemed to be having second thoughts and turned to leave. Brodie caught him by the arm and shoved him forwards. Carried by the momentum of the shove, the second man staggered into the close.

Boswell turned his collar up to his neck, pulled his cocked hat forward, stuffed his hands deep in his pockets and walked past Brodie for a discreet look into the close. The fat man was kneeling before a third figure, who remained hidden in the shadows.

As Boswell strained his eyes to see, he was struck from behind with a blunt, heavy object. He tried to turn, only for the earth to sway, then come rushing headlong to meet him.

*

After the initial shock had worn off, Johnson studied the creature before him with a detached, professional curiosity. Where its nose had been eaten away, only two snuffling holes remained. The lips were gone, giving the creature a malignant, unsettling grin of teeth filed to sharp points. The eyes were coated in a film of yellowish-white viscosity, with grey, parchment-like skin stretched too tightly over the ruin of a face. A broad hood was employed to disguise its abhorrent features, though the smell of death and rotten flesh was enough to scare anyone off.

The intruder reached out a desiccated hand, seized Johnson by the neck, and began to squeeze. The shock of having his airways constricted spurned Johnson to action. He tried to prise the fingers from his throat, but it was an unequal match. He might as well have tried to prise a tree from the ground by its roots. Forced backwards over the cabinet, Johnson was fading fast. How easy it would be, he thought, just to slip away, away from that horror of a face, away from the pain, and into the arms of oblivion.

Another, more forceful part of Johnson's psyche now asserted itself: the part of him that wanted to live. He reached back, feeling across the top of the cabinet until his fingers found the marble bust.

It had been a present from Boswell; a joke, really. Voltaire was an atheist, the very antithesis of Doctor Johnson. The bust was smallish, not much bigger than a fist. Johnson's fingers curled around it. The intruder strengthened its grip and pulled its head up close to his. That horrifying face was pressed to his own in a kiss of death. He could smell the rank, fetid breath. Before Johnson's consciousness ebbed away, he summoned his every last ounce of strength and swung the bust in a huge arc, striking the intruder full force across the side of the head. As it staggered back Johnson struck again. And again. Blood splattered the walls. *It bleeds*, he thought exultantly. The creature collapsed with the side of its head caved in. Johnson looked at the murder weapon, his knuckles dripping with gore. Ironic, he thought grimly, that his intellectual nemesis should be the instrument of divine providence that preserved his life. With that thought he doubled over and vomited, gasping and choking for breath.

Johnson's travails were far from over. A second hooded figure flew in through the door and launched itself at the unhappy man. Johnson had no fight left in him. This second intruder placed its thumbs over his eyes and pressed. Bolts of pain shot from Johnson's eyes to the centre of his brain. Pain blocked everything; thought, willpower, reason, and he found himself praying for a quick and easy end.

Then, just as death seemed like an increasingly enviable prospect, a sudden rush of air parted his wig. All at once the pressure was gone from Johnson's eyes, and a great weight lifted from his chest.

Like a cat correcting itself, the intruder flipped onto its haunches and hissed at the two soldiers standing slack-jawed with disbelief in the doorway. With one great bound it crashed through the window and onto the street, leaving a thick trail of blood as it fled. Passers-by screamed in horror as the thing loped towards the nearest close and disappeared.

Johnson looked up at the two soldiers in the doorway with smoking rifles clutched in their still trembling hands. 'What kept you?' he gasped.

*

'Halloooo? *Halloooo!?*'

Boswell awoke to darkness, and someone yelling in his ear.

He was in an uncomfortable sitting position with his hands tied behind his back. His ankles were bound. It was cold, dark, wet, and his hair was matted with something warm and sticky.

It was not, it was safe to say, how he usually chose to spend his Saturday nights.

Hallloooo?

Slowly, painfully, Boswell turned his head. It was the fat man from earlier that evening, the foppish one who had accompanied Brodie from the bar to the alleyway.

'Pipe down, will you?' Boswell groaned. 'I feel like the Royal Scots Greys have been riding through my head. How long have we been shackled here?' The binding around Boswell's ankle bit into the flesh, causing it to throb painfully.

'Who knows?' said the fat man. 'That blackguard took my fob watch. Two, maybe three hours? What does it matter? We're going to die here! Help! *Help!*'

'*Stop it!*' hissed Boswell through gritted teeth. 'You aren't helping matters by wailing like a damned baby.'

The fat man gave Boswell a despondent look of dismay mingled with despair, then regained his composure. 'You are right, of course... I'm sorry...'

'Now let me think,' said Boswell. He could remember only fragmented images: the rain, the cold steps, the warmth of the whisky, the leering face of Deacon Brodie emerging through the rain; then as if from a dream came the fat man, the alleyway, and the hooded figure from the shadows. Boswell looked suspiciously at his cellmate. 'What were you doing with Deacon Brodie?'

'What was I...?' the fat man spluttered defensively. 'I was...he was... Now listen, what makes you think I was with Bro... with that man?'

From the corner of his eye Boswell could see the man puffing up with self-righteous indignation, the sure sign of a liar. 'Because I followed you from the tavern,' he said with a weary sigh. 'I saw everything.'

The fat man seemed to deflate. 'I was going to meet a lady, if you must know. Brodie told me he knew where I could meet the finest fillies in all of Edinburgh. Discreet, too. And why shouldn't I? I'm a red-blooded man, after all. My wife doesn't fully understand my n—'

'I don't give a damn about your wife, or your bloody tarts,' snarled Boswell. 'What happened next?'

'He threw me down a close, told me to pay the man there half a crown. He... I... *Oh... Oh God! That face! Oh God Oh God Oh God....*'

'*Quiet!*' hissed Boswell. The fat man bit his lip, emitting gentle, hiccupping sobs, like a chastised child in the throes of self-pity.

'Quiet, damn you!' hissed Boswell. 'I'm trying to listen.' Boswell thought he could hear movement overhead and strained to listen. A big plop of freezing water rolled down the back of his neck. Sure enough, he could sense the faint trundle of carriage wheels, and the vague suggestion of a brickwork arch high above. 'Of course!' he cried. 'We must be in a vault under the High Street. Listen, can you hear?'

'What of it?' whined the fat man. 'We're going to die here, whether we're under a road, or St. Paul's bloody Cathedral.' He started to sob again, until Boswell wished he were free just so he could beat the wretch to a bloody pulp.

He decided to try a different tack. 'Look,' Boswell said, 'what's your name?'

This new kindness in Boswell's voice seemed to have a calming effect on the man, and he stopped sobbing long enough to speak. 'S-Simon. Simon Carruthers.'

'Listen, Carruthers. My name is James Boswell. I have friends in very high places who may be able to help us. Have you heard of Doctor Johnson?'

Carruthers' ears pricked up. 'The Dictionary Johnson? Clever chap, they say. What about it?'

'Clever? Only the greatest mind in all of England. He is a good friend of mine, and he will be looking for me right now. D'ye hear?'

Carruthers tried to stop his teeth from chattering. 'Y…yes.'

'Carruthers, can you move?'

There was a noisy rattle of chains. 'No,' came the defeated reply.

'How are you tied?'

'My hands are bound with something. Twine, I think. And my ankles are chained together good and proper.'

Boswell's chin slumped onto his chest. It was the same with him. But he was not to be deterred. 'What are you sitting on?'

'Rubble, I think.'

'Feel around with your feet a bit. Are there any boulders? Rough ones, preferably.'

Boswell heard a clink of chains, a scurrying scraping sound, and then, 'Yes, I think so. Just at the end of my reach.'

'How big is it?'

'I think I can get it with my heels. Wait there.'

'Good stuff, Carruthers!'

'Right, I'm holding something with my feet, but I can't get it towards my hands. I'm going to try to throw it your way.'

'Right Carruthers. Careful now, this could be our only chance…'

Carruthers gave a heave, and something landed on Boswell's lap.

He looked down and gave an agonised groan.

The whiteness of the skull told Boswell it had only recently been stripped of flesh and sinew. In places, dried flakes of skin remained. Shallow grooves and scratches on the scalp suggested someone had been at it with a sharp implement, scraping away at the flesh with a knife or a piece of flint.

'Did you get it? What is it?' said Carruthers excitedly.

'It doesn't matter,' said Boswell, his heart sinking through levels of horror he didn't realise existed. His voice sounded strange to himself; detached and far away. 'It doesn't matter...'

*

Doctor Johnson found himself surrounded by pale faces and muffled voices: the two dragoons who had rescued him in the nick of time, a magistrate whose job it was to contain the situation, and a few important-looking gentlemen he had never seen before. 'Stand back,' the magistrate told the others. 'Let him have air.'

Johnson grabbed instinctively for his neck and groaned as memory came flooding back.

His head pounded miserably, and every rib in his body sang with pain. Lord Chalmers the magistrate, a man almost as big as Johnson in height and girth, helped the Doctor to his feet, and supported him as he hobbled to a chair. Johnson looked gratefully at the high-ranking official. He had a kind face, with the red nose of a habitual claret drinker.

'You there,' said Chalmers to one of the constables. 'Bring this man some water. And for pity's sake find a doctor.'

Fifteen minutes later, a local physician was admitted from among the crowd gathering outside. With impressive efficiency he tended to Johnson's wound, binding his ribs and administering laudanum for the pain. 'You've had a nasty shock,' he told Johnson. 'You also have two cracked ribs and some bruising, and you'll have a headache and a pair of black eyes for a few days, but otherwise, you'll live.'

'Thank you. Doctor...?'

'Grant.'

A fine mist of rain blew in through the broken window and settled like dew on the bludgeoned corpse in the middle of the floor. Johnson felt a shiver course through his body. *Somebody walking over his grave*, his mother used to say.

Two extra men had been posted outside to block the entrance from curious passers-by. Rumours were flying about walking corpses, and the last thing the authorities needed was a riot on their hands.

Johnson winced as he turned to face Lord Chalmers. 'Where is Mr Boswell?'

'No sign I'm afraid.'

Doctor Johnson nodded grimly as he buttoned up his shirt. He motioned towards the corpse and asked the two soldiers to lay it out on the table, then rose to his feet using the back of the chair to steady himself. He turned to Grant. 'Have you ever seen anything like this before, Doctor Grant?'

Grant leaned over the body. 'The flesh shows signs of necrotic degeneration, and yet the general nervous system and musculature seem intact.' He lifted an arm and let it drop back onto the table. 'He could almost be a healthy specimen, apart from the disfigurement.'

'So what is it, in your opinion, Doctor?'

'Beyond my level of expertise, I'm afraid.' Grant moved across the room to the bureau, hastily scribbled something on a piece of paper, then crossed over to the broken window and peered outside. 'You boy!' he cried to a face in the crowd. A little boy stepped out from the row of curious observers.

'Do you know the Royal College of Physicians on Fountain Close?'

'Aye, sir.'

'Good lad. Here's sixpence.' The doctor wrapped a coin in the note and tossed it through the broken window. 'Go there and ask for Sir Joshua Hunter. Show him this note. Tell him Grant of Corstorphine sent you. If you're back within the hour, there's another sixpence in it for you.'

'Jo-shoo-ah Hunter. Righto, sir!'

The Fall of the House of Thomas Weir

Fifty minutes later, the boy returned to claim his prize. The constables admitted a tall, slightly stooped gentleman carrying a leather bag. Johnson recognised him at once as a Knight of the Cape. Sir Bones, they had called him. He had obviously dressed in a hurry, with his collar unbuttoned and his dark grey wig unevenly powdered, traces of it dusting his shoulders.

'Doctor Hunter,' said Grant. 'Thank you for coming at such short notice.'

'Doctor Grant,' said Hunter, nodding with professional courtesy. 'Where is the patient?'

'I'm afraid it's a bit late for that,' said Grant, pulling back the sheet to reveal the grotesquely disfigured corpse stretched out on the table.

'A leper, eh?' said Doctor Hunter with a cursory glance at the body.

At the mention of leprosy, every man in the room except for Johnson and Grant took a step back.

'You surprise me, Doctor,' said Grant. 'This body shows none of the tell-tale signs of internal tissue corruption.'

'Nevertheless, the outward lesions bear all the hallmarks of an advanced stage of leprosy,' said Hunter, approaching the body. Though his figure was ungainly and his angular limbs curiously uncoordinated, Doctor Hunter evidently took some pride in his hands, which were immaculately clean with neatly clipped fingernails. They were the hands of an artist, decided Johnson, the long white fingers poised elegantly over the body like a harpsichordist about to play a technical piece by Bach. 'Though I must confess,' added Hunter, 'I have never seen anything quite like it. This man was in the prime of his life. Just look at those shoulders! I would need to take the body back to my laboratory for further tests, of course.'

'Yes of course, Doctor Hunter,' said the magistrate.

The two soldiers wrapped the body in its sheet and carried it outside. The crowd swarmed round, trying to catch a glimpse as the men placed the body in the back of a cart. Hunter jumped up alongside, eager to dissect his new toy from the comfort of his laboratory.

Doctor Grant turned to Johnson and extended his hand. 'Well sir, I have patients to attend to. Please don't exert yourself unduly, and take a little laudanum if the pain gets too bad.'

Johnson pressed the doctor's hand. 'Thank you, sir. Your assistance in this matter has been invaluable.'

'Yes. Well, don't hesitate to call if you need anything else.'

After Grant and the others had left, Johnson approached the two dragoons posted outside his door. 'Gentlemen,' he said, 'I seem to have misplaced a Mr Boswell, and I have no wish to concern Mrs Boswell unduly on her return.'

Relieved to have something useful to do, the two dragoons clattered off down High Street to search for the missing man. Johnson climbed into bed fully clothed, and was asleep before his head hit the pillow.

Chapter 9

As Above, So Below

Electorate of Bavaria, 1764

Most Esteemed Colleagues,

In Rastaban we have lost a capable Beta, who with his penetrating mind and great wisdom might have proved an invaluable ally in the struggle to come. Alas! his paltry Christian scruples have made him an enemy of our Order, and the Great Work must now be completed without his guiding influence.

Already have I chosen a suitable replacement from among the ranks of the Masonic Brotherhood, a worthy Knight who shall henceforth be referred to as Brother Athebyne. With this addition we are five once more, and, with the circle complete, the other elements will invariably fall into place.

The sacrifice must be a chaste virgin, preferably a child of Nordic extraction. The location of the Ritual will be disclosed in due course. Let us prepare with due diligence through meditation and fasting, that our bodies may be ready to receive the Dark Gift.

Gentlemen, let us not flinch in our resolve, nor be distracted by foolish notions of morality. The Son of Man, that false redeemer, has had his day and has failed. We must now give our allegiance to a greater power; a power which will deliver us not to some intangible future glory, but to paradise here on earth!

And so, my brothers, let us rise up as one with a noble fire in our veins, and be the first to usher in this new age of Kali Yuga!

I remain, your servant &c.

Brother Thuban

Alpha Draconis.

Sister Grace nervously straightened her habit, then rapped firmly on the door to Sister Daphne's office. 'You may enter,' came the imperious reply.

Grace opened the door to find Sister Daphne sharing a glass of sherry with her superior, Sir William. She had obviously been laughing at some shared joke, her face flushed with pleasure. 'Well?' she said, as if irritated by this intrusion on an otherwise pleasurable evening.

Sister Grace cleared her throat to address her superior. 'It's Mrs Boswell, ma'am. She came to speak to Sir William this afternoon, begging your pardon sir, but I haven't seen her since. That was six hours ago now. Poor little Veronica is beside herself.'

Sir William listened to Sister Grace's concerns with puzzlement etched on his face. When she had finished, he merely said, 'Mrs Boswell? Who is that?'

'Mrs Boswell, Sir William. She arrived here this afternoon with gifts for the girls.'

Sir William shook his head and released his breath through pursed lips. 'I have no recollection of a Mrs Boswell stopping here. Do you, Sister Daphne?'

'No, Sir William,' smirked the Mother Superior.

Sister Grace could only gape in amazement. 'But... She...'

'Sister Grace,' said Sir William. 'Are you sure you are feeling quite yourself?'

The Fall of the House of Thomas Weir

'Perhaps she has been at the sherry again, Sir William,' suggested Sister Daphne, which prompted snorts of laughter from both of them. Sister Grace could only continue to gape slack-jawed with confusion. Suddenly the mirth left Sir William's face; he consulted his pocket watch. 'Sister Grace, you may not have noticed, but I am a busy man with people to meet and appointments to keep. You will help Sister Daphne to assemble the girls for selection at once.'

'But Sir William,' Grace tried again. 'You must rem—'

'That will be all, Sister Grace!' snapped Sir William.

Her head bowed, Sister Grace followed the huge form of the Mother Superior down the corridor, a sinking feeling of horror in her heart. When they reached the girls' dormitory, Sister Daphne flung open the door and placed her hands on her hips. The girls inside were all gathered round the Boswell girl, comforting her and stroking her hair. Veronica looked up, her cheeks stained with tears.

One little girl, a bold redhead called Rachel, was fervently grasping Veronica's pale hand. She looked up defiantly at the looming figure of the Mother Superior and scowled, undaunted. 'Where is Veronica's mummy?' she said, then pursed her little lips.

Sister Daphne inclined her head to look at Veronica like a monitor lizard contemplating a fly, then slowly, mechanically, a look of benevolence softened her features. 'Poor little Veronica,' she said in a singsong voice. 'Where do you think your mummy has gone? Why do you think she brought you here? She has flown away, my little starling. She doesn't want you anymore. Nor does your father. You are an orphan now, just like all the other little girls.'

Veronica cast a defiant look at the Mother Superior, then her bottom lip began to tremble and she burst into tears, burying her head in her hands.

'There there,' said the Mother Superior, taking a step forward. 'Don't cry dear! Perhaps Sir William will choose you, and you can have a new family! Maybe even a richer family than your old one!'

'I d...d...don't w...w...want a new family!' Veronica wailed.

'You're a liar!' cried Rachel, and she charged at the Mother Superior, launching a kick at her shin. Sister Daphne picked the girl up by the scruff of the neck, her little legs still kicking, and tossed her across the room with a grimace of distaste. She rushed forward with her cane raised, ready to strike. Sister Grace was on her immediately, wrestling for the cane. 'Sister Daphne!' she cried. 'What are you doing!'

Sister Daphne spun round and struck Sister Grace so hard across the face one of her teeth flew out. Several of the girls began to cry. 'Now enough silliness, girls,' said Sister Daphne, straightening her habit as if nothing were amiss. 'Wash your faces. We don't want to keep Sir William waiting, do we?'

*

James Boswell sat with a broken jawbone clamped between his boot heels, working away with furious concentration on the binding to his wrists. It was a near impossible task in the dark to see what he was doing, and after a while his wrists began to burn without troubling his bindings in the slightest.

'Give over, won't you?' said Carruthers. 'You're never going to cut through that rope.'

'You're right,' said Boswell, conceding defeat. With a grimace of disgust he kicked the bone as far from him as he could, then turned to Carruthers with barely concealed ill-humour. 'Listen, what are you doing here anyway, Carruthers?'

'If you can think of somewhere else I should be,' said Carruthers drolly, 'then by all means call me a carriage.'

'I didn't mean *here*. I mean, you seem like a decent sort of chap. Don't you have a family at home?'

'Ah, yes, but one does get intolerably lonely on the road. I am a traveling salesman, you see, and in a moment of weakness I... I...' Carruthers clenched his fists as the tears sprang from his eyes. 'But I swear, if ever I get out of this place, I will fall down at my dear

Florence's feet and *beg* her forgiveness. I-'

'Shhh,' hissed Boswell. 'I think someone's coming.'

Chains rattled and a set of wooden doors swung open, and the two prisoners peered blinking into the pale morning light.

'*Stand uck,*' said the creature standing in the vault entrance. He stood at around six foot three in a rough monk's cowl of sackcloth, with a cudgel attached to the belt around his waist. Not a man to argue with, in other words. As Carruthers and Boswell staggered to their feet, the figure came forward and bent to unshackle their legs.

'Water,' gasped Boswell.

'*You see the nassssster, then we will drink and eat all. Oh yessss. Cun.*'

The vault opened onto a cobbled backstreet in the shadow of High Street. Trembling with fatigue and hunger, they followed the hooded figure across the shaded tenement alley to stop before a wooden coal hatch. The revenant stooped to open the padlock with a rusty key he took from his pocket. Boswell glanced up the empty street towards the busy Cowgate, which seemed both tantalisingly near and hopelessly far, and played his last, desperate card.

*

Eight storeys up, Mrs Irene Miller of 5 Niddry Street and Mrs Brenda Cunningham of 8 Niddry Street sat by their scullery windows, elbows resting on sills. It was their favourite part of the day. With kitchens facing one another from opposite sides of the street, such was the narrowness of the passage at that height that they could almost shake hands, had they been so inclined. Yet these two women were by no stretch of the imagination friends.

Their long-suffering menfolk Mr Forbes Cunningham, an undertaker by trade, and Mr George Miller, the tobacconist, were boon companions who liked nothing better than to share a tot of rum of an evening in the Jolly Judge, and sometimes more than a tot, while their little ones played on the cobbled streets outside.

With both families anticipating the forthcoming nuptials of their eldest two—Billy Miller and Nell Cunningham—the proud fathers had plenty to celebrate.

Unfortunately none of this mattered to their warring wives, who had nurtured in their hearts an enduring and bitter rivalry for most of their adult lives. Nobody could remember how it had started, least of all these two beldames, but the simple truth was that their mutual animosity had sustained them through multiple childbirths, harsh winters and deathly poverty, and they wouldn't have missed their daily altercations for the world.

Each morning at precisely six o'clock the two women leaned out of their windows to scowl at one another and heave accusations back and forth across No Man's Land.

'…Your George was out to all hours last night. Probably got a fancy woman shacked up somewhere…'

'…Is that right? You're just jealous you can't get that lazy good-for-nothing bessom of yours to leave the house….'

'…Was that your wee Alastair I saw doin' the goat's jig wi' thon wee wagtail Mary Docherty up the close last night? Goin' at it like a pair o' oxen they were…'

'…At least he has wick in his candle, unlike your James…' and so on *ad nauseam*, until some long-suffering neighbour fresh off the nightshift would yell up, at which point both women would unite in their opprobrium, using language to make a dockside tough blush.

That morning, however, there was a temporary armistice as the two women bore witness to a curious scene unfolding on the street below. A well-dressed young man in his mid-thirties, his fine clothes spoiled—presumably from a night on the tiles—was tearing down Niddry Street, bellowing from the top of his lungs. Hot on his heels was a tall figure clad in what appeared to be a monk's cassock and hood. The former had just reached the busy intersection at Cowgate and freedom when his pursuer seized him by the scruff of the neck, hauled him back down the street and bundled him into a coal cellar. This dramatic scene lasted all of five minutes. Mrs Miller and Mrs Cunningham looked at one another, shrugged their shoulders, and resumed hostilities.

*

The narrow staircase descended steeply into darkness. The prisoners were pushed downwards for an interminable length of time, harried and confused, until at last they reached level ground. With the hooded stranger driving them onwards, they moved along a tunnel far beneath the city streets, the claustrophobic atmosphere of the passage heightened by the almost complete lack of light.

Suddenly the ceiling disappeared, and Boswell and Carruthers looked up to see grey daylight through a grate maybe fifty feet above their heads, with rainwater splashing down.

Their captor lifted his hood to let the water splash onto his ruin of a face.

Perceiving Boswell's disgust, the revenant slowly turned its head and fixed the prisoners with a hideous, lipless grin. With a gasp of horror, Carruthers fainted dead away.

'*Kick hin uck,*' rasped the revenant like a poorly trained ventriloquist.

Boswell reached down and helped Carruthers to his feet.

'*Drink,*' said the revenant, and stood back. The two men dutifully placed themselves under the grille, letting the rainwater splash over their faces.

Their captor reached into a pocket and withdrew a handful of broken biscuits. '*Eat.*'

The biscuits were dry and tasteless, but Boswell and Carruthers made them disappear in seconds. Whatever was in those dry biscuits, they provided the prisoners with enough energy to go on.

They laboured for perhaps a quarter of a mile through a channel of rock so narrow Boswell could touch both sides with his hands, until with one final shove they reached their destination.

All the dark crafts of Bruegel or Hieronymus Bosch, even in

their most fevered states of demented inspiration, could not render half so effectively the scene of horror that confronted them. If there was a Hell, thought Boswell, then surely they had arrived.

In some ways it resembled a normal street scene, tenement buildings leaning together like drunks for support, smooth black cobblestones underfoot. Light was supplied not from the sun, but from flickering torches affixed to the walls. The air was thick and stuffy, and yet there must have been oxygen coming from somewhere or the torches would have failed. High above their heads, where there should have been a blue strip of sky by day and the starry firmament by night, there stretched a high-vaulted canopy of soot-black brick. It was a hideous inversion of the world above. People of sorts could be seen peering from windows, sitting on street corners or going about their day-to-day business, but with a marked difference. Some bore only a vague suggestion of death: a grey pallor, a face covered in welts and boils, a malodorous presence. Others were in an advanced state of decomposition, with rotting flesh and missing noses, ears, lips, fingers and other extremities. All had that same milky-white viscosity covering their eyes, and yet from the way they moved it appeared that their infirmities or lack of vision little affected their perceptions.

As the two men were led down the street, passers-by paid them scant attention, except to regard them with a kind of cold curiosity. Boswell staggered on, numb with shock, while Carruthers whimpered to himself like a tired and frightened child. At the end of the gloomy street they came to a subterranean crossroads, a cobbled square where four ways met. In the middle of this square was a well, in front of which stood a stone pillar, square shaped at the bottom and tapering slightly towards the top, a brass crucible, and a stone altar upon which various items of occult paraphernalia; a gold chalice, a black candle and a silver dagger had been placed. The two men were strapped tightly to the pillar, back to back, drawing a curious crowd. Some revenants approached to pinch an arm or a thigh, and Boswell was reminded for one horrible moment of a cattle market. The children crowded round to complete the nightmare, their disfigured little faces peering up at them with open curiosity.

Boswell glared at their ugly faces and started to laugh: a high-pitched, fevered and hysterical laughter that frightened even himself.

*

Doctor Johnson rose early and climbed the stair to see if Boswell had returned. He had not. Not even Boswell's loyal manservant, Joseph, was there to greet him. The place seemed devoid of life without the Boswells' cheerful influence, and Johnson almost felt like an intruder in the deserted apartment.

He had just thrown some bacon on the stove when there was a knock at the door. The two dragoons from the previous night had returned, though regrettably with no news of Boswell.

'I am sure you did everything in your power,' said Johnson with a sigh. 'You must be hungry. Come in.'

'Much obliged to you, sir,' said the larger of the two, removing his bearskin hat and stepping inside.

As the men took their places at table, Johnson threw some more bacon onto the griddle and served it with a warm loaf of bread and a generous pat of butter. The two men enjoyed their unexpected feast while Johnson questioned them on various subjects, always courteously, inquiring after their health and that of their families, slyly consulting them on practical matters, which flattered the soldiers' opinion of themselves and raised their host even higher in their estimation.

The first, a strapping red-headed Highlander named James Douglas, had a gentle nature despite—or perhaps because of—his powerful frame, whereas the second, a slight, narrow-shouldered Lowlander with quick, darting eyes, Hector Gillies, was considered the finest shot in his regiment.

After securing their promise to keep a lookout for Boswell,

Johnson took leave of his new friends on the street outside, then hastened down High Street to Fountain Close, where the Royal Society of Physicians kept their headquarters.

The secretary who took his name led a breathless Doctor Johnson into an oak-panelled lecturing theatre. Light streamed in through a glass cupola overhead, illuminating the stage, where a solitary figure was hunched over a microscope.

The corpse was spread out on a table beside the man with the microscope, covered in a blood-stained sheet. As Johnson approached the dais, he had the eerie feeling the body would move, sliding away the sheet to reveal that terrible face from the night before.

Hunter looked up from his work. From his bedraggled, unshaven appearance, Johnson could see he hadn't slept. Despite his exhaustion, he was visibly excited by something.

'Ah, Doctor Johnson. I really must thank you for providing me with this remarkable specimen. Take a look.' He gestured towards the microscope, an elegant piece of equipment with a brass body and solid mahogany base. Johnson peered through the eyepiece onto an alien world, where countless little sausage-shaped particles swarmed and multiplied before his eye.

'Incredible. What is it I am looking at, Doctor Hunter?'

'Leeuwenhook's wee beasties, Doctor. Gigelorum. Or to use a more scientific term, *animalcules:* organisms small enough to inhabit the ear of a mite. The animalcule which causes leprosy is parasitic, ultimately resulting in the disintegration of the human body. But in the case of our friend here, the invading parasite has transformed into something quite extraordinary. Both parasite and host appear to exist in a mutually beneficial, symbiotic relationship. The subject's lungs were intact at the time of death, with no indication of the complications common to leprosy such as joint weakness or paralysis.'

'Fascinating,' said Johnson, looking at the organisms swarming before his eye with fresh wonder. 'But what about the corruption of the flesh? Surely you don't mean to say that thing on the table is healthy?'

'Well, it's not pretty, that's for sure. But from a biological perspective he's perfectly suited to his environment.' Doctor Hunter walked over to the corpse and flung off the sheet. 'A common misconception is that leprosy *causes* the body to decay, but that is most emphatically not the case. Leprosy kills the nerve endings, rendering the sufferer insensible. These sores, lesions and missing extremities are a result of repeated injuries, or infections caused by unnoticed wounds; much in the same way an opium addict might chew off his own tongue or burn himself by sitting too close to the fire.'

'You mean those things that attacked me last night can't feel pain?'

'Precisely so. But there's more. Do you see the white film over the eyes here?' Hunter raised the creature's eyelids with his thumb.

'Was he blind?'

'To all intents and purposes, yes. But nature supplies the deficiency of one sense by improving the quality of the others. Smell and hearing, for instance, as in a bat or a mole. This man had poor eyesight, because he is accustomed to an environment where sight is unnecessary.' Hunter held up the creature's fingers for Johnson's inspection. 'Look at the sandstone residue here.'

Johnson leaned forward, observing the dirt particles under the creature's ragged fingernails.

'It is my guess that this man has spent a significant amount of time, perhaps all of his life, groping in darkness. His upper body strength is immense, his hands large and spade like with hard callouses, ideal for burrowing.'

'Doctor Hunter, do you think it possible there are more of these creatures, lurking in the vaults and tunnels under the city?'

'Good God, man. I certainly hope not!'

'Why do you say that?'

'Because,' said Hunter, removing his spectacles and looking levelly at Johnson, 'I happened to examine the contents of his stomach.'

*

A crowd had gathered round the subterranean square, filling the four streets and leaning out from blackened, empty window sockets above. They were making an excited hubbub, chattering among themselves, while children ran around the base of the column, chasing one another with sticks. Boswell was reminded of the restless sense of excitement before a theatre performance. He turned his head as best he could. 'Are you still there, Carruthers?'

'Yes,' replied Carruthers blandly. The absence of fear in the man's voice worried Boswell in a way his most hysterical outbursts could not.

'Chin up, Carruthers. There must be a way out of this. Granted, things do seem a bit bleak.'

'If you say so...' he said morosely. Then, 'Boswell, if you survive this accursed place, will you do me a favour?'

'Don't speak like that,' said Boswell. 'We'll both get through this somehow.'

'No,' Carruthers replied in the same flat tone. 'Promise me you will find my wife Florence in Bethnal Green. If I could do it all again, I... I... Tell her I love her, Boswell, and I was always true to her, after a fashion. And kiss my daughter once for me.'

'I promise, Carruthers.'

The unearthly blast of a horn cut through the noise; the crowd parted as a revenant approached the square. It seemed to Boswell that the hooded ones in sackcloth, whose faces were the most disfigured, were the elders of that hellish crew—the High Priests, so to speak—and as such were afforded the most respect. There were a number of them spread out among the crowd, taller than the rest, with an aura of fear and death surrounding them. The others, the worker ants of the colony, gave them a wide berth. This one held in his gnarled claw a staff curiously formed like a shepherd's crook, with what looked like a bell at the top. The revenant stopped at the base of the ruined well and tapped his staff three times, causing the bell to ring. He took a few steps back, and a dead silence ensued.

Boswell turned his head to look. A blood red mist, thick and reeking, came billowing over the lip of the well.

There were deeper, fouler places in the bowels of the earth than the revenants' domain. Had Boswell the means of climbing down that vertical shaft, he might have borne witness to vast, yawning cavities of staggering complexity, towering stalagmites, subterranean lakes of fire and glittering caverns where the terrible lizards once held dominion. He might have seen the ruined cities raised by unseen hands, or witnessed their direful inhabitants, though he would not have lived to tell the tale.

The atmosphere was electrified. Boswell became aware of the same throbbing, humming, *shuddering* sensation that so distressed him on Arthur's Seat, but this time dramatically intensified. The well was now belching smoke, illuminated from some hellfire below, and for one breathless moment Boswell was reminded of Faust, and the hush that descends before Mephistopheles himself emerges from a hidden trapdoor centre stage.

The cobra-hooded figure that crawled out of the abyss must surely have numbered among Satan's most trusted lieutenants. Resplendent in a scarlet cloak of silk emblazoned with mysterious golden symbols, it stood seven feet tall and exuded an inhuman, diabolical aura.

Slowly the creature turned its head, looking from Boswell to Carruthers and back again, before stepping down from the rubble and approaching the obelisk.

The demon brought its head close to Carruthers' and breathed in deeply through its nasal cavity.

'Fear...' it hissed. '*Goooood... fear makes the blood so much richer.*'

The crowd had fallen away into silence. Carruthers rolled his eyes until only the whites were showing. His face was covered in a sheen of sweat, and he began to make strange drowning noises, '*uuuub....uuuub...*' in the back of his throat, his leg twitching like a man in the throes of an epileptic fit. He was in a paroxysm of terror.

The scarlet demon turned to the stone tablet on which had been placed the occult paraphernalia, reminding Boswell for one ludicrous moment of a surgeon about to perform an operation. The demon took up a dagger, testing it for sharpness on one clawed finger, then turned to Carruthers and teasingly cut each button from his shirt, all the way to the neck. Next the creature took up the goblet and raised it to the crowd. Quietly at first - just a murmur - the spectators began to chant: '*Ho Ophis Ho Archaios, Ho Drakon Ho Megas…*'

It was a harsh, guttural language Boswell half-recognised, though he couldn't quite place it.

As the chanting rose to a crescendo, the Scarlet Demon turned its attentions back to Carruthers, and in one fluid movement cut the victim's throat from ear to ear. The twitching stopped, and the monster caught the flow of blood in the cup. Blood pounded in Boswell's ears, until the noise of the crowd was a muted roar. Raising the chalice in both hands before the braying crowd, the demon tilted back its head and poured the warm fluid down its throat.

But the horror had yet to reach its blood-soaked climax.

The beast cut out Carruther's heart and held the pulsating organ aloft, then dropped it in the crucible, watching it spit and crackle as it roasted in the flames. Its movements were clinical, methodical, like an anatomist conducting a post-mortem. The demon retrieved the burning heart with one clawed hand, held it up to the crowd who were now in a state of orgiastic frenzy, and bit into the charred, blackened organ as if it were a juicy red apple.

'Poor old Carruthers,' thought Boswell, quivering on the very edge of sanity.

The hooded one was not finished with Carruthers. Two revenants stepped forward and cut the body from the pillar then threw it onto the stone altar. The scarlet demon approached the body and hacked off the limbs with all the ease of a master butcher. It threw quivering body parts into the crowd, who fought over their prizes like a pack of hungry jackals.

As they revelled in their revolting feast, Boswell vomited down his shirt and, mercifully, passed out completely.

Chapter 10

Ring-a-Ring-o'-Roses

Four men—Doctor Johnson, Lord Chalmers, the Duke of Queensberry and Doctor Hunter—sat around a table in a private booth of the Jolly Judge Inn, with four tankards of ale before them. Doctor Johnson, who had information of some importance to convey, started the proceedings.

'Let us look at what we know, gentlemen. Brodie's fingerprints are all over these crimes. He must be working with the individual who broke into Boswell's apartment last night and attacked me; the same *"Ghoul of Greyfriars"* who was seen heading towards the MacKenzie crypt. The night watchman mentioned the wretch carried a sack full of "lost souls struggling to get out", which struck me as odd at the time. I believe these villains—for there are several of them working in tandem—are ransacking households all over Edinburgh, and depositing a portion of the booty in the MacKenzie crypt for Brodie, who supplies them with keys. We will go directly to the cemetery. That is where you will find your belongings, Your Grace, and if we're lucky, catch Deacon Brodie in the act.'

Queensberry slammed his hands down on the table and shot to his feet. 'Right! I'll kill him.'

The Fall of the House of Thomas Weir

'Just one moment, Your Grace,' said Lord Chalmers, placing a restraining hand on the hot-headed duke's arm. 'We have not quite thought this through. What if Brodie's been there already, and cleared away all of the evidence?'

'That is a distinct possibility,' said Johnson. 'But something tells me that Brodie has been waiting for things to settle down before he makes his move. This *"Ghoul of Greyfriars"* has been causing quite a stir recently, and the last thing Brodie needs is to draw attention to himself or his nefarious activities.'

'Do you think anyone else is mixed up in this?' said Chalmers.

'Almost certainly,' Johnson confirmed. 'This Brodie is a crafty weasel, but I don't think he has the capacity to mastermind an operation of this size. We find Brodie, we find out who is pulling his strings.'

'And what of Mr Boswell,' asked Chalmers. 'Will Brodie be able to tell us his whereabouts?'

Johnson tilted his head thoughtfully, then peered through the window towards the dark side of the street. He made a beckoning gesture with his finger, and the same boy who had fetched Doctor Hunter the previous evening suddenly appeared at the door.

'Tell me, boy,' said Johnson, smiling amiably at the lad. 'Do you know who Lady Colville is?'

'Lady Betty? Of course, sir. Everybody knows her.'

'Good. Here's a sixpence. Tell her to meet us this evening at Queensberry House.'

'Queensberry House. Right, sir!'

Doctor Johnson turned to his co-conspirators and shrugged. 'Something tells me we will need all the help we can get before the night is through.'

*

Deacon Brodie locked the door to his warehouse and took a deep breath. What he had to do next was distasteful, but a necessary part of the job. He kept close to the walls as he made his way

95

down the High Street, ducking down closes and alleys to avoid being seen, weaving around drunkards and streetwalkers, hopping over sleeping or unconscious bodies. A small and unassuming man, he could be discreet when he needed to be: a necessary part of the job. How else had he been able to maintain a double life for so long? By day a pillar of the community, with a regular seat on the city council and a respectable trade, he played the part of responsible citizen to perfection.

Come nightfall Deacon Brodie was a different beast altogether: drinking, attending cockfights, gaming, whoring, carousing, no vice or escapade was beneath him. He had to pay for this lavish and irresponsible lifestyle, of course. But then again, he had the perfect setup. Some of the richest people in society invited him to their homes, in his capacity as cabinetmaker and locksmith. All he had to do was find out where they kept the valuables and, when the owner had his back turned, he pressed the master key into a piece of clay he kept hidden in his pocket. Sometimes he would even fit one of his own locks as part of the deal.

Brodie didn't work alone. Ask no questions, that was the key to this whole business. Whom he worked for, he had only the vaguest of ideas. Didn't want to know. It was a small mercy his boss kept his face hidden and stayed in the shadows. All he had to do was provide a key and an address. Maybe a diagram showing where the valuables were hidden. That was all. No guilt. No way of linking him to the crime. A few days later he would collect his share of the treasure from one of the allotted places.

In return, all he had to do was pick up some unwitting victim from the tavern, send him down a close, and... that was it. Simple. He never knew what they did with the bodies. Didn't care, as long as they paid him. Ask no questions, that's what kept him sane. The next day he would go to one of the many pick-up points around town, somewhere the average passers-by avoided, maybe a house with a haunted reputation or a graveyard, and there would be a fob watch, a handful of coins, perhaps a gold ring or two for the taking. The house break-ins were more lucrative, of course. But still he had to send them a live one every now and then.

Brodie scrambled over the broken part of the cemetery wall using the familiar footholds and handholds. When he first came here, he had been terrified. But that was the beauty of it. Who would come to a cemetery at this late hour? Even the old watchman kept away from the MacKenzie Crypt after dark.

When he reached the mausoleum he fumbled in his pocket for the key. As quietly as he could, he fitted the key in the lock then swung open the iron door.

Once inside the crypt, he raised the nearest coffin lid to look inside. My God. The casket of jewels alone was worth hundreds. Then there was twice as much in unmarked bills, and a stack of documents bearing some sort of government insignia. Blackmail it was, then. That was a new one, even for him; the thought of the power he could wield over another soul gave him a thrill of excitement. He would squeeze that arrogant, overbearing brute Queensberry till he shat gold. There would be more than enough to pay off his gambling debts. Enough to retire. He'd never need to work for those creepers again. He would take his favourite mistress and leave; perhaps get a ticket on the next boat to the New World. He, the one they called the Master, would be furious. He would send his people after him. But if he left first thing in the morning...

Deacon Brodie filled his sack, then stepped outside and swung the mausoleum door shut behind him. As he turned the key in the lock, he had the creeping sensation of being watched. Yes, there was a movement in the darkness beyond the gravestones. Something was approaching.

'*Who's there?*' he hissed into the cold night air. Was it one of them? Could they read his mind?

Brodie watched a portly figure step out from the shadows. It was the fool from yesterday. The one with the inheritance. Sir Loin. He must have cottoned on to his little plan. With a sigh of relief, Brodie slung the sack over his shoulder and fingered the cosh in his pocket. He would deal with this one easily enough.

'Put your hands in the air, sir,' said the Englishman.

Brodie was about to laugh in the fat fool's face when five other men stepped out from behind him. That dull-as-dishwater Doctor from his club, the magistrate lord something or other, the city guard, and the Duke of Queensberry himself.

Christ, thought Brodie.

'I would do what he said, if I were you,' said the magistrate. With an audible click the two guardsmen cocked their pistols. Deacon Brodie dropped the sack containing the Duke of Queensberry's valuables and raised his hands in the air.

*

Boswell opened his eyes to find himself in a dingy cell. He was lying on a pile of rubble, which brought his head almost to the ceiling. He tried moving his legs, only to hear the clink and rattle of chains. So he was a prisoner again. On the opposite end of the chamber, on either side of a stout wooden door, a pair of torches cast their flickering light against the blackened walls of his cell.

His thoughts turned immediately to his captors. How long had they existed in that squalor, feeding on human flesh, while up above the rabble carried on with their daily existence, like cattle, oblivious to the threat swarming beneath their feet?

Then there was the Thing from the Well. Unlike the revenants, who may or may not have been men at one time, this was something else entirely. The revenants feared their master as a pack of hyenas feared the lion. Poor Carruthers had been terrified out of his wits, but he hadn't screamed. Boswell wondered if he would be so brave when his time came.

As his eyes became accustomed to the darkness, he had the distinct impression of being watched. Shadows flitted from wall to wall, gradually forming themselves into three nebulous shapes before his eyes. Boswell scurried backwards, kicking out at the rubble under his feet. Some of the looser rocks clattered to the bottom of the pile, striking the stone floor with a hollow sound.

The Fall of the House of Thomas Weir

Boswell looked down, and the flickering torchlight revealed a heap of tiny bones. It was a mass grave of children!

He suppressed the urge to scream. He knew that if he started, he would never be able to stop.

The shapes hovering before him were as insubstantial as mist.

'Who are you?' gasped Boswell, rubbing his eyes.

The ragged little girl with the doll couldn't have been more than ten years old, but her face conveyed a weariness and wisdom far beyond her years - a sadness and a beauty that was not entirely human.

'You know who I am,' she said, with a peculiar little smile and a tilt of her head.

'You... You're an angel...' gasped Boswell.

The girl covered her face with her hands and emitted a girlish laugh that reverberated around the dead room.

'Or... Or a ghost.'

'Of sorts,' said the little girl, tilting her head thoughtfully.

The little drummer boy stood proudly to attention beside the girl. He wore a red military tunic with a shiny drum strapped to his belt, though his face was as pale as a winter morning. 'Who are *you*?' asked the drummer-boy with wide-eyed candour.

Boswell's throat was dry, and he had to clear it before he spoke. 'M...my name is Boswell. James Boswell.'

'*Is he one of them?*' whispered the third and smallest apparition, a barefoot chimney sweep in rags. His big, fearful eyes seemed all the more striking as they peered out from a blackened face.

'I don't think so,' said the girl. 'You can tell the other ones by looking at their eyes.'

'The other ones?' said Boswell, amazed that he could be talking to a spirit so matter-of-factly. 'Who are *they*?'

'Blood-drinkers,' said the girl with the doll.

'Shapeshifters,' said the drummer boy.

'The Ancient Ones,' said the chimney sweep.

'You mean there is more than one of them?' said Boswell.

'They dwell in a place far below us,' said the girl in a tremulous voice, 'where no mortal has ever walked, not even in their worst nightmares.'

'Even the revenants fear them,' said the drummer boy, as if reading Boswell's thoughts.

'What do they want?' said Boswell.

'They want to steal your face and use it as a mask,' said the girl.

'My... face...?' said Boswell, his hand reaching involuntarily for his cheek.

'But for that they need your blood,' said the sweep.

'They like the blood of children most of all,' said the girl. 'That's what gives them their power. But a full grown man will do. Especially a frightened one.'

'They'll get round to killing you sooner or later,' said the drummer boy matter-of-factly, 'but you're not frightened enough yet. That's why they brought you here. To let you stew awhile.'

'I'm not afraid,' insisted Boswell.

'You ought to be,' whispered the chimney sweep.

'But who *are* you?' Boswell cried. 'How did you end up... like this?'

Wordlessly the apparitions closed their eyes, and all at once Boswell's head began to spin. He shut his eyes against the swaying of the room. Perhaps it was a vision induced by hunger and exhaustion, perhaps the ghosts had somehow managed to find a way into his skull, but when Boswell opened his eyes again he was no longer in his cell.

He could see soldiers dressed in bright red military tunics uncovering a tunnel beneath the castle parade ground. The style of their uniforms told Boswell this happened a long time ago. The soldiers were grasping a rope, lowering a small boy into the tunnel. The little drummer boy's legs kicked frantically until his feet touched solid ground.

The soldiers followed the faint sound of his drum down High Street, listening as the drummer boy ventured deeper and deeper into the tunnel... *rat-tat-tat* went his little drum, *rat-tat-tat*. The drum came to a stop somewhere beneath the old Tron Kirk. The soldiers looked at one another and waited, but they would never hear the little drummer boy's drum again. They blocked up the entrance to the old tunnel soon after that.

Abruptly the scene changed, like the turning of a page, and Boswell saw the tiny chimney sweep in his death agony: stuck in a chimney with his arms pinned by his sides. Boswell could feel the boy's pain as if it were happening to him. It was intense, unendurable. The boy's master lit a fire below his feet to try forcing him upwards, but the boy was stuck fast. He could smell the acrid smoke as his flesh started to blister...

Before Boswell could open his mouth to scream, the page turned one more time and he was watching the little girl with the rag doll clinging to her mother. The mother's head was tilted at an unnatural angle, plague sores covering her waxen face like blood-red winter roses and glassy, unseeing eyes. A doll's eyes. High above them, the circle of light was steadily narrowing, as the men with trowels shut the little girl in with her dead mother. The circle became a pinpoint, and then that disappeared and they were left in pitch darkness.

He opened his eyes with a sharp intake of breath and looked at the innocent faces of the apparitions. Like masks. Like wax dolls. The tears came easily, abundantly. They had all died alone and afraid, without love or a whisper of hope. For centuries they had led their half-existence underground, not knowing if they were alive or dead, fleeing the tread of the Ancient Ones, dreading the well and the flash of scarlet and gold. Boswell felt that his heart would break for them.

'Wait!' he cried. 'Don't leave! Stay, I beg you!'

But the outlines had already begun to fade.

'You have to run,' said the girl, as if from a great distance. Boswell was alone again until, overwhelmed by exhaustion and horror of his situation, sleep overcame him.

He awoke to find someone had removed the chains from his legs. With a rush of wonder he recalled the three children, and felt fresh pangs of pity and sorrow. He needed to get back to Doctor

Johnson and warn him. Back to the light. The last thing the little girl had told him was to run. It seemed like a good idea. But how?

Then, just as he was beginning to think he would die in that cell, the heavy door swung open of its own accord, revealing a corridor as dark as pitch.

Chapter 11

The Fall of Deacon Brodie

Electorate of Bavaria, 1770

On the 23rd April 1765 I received my first visitation from the inter-dimensional being who would come to dominate my every dream and waking hour. Over the course of the next three weeks, this entity, who identifies as male though in truth his species have evolved to render such physical distinctions redundant, dictated to me a series of revelations concerning the nature of the universe and the destiny of mankind.

This being, who will henceforth be referred to as "Nacash", hails from the semi-mythical continent of Atlantis, the precise location of which was revealed to me during the course of three incredible interviews.

(The following transcript has been painstakingly recorded from memory.)

Nacash himself, insubstantial as a shadow, explained to me that he is as yet unable to manifest himself in true physical form, unless his passage be aided by means of a blood ritual, which can only be performed by the initiate after seven days of fasting, when the moon is in its new phase. During the ritual, which involves human sacrifice, the entity known as Nacash may take possession of a human form, though he requires subsequent 'transfusions' on a regular basis in order to maintain it.

What follows is a word-for-word account of intelligence I received whilst in a 'trance' state, and though the voice I heard was not perceived through the natural senses; that this entity has objective reality and is not some hallucination or fancy created by my own disordered mind, was proven to me by the disclosure of certain facts which were impossible to otherwise know.

Interview I

Nacash – Thuban

Thuban: *Please identify yourself.*

Nacash: *My name is unpronounceable in your common tongue, though you may call me Nacash, if you prefer.*

Thuban: *Who are you?*

Nacash: *I am of a race immeasurably superior to man. You may think of me as a God, though not the Yahweh of your Bible. To us, your Christian God is the devil incarnate. The primitive, human mind might perceive my kind as "evil". However, we inhabit and operate within a sphere beyond such paltry dichotomies.*

Thuban: *You said "us". Do you mean there are others like you?*

Nacash: *As I said, we are a race.*

Thuban: *Where do you reside?*

Nacash: *Our dwelling places are deep underground, though once we reigned this earth as Kings of Atlantis.*

Thuban: *What is your agenda?*

Nacash: *We wish to walk among you as of old, to direct and guide you on the true path to enlightenment, to establish heaven on earth, and to allow you to share in this knowledge.*

Thuban: *And how is this achievable?*

Nacash: *We require blood sacrifice. We need host bodies, who must be fully mature adults. However we also desire the blood of children, whose blood is indescribably exquisite to us.*

From *the Journals of Professor Adrian Weber*

The Fall of the House of Thomas Weir

Mrs Boswell awoke with a lead weight in her belly and a gnawing intuition that something was terribly wrong. When she opened her eyes that intuition became a horrible certainty. She was shut up in the gloomy attic Sister Grace had shown her earlier. Her first thought was for Veronica. Mrs Boswell ran to the door and grasped the handle. It was locked. She rattled the door and called out for help. No reply.

How had this happened? The last thing she remembered was Sir William's office... *The sherry*. Something must have been put in her drink. But why would anyone drug her? Sister Grace had been talking about some sort of conspiracy involving the children. If that were true, then perhaps Sir William.... No, surely he was blameless in all this. The president of the orphanage was a good man. A moral man. Then she remembered how he had fawned over Veronica, and the way he had watched her as she drained her sherry. He had all but licked his lips...

Oh God, Veronica.

Mrs Boswell shook the door again and yelled. They had locked her in for sure. She looked around for something heavy, then picked up a chair, smashing it repeatedly against the lock. When she stopped to catch her breath she heard footsteps coming up the stairs towards her. Thank God. It had all been a terrible mistake. They would release her and return her daughter. No harm done.

A small panel she hadn't noticed in her panic, a horizontal slot no bigger than a letterbox, slid open to reveal the stern eyes of the Mother Superior peering back at her.

'What is the purpose of all this racket?'

'Sister Daphne! Thank goodness you came,' gasped Mrs Boswell. 'I've been locked in this room, and... and... Well, I'm sure it's all been a misunderstanding. Let me out, please. I need to find my daughter.'

'Don't worry. Your daughter is quite safe—for the moment,'

said the nun tersely.

'What do you mean... *for the moment*? Let me out, please.' She rattled the handle.

'There's no use your trying to force your way out. The door is barred from my side. You will remain here at our convenience, for the time being, at least.'

'What do you mean! Are you mad?' raged the captive. 'I demand to see my daughter. My husband will hear of this!'

'Your daughter is a very lucky little girl.' The Mother Superior's eyes searched Mrs Boswell's face, drinking in her fear and confusion. 'She has been chosen. It is a great privilege. If you behave yourself then perhaps you will be permitted to watch. And who knows? Perhaps the Master will afford you the same honour.'

The panel slammed shut, and Mother Superior descended the stairs, deaf to the screams of terror and anguish coming from behind the locked door.

*

'Mr Brodie,' said Johnson. 'I urge you to talk. So far we have treated you as a guest, but if you choose to remain silent we will hand you over to the Duke, who I assure you, is not so patient as I.'

Deacon Brodie was seated in the middle of the drawing room of Queensberry House, surrounded by the grim faces of Doctor Johnson, Lord Chalmers, Doctor Hunter and the Duke of Queensberry, with two soldiers standing guard at the door. Queensberry was delighted over the return of his valuables, eager to teach the culprit a lesson he wouldn't forget in a hurry.

'I told you before,' replied Brodie dully. 'I don't know where your friend is.'

'Who do you work for?' demanded Johnson.

'Myself,' said Brodie. 'I work alone.'

Johnson gave a sigh, and nodded to the Duke of Queensberry.

'Right boy,' said the Duke, rolling up his sleeves. He seized Brodie's arm and bent it up behind his back.

The Fall of the House of Thomas Weir

'Who do you work for?' Johnson demanded again.

'No one...' said Brodie through gritted teeth.

'Where is James Boswell?'

'I... *Argh!*' Queensberry yanked his arm a little further. 'I don't know!'

Johnson shook his head. 'Mr Brodie. We aim to have this information out of you by hook or by crook. If you do not cooperate, Lord Chalmers here will personally see to it that you hang by the morning. Now one more time. Who do you work for?'

'Answer him, boy,' growled Queensberry before slamming his fist into Brodie's stomach. The prisoner doubled over, gasping for breath, but kept his silence.

'Right,' said Queensberry and, grabbing Brodie by both lapels, he half-lifted, half-dragged him over to the open window, where he dangled him four storeys above the cobbled courtyard.

'If your friend is with *them,* he's dead already!' cried Brodie. 'There's a whole network of tunnels down there. Miles of them! I've never been down there. Nobody has, unless you're one of them.'

'A name,' snarled Queensberry.

'I've never seen his face. I don't know! The others only speak of him in fearful whispers.'

'A name!' cried Queensberry again.

'I can't... He'll kill me... Or worse...'

Johnson looked disgusted. 'That's enough,' he said. Queensberry heaved Brodie back in and threw him to the floor. Brodie curled up in the corner, whimpering fearfully.

Johnson gestured for the three men to join him in a corner of the room. They leaned together and spoke in lowered voices. 'Whoever Brodie answers to,' said Johnson, 'he operates an extensive criminal network, using these revenants to do his dirty work. This Brodie is scared half to death. If we push him further, there's no telling—'

Johnson's train of thought was cut short by a sudden rush of footsteps. The three men spun round, only to find Brodie's chair empty. They ran to the window and looked down on the cobbled courtyard below, where Brodie's broken body lay sprawled in a spreading pool of blood.

'My God...' said Lord Chalmers.

Johnson shook his head and crossed himself. 'Poor devil.'

'There goes the last chance we had of finding who's behind this,' said Queensberry.

'Not necessarily,' said a voice at the door. The four grim-faced men turned as one to face the beautiful young woman standing in the doorway. Her face was perfection, her hair a mass of auburn curls swept up at the front, with a tartan shawl thrown over her shoulders to protect her from the chill Edinburgh night.

'Lady Colville,' said Johnson, bowing deeply. 'What kept you?'

*

Boswell peered out onto a high-arched close complete with weathered steps, darkened doorways, and supporting buttresses overhead. Sleeping bodies lay everywhere, some still grasping the remains of a half-gnawed rib or something worse. A primal fear, raw and suffocating, came clawing its way from Boswell's belly to his throat. The scene before him was the stuff of nightmares, but the fear of never seeing his wife and child again was stronger still, and galvanised him to action. With a deep breath he stepped out into the passageway. He picked his way between the snoring bodies, stealing his way up the cobbled lane. He walked on a knife edge: the slightest noise and he would suffer the same dreadful fate as Carruthers.

The faint tread of footsteps echoed down the darkened close, getting closer with each step. Something was coming, and fast. Boswell looked frantically around, spying a nearby doorway. He ducked inside, feeling his way around a pitch-dark vault until his hands found something solid; it was a barrel. He flung off the lid, relieved to find it was empty, then climbed inside and ducked down. He held his breath as the footsteps came to a halt outside the door.

The Fall of the House of Thomas Weir

Boswell peered through the slats of the barrel at the tall silhouette filling the doorway, blocking out what little light remained. Then something utterly strange occurred. The creature in the doorway began to produce a rapid series of clicking noises with its tongue against the roof of its mouth. It sounded to Boswell like a baby's rattle, and it utterly terrified him. The rattling noise increased, until the hunter was standing over his barrel. Clawed hands scratched their way around the rim. Boswell shut his eyes and silently prayed for deliverance. Then the rattle was abruptly silenced, and the creature withdrew. Boswell waited for the sound of footsteps to disappear, then with a sigh of relief he climbed back out of the barrel, scarcely able to believe his luck.

The tenement flats of Old Town had been built on either side of a steeply sloping ridge, so that one might enter the front of a building on High Street, only to find oneself five or even ten storeys up on the other side. Long ago, residents of the lowest levels had taken advantage of this unique situation, digging laterally from their basements into the steeply sloping rock face. The volcanic sandstone was brittle, porous, and easy to excavate; before long the residents had built for themselves an entire network of tunnels extending from their basements into the sides of the hill, enabling them to accommodate their ever-expanding families. These tunnels and chambers joined up with others until the entire ridge was a rabbit warren of activity, a vast network of clans and families living side by side in the dark. When the plague came, there was little that could be done to help them. The authorities sealed up the entrances, bricked over the narrow closes, and that was that. Or so they thought.

As Boswell moved deeper into Castle Rock his surroundings changed. He was no longer moving through subterranean streets and closes, but climbing through a series of interiors, penetrating into the very foundations of the city, trying to put as much distance between himself and his pursuers as possible, and if he was lucky find a way home.

Soon light failed completely, and Boswell found himself

groping in darkness. The walls seemed to grow narrower. It was hopeless. He was starving, exhausted, and his muscles ached in places he hadn't known existed. He sat with his back against a wall and closed his eyes. How easy it would be just to lie down and fall asleep.

A dead silence prevailed. Far above, life in all its multitudinous forms went on. Children were laughing, dogs were barking, cats prowling, sweethearts courting, all the warp and weft of day-to-day existence. Perhaps, thought Boswell with the faintest glimmer of hope, Doctor Johnson was out looking for him. Then again, what were the chances of his ever being found alive again? He might as well have been on the dark side of the moon. Down here in the bowels of the earth, no light entered, no sound reverberated. He tried to remember the taste of whisky, or the face of his daughter, or the smell of freshly cut grass, or the sound the wind makes when it stirs the leaves, or the feel of a woman's caress, but the darkness blotted out all memory and hope.

Perhaps it was fitting, Boswell told himself with a kind of grim irony, to be trapped in this airless vault. Perhaps he was being punished for his many infidelities. Had he not loved life and liberty too much? Had he not jealously guarded his freedom, like a miser with his coins, often at the expense of his own family and responsibilities?

Even Carruthers had expressed remorse in the end. He had confessed his sins, and his love for his family had saved him. Oh, Carruthers! His confession, even to so unworthy and hypocritical a listener as Boswell, had absolved the Englishman in the end. Yes, he had to believe it was so. But who would listen to Boswell, down here in the dark? To whom could he confess his sins, save the dark alone?

An all-conquering wave of despair washed over Boswell's exhausted frame. He hugged his knees to his chest and rocked himself back and forth, whimpering softly like a frightened child. His lips, dry and chapped, moved in silent prayer.

Out of the depths I cry unto thee, Oh Lord! Hear my voice: let your ears

The Fall of the House of Thomas Weir

be attentive to the voice of my supplications…

A voice, speaking urgently in his ear, startled Boswell from his exhortations. It was the voice of the little ghost girl.

She was telling him to get up.

If they catch you, she said, *they will eat you.*

Boswell opened his eyes. A distant blue light glowed somewhere off in the dark. His heart told him it was his little guardian angel showing the way. He picked himself up and staggered towards it.

*

Lady Colville sat in the study of Boswell's home on James Court, the missing man's pocket watch held in the palm of her hand. The men looked on: Queensberry and Doctor Hunter with barely concealed scepticism, Lord Chalmers with mild curiosity, while Johnson watched with a kind of intense fascination.

'So what happens now?' said Queensberry.

'Now we wait,' said Johnson.

Lady Colville closed her eyes and sat perfectly still. She seemed a statue of marble, the only movement the faint rise and fall of her chest, her face pale and drawn in the flickering candlelight.

After about ten minutes, Queensberry gave a sigh. 'I knew this was a waste of time. You've had your fun, now let's—'

'Shh... Her eyes are moving,' said Lord Chalmers.

When Lady Colville spoke, all four men started. 'I see him!' she gasped. 'I see Mr Boswell!'

'Where?' demanded Johnson, seizing Lady Colville's hand. 'Where is he?'

'Hard to say. He is lost in shadow. He is running. Something pursues him.'

'What is it?'

The last vestige of colour drained from Lady Colville's face, and her eyes rolled up in their sockets to expose the whites. She looked ghostly in the candlelight. 'An eye. An eye surmounting a pyramid. A serpent's eye! It sees me! It sees me!' Frightened, Lady

Colville raised an arm to cover her eyes. 'I must hide. I am naked in His presence...'

'Wait!' cried Johnson. 'Look closely. Nothing can harm you here. Who is it? Who do you see?'

Lady Colville slumped back into her chair, her brow furrowed with concentration. 'I see a beast with the body of a lion,' she announced, 'and the wings and head of an eagle.'

'A griffin,' said Johnson.

'Yes that's it,' said Lady Colville softly. 'A griffin. It is fighting with something. An eagle, I think. Yes. It is a monstrous eagle. They are grappling one another. The eagle has the griffin in its talons, and the griffin is clawing at the bird. There is blood everywhere. So much blood!'

Lady Colville's eyes shot open and she cast a bewildered, frightened look around her.

Johnson placed a gentle hand on Lady Colville's shoulder. 'Thank you, Lady Colville. You have been of the utmost assistance. Come, you must rest now.'

After escorting Lady Colville from the room, Doctor Johnson returned to check behind the drapes. He blew out all the candles apart from one, which he left burning on the table before them.

'So what did you make of that?' said Lord Chalmers.

'All nonsense, of course,' said Queensberry.

Hunter agreed. 'The lady spoke in riddles.'

'On the contrary, gentlemen,' said Johnson. 'There is much we can glean from Lady Colville's vision.'

The three men looked curiously at Johnson. 'Then enlighten us please, Doctor,' said Lord Chalmers.

'An all-seeing eye, surmounting a pyramid wreathed in flames,' said Johnson. 'The Eye of Horus. What does the symbol mean to you, gentlemen?'

'The Eye of Horus is a Masonic device, is it not?' said Hunter.

'In part, yes,' said Johnson. 'But it also has more sinister connotations.'

'Then I'm afraid you have lost us, Doctor Johnson,' said Hunter.

The Fall of the House of Thomas Weir

'My friends,' said Johnson, searching the faces of the men around the table. 'What do you know of the Order of Draco?'

The three men threw puzzled looks and shrugged at one another.

'The Order of Draco?' said Queensberry. 'A bunch of radicals and lunatics, or so I'm told.'

'I read something about it in the Times,' said Lord Chalmers. 'The Order of Draco were a secret organisation outlawed for unnatural and seditious practices. They believed in abolishing princes and nations in favour of a *One World Order*, or something of the sort.'

'Very good, Lord Chalmers,' confirmed Johnson. 'The Order was established by a Professor Adrian Weber and an associate, though the identity of the associate was never discovered. That associate, working under the alias *Rastaban,* first conceived of the Order on a grand scale, drawing up a manifesto, contriving the means by which their message could be spread to every corner of the globe. *His* vision and intellect were the driving force behind the Order, with Weber—known to the world as *Thuban*—his closest confidant.'

'Yes,' said Doctor Hunter. 'Rastaban and Thuban. I've heard of them. Their correspondence was made public, was it not? Revealed some sort of schism in the group: a difference of opinion. They parted ways after that. Thuban—Weber that is—was arrested for sedition and sent into exile with a pension, which he refused. No one ever learned what happened to Rastaban.'

'He turned his back on the Order, and became their most implacable foe, swearing to flush out and destroy that which he himself had helped to start.'

'This is all very interesting,' said Queensberry. 'But what does any of it have to do with us?'

Johnson gave a sigh, and for the first time the three men around the table noticed how tired he looked. 'What I am about to share with you gentlemen is something that I have never told anyone before. When I have finished, you may look on me in a different light.'

The men all cast startled looks at one another. 'I believe I am not alone when I say that whatever you have to share with us here tonight will not affect your standing as a man of the upmost integrity and honour,' said Lord Chalmers.

'Hear hear,' said Queensberry. 'Now get on with it, Doctor.'

'Gentlemen,' Johnson said, with the air of a man relieving himself of a great burden. '*I* am Beta Draconis! I am Rastaban!'

Chapter 12

Ordo Draconis

Mrs Boswell was resting with her head against her prison door, desperately reviewing her options. She tried to imagine what anyone could possibly want with her daughter. Was it kidnap? But her husband was not a rich man; how much ransom could they possibly expect? Clearly this Sir William wanted something; if it wasn't money, then what was it? Doctor Johnson must know something. He was the key to all this. Everything had been fine until he came to stay. Clearly he was involved in something, getting himself mixed in with the wrong crowd, attracting the attention from the wrong sort of people... and now his friends were paying the price. Mrs Boswell heaved a sigh. Doctor Johnson was a not a bad man. James loved him. So did Veronica. And she had to admit, she felt a certain fondness for the old bear herself. If Doctor Johnson was in trouble, it was through no fault of his own. It was up to her to fix things.

Mrs Boswell took the brooch from her shawl and knelt before the keyhole. She had heard that house breakers did this sort of thing: how hard could it be? She inserted the pin of the brooch in the hole and started to waggle it around. It was a medium-sized lock, so surely the pin was strong enough. After about ten minutes of this, just when she was about to give up, she heard a resounding click. Success! With a wild cry of joy, Mrs Boswell stood up and turned the handle. She pushed the door. It wouldn't budge. She tried again, putting her shoulder and all her strength against the door. Then she remembered what Sister Daphne had said, that the door was barred from the other side. Mrs Boswell collapsed to the floor in a sobbing heap. She never cursed, but she had learned plenty of curse words from the street hawkers who plied their trade from beneath her window. She used them now.

*

Johnson looked at each man in turn, searching their eyes to measure the effect of his revelation.

There was a long pause.

'What?' said Chalmers.

'Surely you are joking,' said Hunter.

'Yes, come on, Johnson,' said Queensberry. 'This is no time for japes.'

'I never joke. And now, before I continue, I must secure an oath from each of you that what I am about to tell you goes no further than these four walls.'

After the three incredulous men had given their oaths, Johnson began his incredible narrative.

'You must understand, thirty years ago I was a very different man from who I am today, living in a very different political climate. I was still young and idealistic. A poet and a dreamer, with Jacobite sympathies. After the fall of the Stuart dynasty, we had a German on the throne. A foreigner who didn't speak a word of English. I was sick and tired with princes and their lives of unearned privilege. I began publishing articles under the pseudonym "Rastaban". In short, I dreamed of a world free from tyranny, where each man was a light unto himself, answerable only to One God. Like I said... I was an idealist.

'Before long,' Johnson continued, 'a like-minded individual

contacted me through the classified section of the Times, using the pseudonym *Thuban*. This was my first introduction to Dr Adrian Weber, Professor of Canon Law at the University of Ingolstadt. The man who was to become my most bitter enemy.

'Weber and I entered into a lengthy correspondence. We spoke of the abolition of organised religion and the deposition of Kings; in its place, a single world-religion of brotherly love, based on the teachings of Christ, with individual happiness its main goal and *raison d'etre*. I shudder now to think of my own naivety: how I thought I could bring about anything other than sheer anarchy.

'Like the early Christian Gnostics, we took for our sigil the image of the serpent. The snake, to us, was a symbol of eternal life, and Christ himself "the good serpent".'

'Blasphemy!' spluttered Lord Chalmers, who looked genuinely offended. 'The serpent represents Satan. You would turn the world on its head!'

'I do not mean to offend now, and I did not then!' cried Doctor Johnson. 'But I speak of the Christ of Gnosis, rather than the Christ of history. Answer me this: why do you think we call Christ *The Nazarene?*'

'Because he comes from Nazareth, of course,' said Doctor Hunter.

'A common misconception,' replied Johnson. 'The historic Jesus was not born in Nazareth, but in the town of Bethlehem. The Nazarenes were in fact an ancient sect who secretly dedicated their temples and shrines to the image of the serpent. It is said that the infant Jesus, in his flight from Herod, was brought to Egypt, where He was initiated into the secrets of the Pyramids. The Great Pyramid itself is aligned with the constellation of Draco, the Great Serpent, which represents death and rebirth. Consider Christ leaving His shroud behind in the tomb. Is this not akin to the snake shedding his skin? Yes, yes, I see the look of horror on your faces! But understand this: I was weary of wars waged in His name. We resolved to create a new deity, not in our own image but veiled in obscurity, shrouded in an impenetrable mystery: a Christ for the ages, irreproachable, eternal! A Christ that would inspire a sense of awe and reverence. Like I said, the seeds of dissent were already being sown, and I was its unwitting agent.

'I was the group's tactician. It was my idea, for instance, to infiltrate the Freemasons, using previously existing lines of communication to spread our message. The symbols and devices of Freemasonry we adopted as our own. I travelled like a philosopher from city to city, from lodge to lodge and even from house to house, trying to unite the Masons and to get the lodges put under the direction of the Order, through my choice of the master and the wardens. We had a regular network of devoted adherents. We had our own printing press. The word spread like wildfire: or perhaps a more fitting metaphor would be a virus.

'Soon cracks in the organisation began to show. Perhaps inevitably, Weber and I had a disagreement on how to achieve our ends. Weber believed in absolute freedom for the individual: freedom absolved of responsibility, freedom from the shackles of moral or civic duty. Writing under the pseudonym *Thuban* he published a series of seditious articles, each more incendiary than the last. He came to see humanity as a curse: a disease to be eradicated. He spoke at length of the right to commit self-murder; of how to commit genocide on a scale hitherto unheard of using poisonous gases; of how to induce miscarriages through artificial means; there was no abomination too vile he would not consider championing. I was appalled. It became clear to me that Weber was not the committed Christian he claimed to be, but had more... nefarious designs. I thought we were destroying organised religion to replace it with something greater, but Weber delighted only in destruction. New members initiated into our fold ignored the communion ritual that I myself had put in place. Weber, meanwhile, sowed the seeds of discord among our ranks, setting brother against brother. Divide and conquer was his credo. New members were recruited in secret. Weber alone knew the identity of each agent, or where they were at any given time. His motives were not selfless, but base and all-too-human. He wished only to rule. A petty tyrant, as far removed from an illuminated individual as it was possible to be.

'It was only a matter of time before our cherished Freemasonry rituals were subverted to serve more insidious purposes. Reports reached me of illicit midnight masses, of rituals designed to summon demons and, most shockingly of all, of human sacrifice.

'Then I discovered that Weber had conceived a child out of wedlock, abandoning mother and child to the disapprobation of the public. I sought out Weber's family with the intention of helping them, only to find that they had been cruelly murdered. I confronted Weber. We had a terrible argument, but I was unable to prove anything. I washed my hands of the Order there and then. Ever since, I have made it my life's work to seek out and expose this insidious organisation wherever I find it.'

By the time Johnson had finished talking, the room had grown so quiet his audience could hear the candle flame flicker in the dark. It was Lord Chalmers who broke the silence.

'And you say you have severed all ties with this... Order of Draco?'

'Yes, Lord Chalmers. Their tenets I reject utterly, and study them only to discover a means of destroying them. Alas, I have found that, like the hydra, where one head is severed another two grow in its place.'

'Then I think I speak for all of us,' said the good-hearted Lord Chalmers, 'when I say that whatever foibles you may have committed in the past may be put down to the folly of youth. Your conduct in both public and private spheres has more than absolved you of whatever taint an association with this organisation has engendered.'

'Hear hear!' cried Queensberry. 'I shudder to think of all the bloody fool things I got up to when I was a lad.'

'You have done no wrong as far as I am concerned, Doctor Johnson,' said Hunter.

Johnson lowered his head, clearly moved by the delicacy of feeling shown by his colleagues.

'So this Weber fellow.' said Queensberry. 'You say he is still alive?'

'The last time I encountered Adrian Weber he was attempting for a second time to summon the entity which calls itself "Nacash", a Kundalini demon of considerable potency. It ended disastrously for Weber.

'I tracked him to the Swiss Alps, where he had rented a cabin to perform his unspeakable rites. By the time I arrived with the local militia, it was too late. His acolytes we found gibbering in the corners of the cabin or cowering under beds, driven to the point of insanity. Other poor souls had run naked into the snow to die of hypothermia; anything to escape what they witnessed in that cabin. Weber himself barely escaped with his life. I committed him to a mental institution, but a year later he managed to effect an escape. I'm afraid he is quite mad, and will no doubt try a third time to complete the ritual. If Lady Colville's vision is accurate and he is indeed in Edinburgh, then he must be recruiting agents from among the Scottish Brotherhood. I assume he will be using the Scottish Rite of Invocation, which when subverted for evil purposes is dangerous in the extreme. Weber will try to impose his will upon the demon, but the demon will ultimately impose its will upon the man.'

'But what of the rest of Lady Colville's vision?' said Lord Chalmers. 'I mean about the griffin and the eagle?'

'That is easy enough to interpret,' replied Johnson. 'The fighting griffin and eagle can be found on the coat of arms of the Earldom of Roswell.'

The men exchanged astonished glances.

'But the current Earl of Roswell is Sir William: Lord Sinclair,' said Lord Chalmers. 'Surely he is not mixed up in this? His reputation is unimpeachable. King George himself would vouch for him.'

'Yes, come off it, Doctor Johnson,' said Queensberry. 'The man's practically a saint. He's president of St Agatha's Orphanage, for God's sake!'

The Fall of the House of Thomas Weir

'Not to mention a respected Knight of the Cape, a Grand Master Mason, and a damned fine fellow,' protested Doctor Hunter.

'All the more reason to suspect this Lord Sinclair is a secret operative, a *Scotch Knight* entrusted to watch over the interests of the Order within his district, and to fill their coffers.'

The room had become stuffy, and Johnson moved to the window to let in some air. The streets below were empty, and in the lull that comes between the clatter of evening traffic and the cry of the morning-traders an eerie silence prevailed. A black cat, sleek and sinuous, prowled the cobbled lane, then pouncing, seized a mouse in its claws. The predator toyed with its prey, releasing and catching it again, before snatching it up and vanishing into the cruel night.

'Clearly Lord Sinclair is financing Weber's endeavours,' murmured Johnson, 'using these revenants to do his dirty work…' He turned from the window and snapped his fingers together. 'Of course! *Misdirection.*'

'Miss… who?' said Chalmers.

'Misdirection,' Johnson repeated. 'It's a classic card-sharp's move. The attention of the audience is diverted with one hand, while the other hand makes its play.'

'But I fail to see the connection…' said Lord Queensberry.

'Think of it,' said Johnson. 'All those places people avoid— the darkened alleys, the haunted houses, the crypts, vaults, underground passages and graveyards of the city—our friend uses to his advantage. He exploits the superstitions of the weak, using them as a cloak, while he moves his army of lepers like pawns on a chessboard. It's perfect, really: using fear and darkness as a cover. One wonders if he was not the first to whisper rumours of dark things lurking in hidden places, in order to move his stolen treasure from cavern to crypt unmolested.'

'It all makes a strange kind of sense,' said Chalmers.

'And Deacon Brodie?' said Queensberry.

'Deacon Brodie was the key, in more ways than one, acting as an emissary between the living and the dead. Sinclair let Brodie believe he was profiting from those creatures, meanwhile fleecing him at cards, playing with him, as a cat plays with a mouse. And make no mistake, sir. Those foul revenants may be victims of a disease best studied in a laboratory, and to be pitied in their way, but dead they are. Dead to decency, dead to common feeling, dead to Christian values, and ultimately, dead to the Light.'

'Then there is only one course of action available to us,' said Doctor Hunter, rising to his feet. 'We must lay hands on Sinclair—Weber too, if we can—and put a stop to this diabolical madness once and for all.'

'I expected no less,' said Johnson. 'But I must warn you. If Lord Sinclair is part of Weber's inner circle, I cannot ensure your safety. Weber is as dangerous as they come.'

'Danger is my beer,' scoffed Queensberry, rising to his feet.

'I'll drink to that!' roared Lord Chalmers, rising also.

As the men turned to leave, Lady Colville appeared at the bottom of the stairs to block their way. 'You're not going anywhere without me,' she said, drawing a shawl across her shoulders. Though her face was pale and drawn, her countenance was not without firmness or resolution.

'Nay, Lady Colville,' said Johnson. 'With all due respect, this is far too dangerous a business for a lady to get mixed up in. I have a far more important task for you.'

Chapter 13

King of Bones

Interview II

Thuban: *Yesterday you spoke of the continent of Atlantis. Where is this located?*

Nacash: *Atlantis of old was destroyed. All that remains of our once great civilisation lies far beneath the Atlantic Ocean, some three score and ten leagues east of the Outer Hebrides. The group of islands you call the Faroes once constituted the Northern Territory of Atlantis, a mountainous region whose uppermost peaks are all that remain.*

Thuban: *When was it destroyed?*

Nacash: *Many aeons ago. Though this is not our point of origin.*

Thuban: *Where, then, are you from?*

Nacash: *We hail from the third planet orbiting the binary sun of Eta Draconis.*

Thuban: *How did you travel here?*

Nacash: *We have technologies that allow us to travel across vast chasms of space in the twinkling of an eye, though since the destruction of Atlantis we have lost the art. Nevertheless, we still possess technologies which would astound your primitive mind, technologies that we will willingly share, provided you facilitate our assimilation.*

Thuban: *What happens to the human host after assimilation?*

Nacash: *It will achieve blissful, harmonious Union with that of the Guest.*

Thuban: *Do you have physical form?*

Nacash: *Yes, we possess a corporeal presence, but our elemental particles, or* atomos, *vibrate at a different frequency to yours. This means that we cannot be seen unless we choose to reveal ourselves. We enter your dimension by creating a breach in the fabric of time and space, which you commonly experience through a vibrational disturbance in the atmosphere around you.*

From *the Journals of Professor Adrian Weber*

Ghosts.

Ghosts everywhere.

Boswell had never seen so many ghosts.

Actually, until today he had never seen a ghost in his life.

Down there, though, they were as common as candlesticks on Candlemaker's Row. And though they filled him with an unholy dread, Boswell admitted to a certain degree of professional curiosity. *If only Johnson were here to see this*, he marvelled, as a procession of spectral beings passed before his eyes, a swarming mass of ethereal energy whose tendrils curled and wove themselves into shapes resembling real people. The sheer magnitude of paranormal activity staggered Boswell. Perhaps they were drawn to that demon from the well like moths to a flame, or perhaps they had always been here, moving in darkness, with no one around to witness their passing. Each apparition was possessed of its own faint light: some presented little more than a vague outline—the curve of a shoulder, the tilt of a head—others were more substantial. Mostly they were unaware of Boswell, unaware even of their own non-existence, as they went listlessly about their business; like actors on a stage, playing their roles to a darkened and empty auditorium.

The murderer was a stocky man in big brown boots and loose-fitting smock, his eyes dead as coffin nails, cord-like veins bulging from his neck and arms as he choked the life out of his victim, a poor serving girl. Boswell cried out, but the killer could not or would not heed him, condemned as he was to act out his terrible crime until the very walls of his prison collapsed and the vaults were exposed to the blinding light of day.

During the plague years, a substantial portion of the Old Town had been bricked up: men, women and children, young and old, diseased and non-diseased alike, all were condemned to suffer the same terrible fate. Row after row of narrow closes and tenement flats were used as foundations for the "new" Old Town, which was itself over a hundred years old.

As Boswell ventured further into the foundations of the city, following the faint bluish light that seemed to flit around every corner, he noticed the walls and doorways no longer resembled those above ground, but seemed hewn from the very rock itself, not laid out with geometrical precision, but crooked, winding, labyrinthine in design. This, Boswell realised, was the underground city of legend, a maze of tunnels and chambers excavated by basement-dwellers digging into the steeply sloping rock face, then expanded and extended by a new breed of tenants, the revenants themselves.

Here and there Boswell passed traces of former habitation, with discarded items strewn haphazardly around, suggesting someone had abandoned their homes in a hurry, perhaps a long time ago—an overturned pot among the ashes, a leather strap half buried in the rubble, a forlorn-looking doll, an old man's cane still propped against the wall—the spectral light revealed each sad tableau as Boswell groped his way from one hovel to the next.

At first glance, the dark silhouette standing motionless in the corner appeared as nothing more sinister than a cloak and hat hanging from a hatstand. As Boswell crossed the chamber it tilted slightly, then turned to reveal a menacing figure, its face obscured by a grotesque leather mask with goggles for eyes.

The plague doctors had been summoned by the City Council to contain the threat of the disease, sloshing through the sewers in their galoshes, beak-like plague masks stuffed with healing herbs, brandishing axes to dismember the infected and remove them from the city.

Boswell shut his eyes and waited for death. He felt a cold shudder pass through his body. When he opened his eyes he was alone again.

He moved on, feeling his way from room to room. The apparitions were terrible, but they could not harm him, or so he told himself. A fear more tangible propelled him.

A great hue and cry had erupted from somewhere back there in the darkness.

The revenants had awoken.

*

The Ossuary, a charnel house constructed entirely from human bones, lay buried under layers of earth in the former churchyard of St Giles Cathedral, conceived, as with most Ossuaries, during the plague years, when the City Fathers had had to contend with an excess of cadavers clogging up their streets.

In later years the churchyard was swept away to make room for Parliament House, but the Ossuary remained, sealed within a forgotten crypt beneath the Court of Session, a Hall of Hades untouched by light of day, while robes of state swept the polished floors above.

The Ossuary was a masterpiece of gothic ingenuity. A huge chandelier hung from the centre of the chamber, with candles of boiled human fat providing illumination. Spinal columns hung like garlands from the ceiling, while the walls were panelled with femur, tibia, fibula and clusters of skulls. At the far end of the hall, on a raised dais, there stood a tall throne constructed from every conceivable human bone. It was not empty.

The Fall of the House of Thomas Weir

The two ragged supplicants entered the Ossuary by means of a low tunnel, crawling on their hands and knees, then dusting themselves off as they stood before their sovereign father, the King of Bones himself.

Tall, gaunt and grim, the Bone King seemed the mummified corpse of some long dead monarch, but there was a steady fire burning deep within those twin orbs of sight. On his lap rested a human skull, an Imperial Orb worn smooth and shiny as marble from frequent handling over the years, a silent confessor and *memento mori*—as if one were needed—in that godforsaken chamber which had become his living tomb.

Weary of the hunt, weary of companionship, weary from bedsores he couldn't feel, and from the greater pain of living, he rarely moved anymore; only when his subjects brought an offering of human flesh did his thin hands clutch the arms of his throne, only then did the old hunger stir within his belly.

The Bone King leaned forward to address the two supplicants trembling before him. 'Well?'

'Sire,' said the first. 'We lost the meat.'

'What do you mean: lost it?'

'Just as I said, sire. The meat's up and gone.'

'Fool!' barked the Bone King. 'Who was responsible for its storage?'

The two supplicants exchanged nervous glances. 'The High Priest, sire. Cardinal Bone. Tied it up good and proper. Some 'un musta unlocked the chains and set it free.'

The sovereign's thin lips narrowed even further, and he spoke with barely concealed ill-humour. 'Well you shall just have to fetch it back then, hadn't you?'

'How, sire? It has four hours head start.'

'You have a nose, have you not? Well use it!'

'What will we do with it?'

'Cut off its feet and drag it back. I want its liver for my breakfast. And keep it to yourselves. I don't want any o' them downstairs finding out. Last thing we need's Ancient Ones poking their snouts around where they don't belong.'

Dismissing his subjects, the Bone King slumped back on his throne. He looked suddenly weary, crushed by the weight of a hundred years. He stroked the relic on his lap absent-mindedly, gazing wistfully into its empty eye sockets.

How had it come to this, he wondered?

How he missed the old days, the days before *they* had awoken. His family had enough to eat, had they not? Had he not always provided for his children? Maybe the meat was a little tough, yes, a gnarled crone here, a pickled drunk there, but at least it was honest gain.

He thought of the Ancient Ones and suppressed a shudder. He should never have made a deal with them. They usurped his authority, humiliated him before his people, broke rules. Never go upstairs before dark, that was the Law. That was how he had kept his people safe for so long. And never take chillun. That was rule number two. In the old days chillun were strictly off limits. But with *them*, anything was permitted. That is not to say the young ones weren't tasty. Truth be told, they were prodigiously tender. But the Bone King had his principles, and the taking of chillun did not sit quite right with him.

With a long sigh he cast his mind further back, back to when he was a man, and walked proudly under the sun. He had riches then, and status. But his appetites were considered… unnatural.

Stripped of his honours, shunned by his family, feared and loathed by the townsfolk, he was driven from the light. He knew what it felt like to be hunted and despised.

After years of hiding in the shadow, years of snatching what he could from the gutters and graveyards, he had started a family of his own, teaching his offspring how to hunt. They burrowed into the rock like maggots into the hide of a carcass, far from God's eye, down in the bowels of the earth where it was safe and warm. And dark.

But they had dug too deep, and awoken something that should have been left well alone.

The Fall of the House of Thomas Weir

The Ancient Ones. Them downstairs.

At first they had lived in relative harmony, sharing their ill-gotten gains. But before long he felt like a dog that begs for scraps at the table of his master. Was he not King? Where was the respect due to him as lord and master of this realm? It had always been his privilege to receive the first cut of meat, a privilege which had been rudely taken from him. He was like *Toom Tabard* of old—an empty coat—a king in name only. Even his High Priests now looked to them downstairs for guidance.

It was true: as patriarch of a clan of cannibalistic lepers he had to be ruthless and cruel. But no good could come from an association with those lizard-folk. Those demons weren't human. The way they took the faces of their prey, then put them on like masks, it just wasn't sportsmanlike. And that thrumming sound downstairs, night and day. They were up to no good down there, of this he had no doubt. His guess was they were building machines. Huge machines of conquest. One day, perhaps soon, they would rise up. And when that day came it would be all over for his people. Aye, all over for everyone.

The Bone King picked up a femur bone and gnawed with a distracted air.

It didn't bode well. It didn't bode well at all.

*

Boswell didn't know how long he had been running. With no recognisable pattern to the maze of tunnels in which he found himself he ran wildly, instinctively. Sometimes the overhead vents provided a modicum of light, but mostly it was pitch dark. In some places the walls seemed excavated from living rock, in others they were as smooth and as regular as newly laid plaster. Some ways ran straight, others crooked. Sometimes he had to stoop, and in other places he had to crawl on his hands and knees, struggling for breath, dreading to find himself trapped in those coffin-like spaces.

He came to a junction, a parting of ways, and chose without thinking, desperate to put as much distance between himself and the revenants as possible.

With his lungs fit to explode, Boswell stopped to rest against a wall.

He tilted his head to listen. A faint trickle of water was coming from somewhere ahead. Hardly daring to hope, he crawled forward on his hands and knees until he found the source. Boswell cupped his hands to collect the water trickling down the walls of the cave, raising it to his nose before tasting. It was rainwater, good and clean. Boswell drank greedily, until he could take no more.

I will rest here a while, he thought to himself, laying flat against the rough ground.

You mustn't, said the voice of the girl in his head. *They will be here very soon.*

With a groan, Boswell clambered to his feet and forced himself to move.

Finally the tunnel came to an end and he could go no further. He was trapped. He could hear the same infernal clicking noise he heard when he was hiding in the barrel, but this time multiplied a thousand-fold. His pursuers must have reached the fork. He hoped they would choose the wrong path, but they could smell him and came trudging *en masse* along the narrow passage he had chosen. Boswell pushed against the wall in pitch darkness, feeling with his hands until they settled on some loose masonry. Frantically, he pulled at the stonework until he dislodged a large chunk. He peered through the hole he had made into a perpendicular tunnel. This one was wider, rounder, expertly made. With the sound of his pursuers approaching, he pulled away more bricks until there was a hole big enough for him to squeeze through.

Boswell dropped down into this new tunnel, landing in several inches of water. From the hole he had just climbed through, he could hear his pursuers chattering amongst themselves. His heart throbbed in his breast as he spied a faint glow of daylight up ahead. He sloshed onwards, daring to hope, even as he heard the splash of his pursuers entering the tunnel behind him.

*

To anyone walking down High Street on a wet Monday afternoon in late July, the older gentleman walking side by side with the fashionably dressed young lady could have been any father and daughter out for an afternoon stroll.

A closer inspection would have told a different story. Their movements were erratic, random, as if marching to the beat of their own drum. The young lady stopped as if to sniff the air, then led her companion off in a new direction, a gentleman's fob watch dangling from her hand. Her movements were more suggestive of a water dowser following the mysterious course of an underground stream than a lady out for an afternoon stroll with her chaperone.

When they reached the castle gates at the top of the Royal Mile, the older man whispered something to one of the sentries, who seemed to recognise him. The sentry, a big burly Highlander, nodded briefly before conferring with his comrade, a smaller man with narrow shoulders. Seconds later, the old man and younger woman were admitted. Once inside, the woman walked uncertainly around the parade ground, before being drawn like water down a plughole towards the centre. She stood over a rusty manhole cover, holding the watch in her hand like a pendulum, allowing it to swing back and forth on its chain. She looked up at the older gentleman with something like triumph in her eyes. 'He is here, Doctor Johnson.'

'Are you quite sure, Lady Colville?'

'Yes, quite sure.'

The older man called for the two sentries, who came striding over with coils of rope. They lifted the rusty manhole cover, and the old man leaned forward. '*Boswell!*' he cried into the darkness, then tilted his head to listen.

*

chug...chug...chug...

The throbbing in Boswell's head was louder now, reminding him of the Thing in the Well or the terror on Arthur's Seat, only here it echoed in the dark and was deafeningly, maddeningly real. The light ahead was faint, coming from a grille some twenty feet overhead.

As Boswell approached, the noise intensified and he felt his knees weaken. He staggered on towards the light, despite the warning in his gut. With his pursuers only a short distance away, he had no other choice.

Beyond the faint light of the grille, Boswell could see someone or some*thing* crouching in the shadows, blocking his way. He squinted, trying to make out its features in the gloom.

'Boswell!' said a familiar voice. 'Thank God you're safe.'

Boswell was dumbfounded. 'Carruthers? Is it really you? Or am I dreaming?'

'Yes! Yes it's me. I managed to escape in all the confusion.'

'But you're dead!' cried Boswell. 'I watched you die!'

The thing with the face and voice of Carruthers reached a hand into the half-light. 'Does this look dead to you?' Boswell looked at the hand. Though pale and waxy, it was made of flesh and bone. Boswell reached out to touch it but it quickly withdrew, like a spider scurrying from the light.

'Come with me,' said Carruthers. 'I know the way.'

Boswell stared hard into the face of his interlocutor. It was Carruthers, and yet not Carruthers; the more Boswell looked, the more the planes of the man's face seemed to shift and lose definition. He took a step back, suddenly afraid. 'You are not Carruthers.'

'What do you mean?' said the imposter, ensuring his face remained hidden in shadow. 'Come on. There is no time.'

'If you are Carruthers,' said Boswell, 'then tell me the name of your wife.'

The Fall of the House of Thomas Weir

'My wife?'

Boswell could feel eyes boring their way into the back of his skull. '*Florence…*' the Carruthers creature hissed, triumphantly, as if he had stumbled upon the name by lucky chance.

'Carruthers, is it really you?' said Boswell with a faltering note of hope in his voice. 'Stand up so that I can see you.'

The creature seemed to unfold and grow, like smoke filling out an empty space. As the entity stood to its full height it resembled Carruthers closely enough, and yet the face seemed lumpy, somehow. Unformed, as if moulded from wet clay, the skin pulsated and rippled as though trying to organise itself into something more closely resembling that of a human being. It was taller than Carruthers had been and, instead of the foppish clothes, this version of Carruthers wore a cloak of scarlet and gold that touched the floor at his feet. The churning, throbbing sound in Boswell's head had reached its apex, and all the air seemed to leave the room, leaving him struggling for breath.

'Wh— What are you?' Boswell finally managed.

The creature grinned down at Boswell, so broadly that the mouth seemed to split the face in two. Rather than a lowering of the jaw, the whole top section of the head moved back as if on hinges, exposing twin rows of hideously elongated teeth while a tongue, red and forked like that of a snake, flickered out and in of the gaping maw. The creature caught Boswell in the vortex of its gaze, the pupils vertical slits like those of a cat, and as hypnotic as a flickering flame. Boswell felt himself being pulled towards the enemy as if by an invisible string attached to his belly.

Suddenly the overhead grille was pulled away, and a shard of light penetrated the gloom like a sword, bathing the tunnel in light. With a hiss of pure venom the creature stepped back. A voice boomed down from above, breaking the last invisible thread that held Boswell in the creature's thrall. '*Boswell!*'

A big head blocked out the circle of light like the moon eclipsing the sun. Only one man owned that stentorian voice, that ponderous cranium. The silhouette of Doctor Johnson withdrew

133

and another figure appeared. A musket glinted. With a loud *whizz* a chunk of masonry exploded beside Boswell's head.

Later, Boswell was unable to recall the exact sequence of events that led to his rescue. Everything was deranged, disordered—a blur of action and reaction—as in a dream.

A second bullet came whizzing out of nowhere, and the creature's head simply exploded mid-transformation, spattering Boswell's face with green blood and gore.

As Boswell stood frozen in terror, three things happened in quick succession. The monster dropped to its knees, its face still madly trying to organise itself; a rope dropped down from above; and the revenants came splashing towards him. The voice of Johnson echoed down through the vertical shaft, urging Boswell to action. Using his adversary's shoulder as a springboard, Boswell reached for the rope with his last remaining ounce of strength, and catching it, was slowly heaved upwards. A tall revenant in a monk's cassock came lumbering into the light and grabbed for his ankles. The rope gave another lurch, and Boswell was pulled clear of its grasp.

*

The shell that the soldiers hauled out of the hole was barely recognisable as James Boswell, the man Johnson had left only a day and a half previously. His unshaven cheeks were hollow, streaks of white showed through his auburn hair, and his sunken eyes had a distant expression, as if life had shown him too much too soon. His whole frame trembled with nervous tension, and he seemed to withdraw from the slightest touch.

'My poor Boswell!' cried Johnson in a rare excess of emotion. He removed his coat and hung it from the traumatised man's shoulders, then led him carefully to the wall where he could sit. The soldiers brought some whisky, and after a second dram Boswell was able to articulate something of his experiences.

'Well, you have been through it!' Johnson exclaimed, slapping his friend on the back in a bullish attempt to raise his spirits. 'What a lucky shot, eh? These dragoons are worth their weight in gold. Still, I doubt if bullets could put a stop to a Kundalini Demon. Come on, let's get you home.'

With Lady Colville and Doctor Johnson supporting him on either side, Boswell made the short walk from the Castle to his apartment on James Court. Johnson helped him up the stairs and into his favourite chair, while Lady Colville plumped up his cushion and put a kettle on the stove.

'We owe everything to Lady Colville,' remarked Johnson, while the object of his admiration bustled around making tea. 'Her powers of divination are remarkable. Truly, she is a formidable ally.' His tone was light, but the concern he felt for his friend showed clearly on his features.

'Margaret...' murmured Boswell.

'She's with your father Lord Auchinleck, old fellow. Don't you remember?' Johnson replied, patting his hand. 'Which is just as well. One look at you and she'd be throwing me on the first carriage for London. And I wouldn't blame her, either. If it wasn't for me sending you after that wretched Deacon Brodie... I am sorry, Boswell. Truly I am. Can you forgive me?'

Before Boswell had a chance to respond there was a loud knock on the door, and the sound of scuffling footsteps in the hall outside. Moments later Queensberry, Chalmers and Hunter entered the room.

'Gentlemen,' said Johnson. 'Any luck with Lord Sinclair?'

'Bugger gave us the slip,' said Queensberry, slumping onto a chair.

'I'm afraid it's true,' said Lord Chalmers. 'We spent the whole night searching his regular haunts, but to no avail.'

'Good Lord,' said Hunter, seeing Boswell for the first time. 'This man is clearly suffering from exposure. Lady Colville, would you be so kind as to bring some more blankets?'

While Doctor Hunter and Lady Colville busied themselves with the patient, the rest of the company withdrew to the drawing room for a conference. Johnson chose his favourite easy chair by the fireplace, while the other two men drew up stools.

'Boswell was delirious when we found him. But despite his ravings I managed to get an idea of the sheer numbers we are up against.' Johnson stoked the fire with a poker that he absentmindedly twirled in his hand as he talked. 'There is something else down there. Something even more terrible than those revenants. A Kundalini Demon, I think.'

'Then God help us all,' said Lord Chalmers, making a fist and punching it into the palm of his hand. He didn't know what a Kundalini Demon was, but he didn't like the sound of it.

'What do we do now?' said Queensberry.

'Lord Chalmers, how many Scots Greys do we have at our disposal?'

'There are perhaps two hundred dragoons billeted at the Castle. The rest of the regiment is dispersed in times of peace. Why do you ask?'

Johnson rose from his chair and waved the poker, which was still in his grasp, like a sword around his head. 'Gentlemen! My friend has been grievously injured by a pack of bloodthirsty scoundrels whose very existence is an insult to God!' he cried. 'By picking a fight with Boswell, they have picked a fight with *me*, and I swear I shall not rest until each and every one of them has tasted justice.'

The sun, emerging from behind a passing cloud, seemed only to affirm Johnson's words, while somewhere down on High Street a child laughed. The three men knew what they had to do; yet at that moment, the threat looming over the city seemed as far removed from reality as a half-remembered dream from the sober light of day.

Chapter 14

A Council of War

Interview III

Thuban: *By what means are you able to speak with me now?*

Nacash: *I am communicating with you telepathically, which is just one of many gifts we possess.*

Thuban: *And is this ability a natural function of the human mind?*

Nacash: *Yes and no. In many cases the power is latent; a dormant energy which must be awoken by a Higher Power. Some use it frequently without even being aware of it. Yet the majority of mankind have no such faculties at all.*

Thuban: *Who has this power?*

Nacash: *We call them the* sennachi. *When we first came to your world we chose only the first-born from the noblest families to breed with, securing our ascendency over mankind.*

Thuban: *Is this bloodline still extant?*

Nacash: *Yes, the sennachi still walk among you, but when we were banished to the lower realms the sennachi were disinherited. They now wander this earth in nomadic tribes, scattered throughout the four kingdoms. Yet they were once a mighty people, who built the great pyramids of Egypt. They have the power of prophecy and the ability to read minds, among other more subtle powers. They were born of the original race of Anunnaki, whose great heights we newbreeds can only aspire to. For this reason the sennachi are highly prized among my race. The Blood of the Gods flows in their mortal veins.*

Thuban: *Will you share this power?*

Nacash: *Naturally. But first we must be summoned by means of the Blood Ritual, the process of which has already been set down. Only by your interference may we gain access to your world.*

From The Journals of Professor Adrian Weber

The three men crossed the highly polished floor of the Advocate's Library on Parliament Close, a part of the City Chambers directly behind St Giles Cathedral. Built on the site of the church's former graveyard, the library was a triumph of neo-classical architecture, with row after row of beautifully bound books shelved under a colonnade of white marble pillars, golden capitals of finely sculpted acanthus leaves supporting a barrel-vaulted ceiling, and an upper-balustrade decorated with ostrich-feather and acorn motifs. Light streamed in through a lavish cupola in the central gallery, illuminating a solitary reading table where students of law might find sanctuary from the hustle and bustle of the world outside. The whole scene evoked a sylvan grove of sacred birch, whose Arcadian avenues the High Priests of Law swept with their robes of state, speaking in hushed voices, nodding together as they consulted the arcana of their profession.

When the men reached the reading table the eldest of the three, a stout gentleman in a shabby coat and ill-fitting wig, took a rolled-up map from under his arm and spread it across the table.

Moments later a tall military man came striding in, his riding boots ringing smartly across the ornately stuccoed hall, impressive with his bearskin hat tucked under his arm, stiffly starched tunic and rows of medals adorning his broad chest. The casual observer might be forgiven for thinking the eldest of the three men hunched over the map outranked everyone in the room, though in fact he was a mere civilian, whereas the military man striding towards them had two hundred men at his command.

The former glanced up and nodded as the captain of the guard approached.

'Doctor Johnson,' said Lord Chalmers, 'this is Captain Grenville of the 2nd Dragoons.'

'Good day sir,' said Johnson, extending his hand. 'Thank you for coming at such short notice.'

'Good afternoon, Doctor Johnson. My Scots Greys are at your disposal. I hear you have been having some trouble with vermin?'

Johnson smiled perfunctorily, then indicated his map. 'Take a look at this, Captain, if you please.'

Grenville approached the reading table and tilted his head.

'We are here,' said Johnson, tapping a chubby finger against the portion of the map representing Parliament House. 'Now imagine, if you will, that Edinburgh Castle is the head of a huge beast, the High Street is its spine, the Old Church of St. Giles its beating heart, and the tip of the tail here Holyrood Palace. To continue the metaphor, these narrow wynds and closes running at perpendicular, sloping angles to the High Street are the creature's ribs.'

'A most evocative metaphor, Doctor. I see you are a man of keen aesthetic sensibilities.'

'*Ahem*... Well, yes. Now if you look at our current location here on High Street, you will notice the removal of several of these "ribs" to make way for the cluster of buildings you are standing in now.'

'Yes, yes I can see that. There used to be five Closes, if memory serves correctly. Mary Allan's Close, Craig's Close, Stewart's Close, Pearson's Close, and Mary King's Close, all running parallel to one another.'

'That is correct. But according to these records they were never completely destroyed. During the outbreak of the bubonic plague in 1645, upwards of three hundred infected and non-infected residents were bricked up in their homes and left to die.'

'You mean there is still something down there?'

'We have reason to believe so, yes. Somewhere underneath our feet lies a perfectly preserved network of basements and tenement closes, structures that eventually became the foundations for this library and its surrounding buildings.'

'This is all very interesting, Doctor Johnson. But why my dragoons?'

'These underground passages are a perfect breeding ground for the criminal fraternity, a very unique breed of criminal, as we shall soon see. Lord Chalmers?'

Johnson's stout companion pulled away the map to reveal an even older one underneath.

'This map is from 1532, for King James' own personal use,' said the magistrate. 'It shows a secret tunnel running between Edinburgh Castle and Holyrood Palace, to be used by the King in times of emergency. What we are looking at here is a system of underground tunnels and chambers as vast and as complex as the city itself, with the King's Passage serving as a main artery to them all. The creatures using these tunnels have been working tirelessly to extend them for years.'

'Who, or what, are we are up against?' asked Grenville.

'A colony of cannibalistic lepers,' said Johnson. 'A pack of bloodthirsty scoundrels using these passages as their own personal hunting ground. We call them revenants. These are no ordinary men. They have some unique capabilities, which makes them a little tougher than your average enemy to kill. They are able to navigate in complete darkness, for a start.'

'How is that even possible?' said Grenville.

'The organ of the eye has become superfluous, and has dropped out of use almost entirely. Their senses of smell and hearing, on the other hand, are heightened to such an extent that they can find their way around in the dark with astonishing rapidity. From what Mr Boswell has told us, we believe these revenants employ a primitive form of echo location, producing a rapid series of vocal clicks to create a kind of aural map of their environment, much like a shrew or a bat.'

'Good Lord!'

'There is another sense lacking in these revenants, the absence of which gives them a distinct advantage over your dragoons. Due to some peculiarity of the disease, they are entirely lacking in pain receptors, which normally serve to warn us when something we touch is too hot, too cold, too sharp, and so forth.'

Captain Grenville gave a nervous laugh. 'You mean they can't feel pain? Come on, Doctor!'

'I am quite serious,' said Johnson. 'The disease attacks pain-sensors, rendering the revenant oblivious to the wear and tear we commonly receive on a day to day basis. And yet these unique abilities are not the greatest challenge your men will have to overcome. Their appearance itself is enough to daunt even the most hardened of warriors. I have encountered two of them myself, Captain. And believe me, you would not want to meet them alone in a darkened alley.'

'I'll be sure to relay it to my men,' said Grenville. 'So how do you propose we tackle the situation?'

Johnson turned to the Duke and gave him the floor.

'There are five points of entry to the underworld that we know of,' said Queensberry, moving his finger around the map of High Street in a rough oval shape. 'Here beneath us at Mary King's Close, a coal cellar at Niddry Street, a manhole at Edinburgh Castle, a dungeon beneath Holyrood Palace, and there is another entrance hidden here at St Margaret's Well, which as you can see is flush against the north face of Castle Rock. We believe that with guards stationed at each exit we will be able to contain the situation, and prevent these revenants from causing any further mischief. Captain Grenville, you will remain at Edinburgh Castle to oversee operations. Meanwhile Doctor Johnson, Lord Chalmers and I will borrow two of your pluckiest dragoons and make our way to Roswell Castle, where we have more immediate business to attend to.'

'Roswell? That is the ancestral home of the Sinclairs,' said Captain Grenville. 'Surely Sir William is not mixed up in this?'

'If Lady Colville's visions are correct,' replied Johnson, 'then I daresay he's in it up to his neck.'

*

Mrs Boswell read through the box of letters for the hundredth time: page after page of girlish banalities, ponies, silk dresses, dances, boys, each different girl expressing the same empty-headed nonsense. Sister Grace was right. They were all written by the same person. If it wasn't the girls, then who? The handwriting was clearly an adult female. The Mother Superior? It seemed likely. More importantly, if an adult had written these letters, then what had happened to the girls?

Mrs Boswell scrunched up the letters and clutched them to her breast; she shut her eyes tightly and heaved a sigh. She knew in her heart that those girls were dead. This wasn't a kidnapping conspiracy, at least, not in the ordinary sense where a ransom was sought. Sister Daphne was procuring girls for Sir William and his cronies. But why? For what? Mrs Boswell remembered back to a conversation she overhead between her husband and Doctor Johnson. She remembered being angry at the time because she thought the subject matter might frighten Veronica, who was sleeping in the next room. They were talking about satanic rites and ritual, pentagrams, summoning demons and such nonsense, and she distinctly heard Johnson remark, on the subject of human sacrifice, that the Satanists favour an innocent child.

So that was it. Sir William and his cronies were Satanists! And they had Veronica.

Mrs Boswell threw back her head and howled with all her might. It was raw and visceral, the sound of an animal in pain, the howl of a mother forcibly separated from her child. And it was filled with such a terrible rage that even Sister Daphne, pacing the floors below, felt her blood run cold.

*

Nine miles south of Edinburgh, hemmed in on three sides by a loop in the River Esk, the ruins of Roswell Castle stood on a high rock overlooking a deep gorge. The keep had taken its fair share of battering in its four-hundred-year history, from domestic fire to siege warfare; yet despite these depredations it had prevailed. The eastern range, being the only part of the castle still intact, had always been home to a Sinclair, the ancient family who had held domicile there since William St. Clair first raised the Great Turnpike in 1304.

The only point of access was from the south, by means of a narrow bridge over the steeply wooded glen. As the riders crossed in single file they looked down nervously, each wondering if the canopy of trees would break their fall should their horses suddenly lose their footing in the mud. Johnson crossed first, closely followed by Lord Chalmers and the Duke, with dragoons James Douglas and Hector Gillies—the two men who had saved Johnson's life in Boswell's apartment—bringing up the rear.

They found the remains of a great bonfire piled against the main entrance by a high shoulder of rock. Johnson climbed down from his mount and poked around the debris with his stick, uncovering the remains of a horse and the charred spokes of a carriage wheel. The Duke, meanwhile, turned over a wooden panel with his boot, revealing a coat of arms emblazoned on the underside. 'Some important people must have been here, judging from this livery.'

Johnson grunted. 'A black goat on a shield beneath a black-and-white plumed helm. It's Weber's crest.'

'But who would do such a thing?' asked Lord Chalmers.

'Whoever it was they were in a hurry,' said Johnson. 'If they didn't want their victims to be recognised, they went about it in a very haphazard way.'

The group cautiously tethered their horses to the iron hoops on the wall and pushed open the doors to the main keep. Cast-iron hinges, each long as a man's arm, groaned open onto a great hall replete with threadbare tapestries and towering oak arches. Grim family portraits and stuffed deer heads stared accusingly down from the panelled walls. The five lawmen searched around to find their initial impression confirmed. The castle was deserted.

A long dining table had been set for supper some weeks ago, judging from the mouldy bread and maggot-infested meat. 'What could have happened here?' said Lord Chalmers, running his finger across the thick layer of dust.

'Something bad,' said Johnson, his eyes glancing warily around.

A second doorway led out onto the fragments of a ruined wall and watchtower, with a crumbling staircase climbing into a starless sky. Semi-collapsed buttresses stood in a row like the skeletal ribcage of some long-dead leviathan. The wind whistled miserably through the empty spaces, imbuing the scene of carnage they encountered in that twilit ruin with a desperate sense of melancholy.

The roofless courtyard, handsomely paved, featured a well in the centre which had only recently been blown apart, judging from the broken fragments strewn around the blast area. Here and there a weather-blasted tree grew from a fissure of rock, stretching skeletal fingers into a slate-grey sky. A large pentagram covered the paved surface of the courtyard, neatly delineated in chalk, with the blasted well at the centre, and hieroglyphs etched around its circumference. The corpses looked as though they had been placed there intentionally, each marking a point on the pentagram.

The elements had not been kind to them.

Johnson only recognised the first cadaver from the tall forehead and grey streaks of hair. The crows that had taken its eyes settled on the battlements to gloat; hulking, glossy beasts that eyed the intruders scornfully, seeming to laugh with their harsh, metallic croaks, their beaks as hard and as cruel as gun-metal.

'Weber,' confirmed Johnson, removing his hat. 'If only he had turned his talents to the betterment of mankind. Alas! he was undone in the end by his own ambition.'

'Doctor Johnson,' cried Lord Chalmers, standing over the second corpse. 'Do you know this man?'

At first glance the features failed to register. When it finally dawned on Johnson, the shock of recognition was like a blow to his heart. 'My God,' he cried. 'The Reverend Baxter is a good friend of the Boswells. Can he really have sunk so low?'

Johnson hardly dared to approach the third corpse for fear of recognising some other former friend or associate. The fact it was missing a head came almost as a relief. The finely brocaded clothes and smart riding boots, however, suggested a man of some influence and power.

The men moved around the courtyard in a clockwise direction, eager to get the identification over as quickly as possible. The fourth corpse was Sir William, Lord Sinclair. Johnson was appalled, though it came as no surprise. He shook his head sadly at the scene of devastation. 'These men have been dead for at least three weeks.'

'But that's impossible,' Chalmers protested. 'I saw Lord Sinclair only two days ago.'

Johnson looked grimly at the magistrate. 'That was not Lord Sinclair you saw.'

'But I swear to you that it was.'

Johnson got down on one knee to examine the hideous gash on Sinclair's throat, using the end of a stick to lift the ragged flap of skin. 'These bodies have been drained almost entirely of blood.'

'What the hell happened here?' said Queensberry.

'Gentlemen, there is only one logical conclusion,' said Johnson. 'Whatever came crawling out of that well drank these men's blood and stole their identities.'

'Nonsense,' barked Queensberry.

'And yet we have the evidence of our eyes,' said Johnson.

'Doctor Johnson,' said Lord Chalmers, who had crossed the courtyard to examine the fifth and final corpse. 'I think you had better come and see this.'

Chapter 15

The Rock and the Maiden

he two soldiers standing outside Mary King's Close on the banks of the Nor Loch were utterly mystified as to why they had been posted there. The subterranean Close ran from underneath the City Chambers on High Street, carrying the effluence of the city across a patch of waste ground and down to the festering, corpse-filled loch. The stink coming from the place was truly awful.

The two men stared glumly at the water. More of a bog, really, with much of it already drained in the name of progress. Folks that lived on the north end of town didn't go out after dark anymore, deterred by rumours of nameless things slithering out of the water and stealing into the town at night, creeping things made of shadow, and disembodied heads glimpsed floating over the Loch like spectral Chinese lanterns. Scientists wrote scholarly articles to newspapers on the subject. They claimed that rotting vegetation on the newly exposed Loch bed released noxious gases with hallucinogenic properties. Other more superstitious souls said that, when they started draining the Loch, the workmen had disturbed something that should have been left well alone. After all, the Loch had at one time been used to drown women accused of witchcraft. The Loch bed was littered with the innocent victims of King James' fanatical purge, a breeding ground for vengeful spirits if ever there was one.

Lance Corporal Patrick Dowie, the younger of the two sentries, was particularly vexed. He had been playing billiards in the mess hall, looking forward to some leave time that afternoon, when the order came through. Now he would have to wait a whole week to see his fiancée.

Not that it was a particularly demanding detail. No one used these old tunnels under the city anyway. Rumours of creeping things had soon put paid to that, and Dowie didn't spook easily. No, the only enemy here was boredom. Still, every time he turned to face the narrow gap between the brooding tenement flats he felt the cold fingers of dread at his heart. It was so dark it almost seemed to *swallow* the light, and with the sun sinking fast behind the Mound, soon the only light would be from a pallid and indifferent moon.

He turned to the man standing next to him, who seemed to accept his fate with his customary stoicism. 'Remind me,' said Dowie. 'What are we doing here again, Sir?'

'Ye ken orders,' replied Sergeant Miller, a tall, grim faced man with broad shoulders and a hooked nose. 'Nobody enters, nobody leaves.'

'Ah ken that,' said the smaller man. 'But for what reason?'

'Ours is not to reason why, laddie. This order comes from Captain Grenville himself.'

That made Dowie feel a little easier. The men all venerated Captain Grenville like a father, and would have followed him to hell and back if he snapped his fingers. Still, just like Old Grenville to leave them guessing. A dark horse, that one. Dowie looked out across the loch and suppressed a shudder. Maybe better off not knowing, he told himself.

A sudden movement off to the right caught the young corporal's attention. Someone was coming down the farm lane that skirted the banks of the loch. 'Who goes there?' he demanded, fingering his musket nervously. A figure stepped out from the shadows, which Dowie recognised as their staff sergeant, an officious little man called Brown.

'New orders,' said the new arrival breathlessly.

'What orders?' said Miller.

'You are to go in there,' he said, pointing into the darkness of the close, 'and light a fire.'

'A what?'

'A fire, sergeant.'

'That's what I thought you said,' said Miller. 'Nobody told us anything about a fire. Our orders were to stand guard here. Nothing else.'

'The new order has been signed by Captain Grenville,' said Brown. 'He says we are to smoke 'em out.'

'Smoke out who, sir?' said Dowie.

'Didn't say. Just said walk ten paces into the close, light a fire, and shoot any bastard that tries to escape. That's the order.'

'Very well,' said Sergeant Miller. He snapped out a salute, and Staff Sergeant Brown ran off to deliver his message to the rest of the guard around the city.

Miller and Dowie gathered armfuls of fallen branches from the banks of the Loch and stockpiled them inside the close. They used the greenest branches to create plenty of smoke, and waited for a favourable breeze before lighting. It was getting a bit chilly anyway, and a fire would be just the ticket.

Just like old *Blood and Guts Grenville*, reflected Miller. He was never one for waiting around. A maverick in that respect, was Grenville. Always rubbing up top brass the wrong way. The only reason he hadn't been court-marshalled was that the men all considered him something of a hero. They loved to hear his tales, like the time he rode so deeply into French lines he became hopelessly separated from his unit and found himself surrounded. He was captured and brought to a tent for a private audience with no less a personage than King Louis XV, who commended him for his courage and embraced him warmly before setting him free.

You had to hand it to those Frenchies, they knew courage when they saw it. Yes, he was a rum 'un, was Grenville, and fearless as an old badger.

Standing in the mouth of that darkened close, Sergeant Miller took the flint from his tinderbox, struck it against the back of his knife, then cupped his hands and gently blew on the kindling. The two men stood back and watched the straw start to smoulder.

*

There has always been a castle on Castle Rock.

At least, for as long as anyone can remember.

In the time of King Arthur and his Knights of the Round Table, a race of Iron Age warriors who called themselves the Votadini established the Kingdom of Gododdin, a huge tract of land that stretched from the Firth of Forth in the north to the River Wear in the south. Their stronghold they named Dun Eidyn, and they built a great fortress there on the hill. *Maiden's Castle* they called her, for they deemed her impregnable by force. For five hundred years the great halls rang with song and laughter and the golden mead ran freely. But eventually the Votadini exceeded their reach, and on a raiding expedition across the border they were ambushed and massacred by a marauding band of Anglo-Saxons.

The stronghold on Castle Rock exchanged hands many times, held first by the Scots, then by the English, then back again in an endless cycle of siege and skirmish.

In the fifteenth century, having been under Scottish rule for a significant length of time, King James II moved his royal court there, and declared Edinburgh the capital city of Scotland. Stone replaced wood, and piece by piece the castle began to assume its present-day form, steadily becoming the bastion of power and authority we are familiar with today.

Captain Grenville was just the latest in a long line of distinguished military leaders entrusted with the defence of the castle, and by extension the entire city. And since it had succumbed to no serious threat since 1745, when Charles Edward Stuart made his triumphant march into town, Grenville's job was more or less a ceremonial one. It was a role he did not relish, being a man of equal parts courage and determination; or rashness and vainglory, depending on whom one believed.

The old veteran stood high upon the watchtower, looking out upon his beloved city. He had personally given the order to light the fires, and would take full responsibility should anything go wrong. Doctor Johnson had advised caution. A worthy man, to be sure, and Grenville did not doubt the stoutness of his English heart. But Johnson was no soldier, and siege warfare was not Grenville's style. His men waited impatiently on the parade ground below. These were good men, brave men, men eager to cover themselves in glory. Who was he to deny them the opportunity? The moment he gave the signal his dragoons would ride out and cut those revenants down to size.

As a little boy he had watched his father smoke out a den of rats. His ghillie lit a fire at each exit but one, then stood back and watched as the rats came streaming out. The men set about the panic-stricken rodents with their clubs one after another: *smack smack smack*. It had been a massacre. This would be no different. This... Boswell fellow, clearly rattled by his experiences, had most probably exaggerated the size of the threat in his report to Lord Chalmers. Grenville would force the vermin out through the only way available to them: here on the Castle Esplanade, where two hundred of his Scots Greys, the creme of His Majesty's cavalry, were ready and waiting.

*

The Wellhouse Tower stood fast against the north face of Castle Rock, in the shadow of the watchtower. Now little more than a ruin, the broken wall fragments protected an ancient well, and a small, thickly fortified door built into the rock face on ground level. Somewhere on the other side of this door, a rough-hewn set of stairs climbed all the way through the interior of the rock to the watchtower. This secret passage was once used by soldiers from the garrison to collect water from the well, but reports of men becoming lost in the labyrinthine tunnels saw to it that the door was locked permanently.

The soldier charged with guarding the door, Lance Corporal Anthony Fordyce, was surprised and more than a little wary when handed a key and given his new orders. Nobody had opened that door in more than twenty years; from then until now, keeping it locked had become something of a tradition within the garrison. Captain Grenville, however, was determined in his folly, and so despite his misgivings Fordyce turned the key and pulled the heavy door open on its rusty hinges. Decades of musty air came rushing out at once, almost knocking Fordyce from his feet. He built the fire quickly, gathering dried leaves and branches scattered among the ruins of the tower, then stepped back to admire his handiwork before he lit the kindling.

As the flames grew higher a vast, cavernous hall of natural rock was revealed, with shadowy passages leading off to the left and right. In the middle, a pyramid of barrels was stacked so high they almost touched the ceiling. Fordyce pulled a flaming branch from the fire and threw it in to see more clearly.

The gunpowder had lain untouched for thirty years, stacked against the threat of a Jacobite invasion. When Charles Edward Stuart and his army entered Edinburgh, 60,000 people lined the Royal Mile to welcome him. But he never did manage to take Edinburgh Castle, and the gunpowder which had been stored underneath to guarantee him a welcome was soon forgotten about.

Despite the age of the powder it was still dry, and highly combustible. Fordyce squinted to spell out the lettering on the barrels. 'G...U...N...P...O...W... *Shite.*' was all he could manage.

The blinding flash was the last thing he knew.

The shock was so sudden not one citizen could register what was happening until it was too late. The explosion shook the foundations of Castle Rock, blasting manhole covers into the air all the way down the Royal Mile to St Giles Cathedral. People above ground lurched to the side or fell to their knees. Searing flames ripped through the spider's web of tunnels under Old Town, enveloping other strategically placed barrels of gunpowder and caches of winter fuel stored by some of the city's more forward-thinking citizens.

Deep within the Castle Rock, something malignant stirred. And just like that, the Great Fire of Old Town had begun.

Chapter 16

Terror from Beyond the Stars

The crescent moon appeared like a pale smirk over the ruined courtyard of Roswell Castle. Night was closing in. The well seemed to have broken its circular encasement, spreading invisible tentacles across the courtyard, enclosing the walls of the keep in its sinister embrace.

Night fell and darkness arose.

Five corpses encircled the well, like the petals of some withered and diseased flower.

Five men bore witness to the scene of desolation.

Douglas and Gillies stood guard at the doors to the main keep, keeping as far from the stench of death as pride would allow.

Johnson, Queensberry and Chalmers regarded with horror the long-dead body of a man they had left in Edinburgh only hours before.

'If that truly be Doctor Hunter,' said Lord Chalmers, eyeing with distrust the emaciated corpse on the ground before him, 'then who is the imposter we left with Boswell and Lady Colville?'

'That is a good question,' said Johnson, 'and one which I intend to answer.'

Johnson left the group and wandered over to examine the ruins of the well. Moments later he stooped to pick something up.

'What is it?' said Chalmers, appearing at his side.

'It is just as I feared,' said Johnson, passing his find to Lord Chalmers.

The magistrate held the scaly substance up to the moonlight. Each turquoise scale was the size of a thumbnail, and shimmered like the stars. 'It looks just like... snakeskin.'

'Not a snake, exactly,' said Johnson. 'Say rather, a distant cousin, an ancestor of that same serpent who seduced Eve in paradise, precipitating mankind's expulsion from grace.'

Lord Chalmers looked askance at his friend. 'Now you are talking in riddles, Doctor.'

'Then let me be plain. The being who shed this skin is not of this world.'

'Not of this world?' repeated Chalmers incredulously.

Johnson nodded grimly. 'After I had Weber committed to the sanitorium, we found among his personal effects certain papers and documents alluding to a mysterious race of beings who call themselves *Drakon*. According to Weber these creatures are shapeshifters, extra-terrestrial beings from somewhere in the Draco system.'

Johnson sat himself on a broken chunk of masonry and began drawing celestial symbols in the dust with his stick. 'Throughout history they have revealed themselves to us in various guises: in the Bible they are the *Nephilim*, a race of giants who fell from the sky, taking the daughters of men for their brides. The ancient Sumerians and Babylonians called them *Anunnaki*, meaning 'sky-born', and worshipped them as gods. To the Celtic druids they are the *Dragon Lords of Anu*, a higher race of beings who hail from Atlantis, and to whom they sacrificed animals and even children.'

'Thank you for the history lesson,' retorted Queensberry. 'But what has all this to do with us?'

'Perhaps everything,' said Johnson. 'At some point in their history these beings were driven deep underground, defeated by a cataclysmic event of devastating proportions. Legend tells of vast, chthonic regions, cities untouched by light of day, and staggering vistas unseen by mortal eye. The Anunnaki—as Weber prefers to call them—use portals such as these to access the surface. It is little wonder that Edinburgh is such a hotbed of supernatural activity, when one considers that Castle Rock itself sits on a 350-million-year-old pipeline, a volcanic vent that leads directly to the earth's core. Even the revenants have only scratched the surface of this infernal region.'

Lord Chalmers sat down beside Johnson and held his head in his hands to stop it from reeling. 'Wait a minute: underground cities? Atlantis?' he groaned. 'I thought you said these beings were from another world?'

'Originally, yes. The continent of Atlantis was colonised some ten thousand years ago by a race of cosmic voyagers… At least, according to Weber's notes.'

'If I didn't know you better,' scoffed Queensberry, 'then I would say you belonged in a mental institution with your bratwurst-munching friend over there.'

Johnson ignored the jibe. 'Let us look at what we know. Five invocants are required to complete the ritual, which must be performed when the moon is in its new phase. Here we have the bodies of four men whom we know of, plus one unidentified male. The next new moon phase is tomorrow night, which means these men were killed twenty-seven days ago, according to the lunar calendar. And yet we all saw Doctor Hunter—or someone who looks and acts just like Hunter—this afternoon.'

'Let's just say that what you are claiming is true,' said Lord Chalmers. 'What do they look like, these beings? I mean, how should we recognise them?'

'The Anunnaki are ostensibly humanoid in form, yet reptilian in nature, and just as cold-blooded and ruthless as their terrestrial counterparts. They require blood sacrifice to appear among us, but must feed frequently in order to maintain the illusion. They abhor the light, especially in their reptilian or transitional phases, but once they have fully assimilated the blood of their victims they may integrate themselves seamlessly into society. At least until the need for blood reasserts itself.'

'You say the ancients worshipped these beings as gods,' said Lord Chalmers, 'and yet you also portray them as hostile to mankind. How do you reconcile such a contradiction?'

'The Atlanteans were founders of a great civilisation, a race of demi-gods who taught humanity much of value, including the fundamental principles of agriculture, mathematics, astronomy, metalwork and architecture. At some point in the history of this great race a schism developed, giving rise to two distinct factions. On the one hand were the Order of Keledei, a sect of warrior priests who followed the Old Religion, and walked in the ways of righteousness. Those who chose the left-hand path, the Sons of Belial, were an order of fallen angels who succumbed to darkness, tempted by material wealth and selfish ambition. A Holy War broke out between these two factions, culminating in the destruction of the four island states of Atlantis. Legend has it that the Sons of Belial were vanquished by an alliance of men and Keledei, and sent into exile, disappearing entirely from the pages of history. And yet the Sons of Belial endured, though millennia spent brooding in the deep places of the earth has twisted and corrupted them beyond recognition. No longer the inheritors of this earth, they have reverted to their original, reptilian forms; thus they have grown bitter, and envious of the world of man, and dream only of conquest.'

'Then what did Weber have to gain by rousing these... things?'

'Weber was led to believe that these beings had some dark gift or secret knowledge to impart but, inevitably, he was deceived in this. By destroying Weber and usurping his identity, the Anunnaki have seized control of the Order of Draco, who in turn control the Masonic Brotherhood, giving these demons a foothold in every corridor of power in Europe. Perhaps even the ear of the King himself.'

'Of course,' said Lord Chalmers. 'As private physician to the King, Doctor Hunter could wield considerable influence.'

'Not to mention Lord Sinclair in his role as the King's Treasurer in Scotland, giving him control over the purse strings,' added Johnson.

'What is it that they want?' said Queensberry. 'Presuming these things are real, of course, and not the product of some deranged opium dream.'

'In a word: chaos,' said Johnson. 'To turn brother against brother, family against family, and nation against nation; to spread riot, disease, disharmony and discord. By their craft and subtlety they wish to decimate and enslave the population once more, and to reclaim their birth right as of old.'

'Is that all?' said Queensberry drily.

'Not quite,' said Johnson. 'In his mad scribblings Weber speaks of a wind from the East, a reign of terror that will shake the Age of Reason to its very foundations. The Hindus call it Kali Yuga, a time of great trouble and strife in the world. Weber also prophesied the coming of Lamia, Dragon Queen of Anu, mother of all Drakon, who will spread her vast wings and cover the world in a second darkness.'

'Then God help us all,' said Lord Chalmers, who found no reason to doubt Johnson even for a moment. 'But when will this come to pass?'

'The prophecy states that first the dead will rise from their graves, and the world will be consumed by fire.'

Lord Chalmers started. 'The revenants!'

'Yes,' said Johnson. 'These revenants are in thrall to the Anunnaki, providing their masters with everything they need to ensure they can establish a foothold in this realm.'

'Is there a way to destroy these lizard men?' asked Queensberry.

'The Anunnaki are virtually impossible to destroy. Unless…'

'Unless?' said Chalmers and Queensberry in unison.

'If we attack them mid-transformation—when their morphology is in flux, so to speak—like we destroyed that creature Boswell encountered under Edinburgh Castle, then I think they are vulnerable enough to be destroyed.'

The Fall of the House of Thomas Weir

'Then we must try!' cried Lord Chalmers. 'If the fellow we took for Doctor Hunter is one of these Anuki…'

'Anunnaki'

'…Anunnaki, then Lady Colville is in grave danger.'

A sudden noise broke Chalmers' train of thought. The three men turned just in time to see a dark shape sliding over the broken ramparts of the castle.

'Somebody has been watching us,' hissed Queensberry.

Johnson signalled to Douglas and Gillies, who darted off in pursuit. The man they dragged back moments later was dressed in the livery of a servant, his clothes hanging in tattered rags from his emaciated frame. His hair was wild and snagged with brambles, as of one long accustomed to sleeping in ditches, and his fingernails had grown into claws. 'Get your hauns aff me, ye carles ye!' he cried, digging in his heels. 'Nah! Nah! Dinnae! I maunna gang thare!'

Thrown roughly to the ground, the prisoner pawed and scraped at Doctor Johnson's ankles, shaking and panting like a cornered beast.

'Calm yourself, man,' said Johnson. 'We mean you no harm.'

The wretch cast a suspicious look at the faces surrounding him.

'Come now,' said Johnson, pulling his leg free and struggling to hide his distaste. 'You are quite safe. What is your name?'

'Whit reck ma name? We are a' deid men gin we bide here a seicont mair!'

Johnson cast a questioning look at Lord Chalmers.

'He said that his name is neither here nor there, and that we are all dead men if we remain here a moment longer.'

'I know you,' said the Duke. 'You are Sinclair's lackey, are you not? Have I not seen you horsewhipped from one end of the Grassmarket to the other for insubordination, you mangy cur?'

The man grimaced at Queensberry and bared a crooked set of teeth in a parody of a smile, then formed a "C" with his thumb and forefinger and tilted it before his mouth, mimicking a glass of water.

Hector Gillies removed his canteen and tossed it to the prisoner, who wrenched off the lid and drained its contents in seconds. Once he had taken his fill he seemed a little easier, and turned on Johnson with a crafty look. 'Eh, ye wouldna happen to hae a wee drap snuff on ye, by ony chance?'

'What?' barked Johnson. 'Snuff?'

Lord Chalmers reached into his pocket and produced his snuff horn. The servant's eyes gleamed as he helped himself, then satisfied, grinned at Johnson like an eager-to-please dog.

'What is your name?' said Johnson.

'Archie Gunn,' replied the man obediently.

'And you were here when these gentlemen met their fates?'

Gunn nodded.

'And you saw what happened to them?'

A pause, then another nod.

'What came out of that well?'

At this point Gunn's courage seemed to fail. He shuddered.

'Come, man,' said Johnson. 'Whatever it was has gone. Speak now, and avenge your master.'

Archie Gunn's troubled eyes fixed on Johnson's and he said one word in his native tongue, then covered his head with his hands and began to shake uncontrollably.

Johnson cast an inquiring look at Lord Chalmers.

Lord Chalmers returned Johnson's look with an expression of equal parts horror and wonder. '*Uilephest,*' he explained. 'It means fabulous beasts. Dragons.'

A chill wind swept across the forecourt. The three men turned to look at the well, which on its swelling of earth appeared as a gaping mouth, and the howling of the wind was its scream.

*

Lance Corporal Patrick Dowie took back what he said about not getting spooked easily. He didn't know which worried him the more: the arched entrance to Mary King's Close behind him, or the mist-enshrouded water before him. The fire had almost burned itself out. Dowie dropped some branches of birch onto the embers, then stood back and watched as more smoke filled the narrow passage. 'So who is it we're supposed to be watching for anyway?'

Sergeant Miller was sitting on a log near the entrance smoking his pipe. 'Revenants,' he said, without taking his eyes from the loch.

'Reve... what?'

'Revenants,' Miller repeated. 'The risen dead. That's what the papers are saying. It started with this Greyfriar's Ghoul, which ye'd know about if you took the time to read the news, instead of just the funny pages. Turns out there's hundreds of them living under the city, just itching for revenge.'

'Revenge?' said Dowie nervously, not sure whether to take his sergeant seriously or not. 'Revenge for what?'

'On the City Fathers for bricking them up a hundred years ago and leaving them to rot. They're plague victims, see, come back from the dead to wreak vengeance on the living.'

Dowie stared hard at his sergeant to see if he was joking or not. He had a dry sense of humour, Sergeant Miller, like the time last year when he told them Charles Edward Stuart had landed at Leith Port ready to march again on Edinburgh. Had the unit riled up for a whole afternoon, the sod. 'Naaaah,' said Dowie. 'It's rats, that's all. Dirty great stinking rats living under the city. Want smoking out. That's what the fire's for.'

Miller took another puff of his pipe and sent a smoke ring across the water. 'Rats, is it? Oh, well. You know best. *Rats* it is then.'

Dowie was beginning to get more than a little annoyed with the sergeant's insinuating tone. He picked up a flat stone from the banks of the Loch and sent it skimming across the surface.

'I wouldn't be doing that, if I were you,' said Miller softly.

'Oh? And why not?'

Miller removed the pipe from his mouth and jabbed the stem

towards the water. 'It's no' the close ye want to be worrying about. Have I not seen ye cast fearful looks at the water when you think I cannae see ye? And weel ye might, Corporal Dowie, weel ye might, because that Loch is an evil place.'

'Oho!' said Dowie, sitting down beside his superior. 'Haunted now, is it? We really did draw the short straw when we got posted to this little beauty spot. A stinking close behind us, and a stinking bog afore us. So go on, then. What's in the water that I've to be afeart of?'

'You name it,' said Miller. 'Murder victims, suicide victims, and then there was the nasty wee case from a hundred years ago of the man accused of incest with his two sisters. They put the three of them together in a barrel, knocked some holes in it, and threw the whole sinful lot of them into the water tae drown. Can you imagine? Aye, the Nor Loch is a reservoir of unquiet souls, whichever way ye look at it.'

'And witches too, I suppose?'

'A common misconception, Dowie. The Nor Loch used to be the location of witch dunking trials. The puir soul suspected of witchcraft would be dragged down the hill, presumably after being interrogated and tortured, and thrown in the loch. If she floated then she was said to be a witch, dragged up the hill and burned at the stake before the castle gates. If she sank she was innocent, but of course by then she had already drowned. Some say that these innocent victims come creeping and a crawling out of the sludgy pit of the Nor Loch each night after sundown, looking for victims to drag down to a watery grave with them.'

'Well, Sergeant Miller, and that is quite the story. Let me make a suggestion. You watch the Loch, and I'll watch the Close, and if by some miracle we survive the night, I will buy the first round in—'

'*Shhh,*' said Miller, tilting his head. 'Can ye hear?'

Dowie stood perfectly still and strained his ears to listen. The stillness of the night was almost absolute. All he could hear was the croaking of frogs from the muddy banks of the Loch. 'I hear nothing, sergeant. What is it I am supposed to be hearing?'

'From inside the close. Voices.'

After a few seconds Dowie could hear it too. A sort of chattering, jabbering noise, accompanied by the soft padding as of many feet running together.

'*Lord ha' Mercy*,' whimpered Dowie.

'Be quiet!' hissed Miller. 'Grab your weapon.'

Miller took his rifle from its perch against the wall and cocked it, getting down on one knee and squinting as he took aim. Dowie was already loosening his kit and letting it fall to the floor.

'What the hell are you doing, Dowie?'

'Getting ready to run, sir.'

'Are you mad? Don't be a fool. You will be shot for cowardice before the castle wall.'

'Better that than being eaten alive,' reasoned Dowie, kicking off his heavy boots.

The chattering noise had now become a wild cacophony. Whatever it was, it was getting close.

'You come too,' pleaded Dowie. 'You will be torn limb from limb!'

'I am a Dragoon of the Royal Scots Grey, soldier. A Scots Grey never leaves his post!'

'Suit yourself,' shrugged Dowie, and with that he was off like a shot, ploughing into the stinking water of the Loch.

Through his terror Dowie heard two loud gun blasts, then seconds later an ungodly sound, as of a man plunged into the extremes of agony. He didn't look back as he ploughed into the water. After a few hundred yards he turned. Miller hadn't made it. The monsters were tearing him limb from limb. With a terrified whimper Dowie turned and moved deeper into the water. The lights of the New Town twinkled in the distance. If he managed to get across the boggy water, he might stand a chance.

The soft mud sank beneath his feet. He tried to lift a leg. It felt heavy. He placed it in front of him with a squelch, then tried to lift the other leg. It wouldn't budge. He struggled in a panic, only to sink deeper into the morass. A crowd of revenants had gathered on the bank to watch. Dowie could hear them chattering and laughing amongst themselves. Damn them. He cried out for help. A group of farmhands appeared on the other side, just visible in the darkness. They were reaching out, trying to get him to catch hold of something. A branch. If only he could reach it. Dowie was waist deep now. He reached out, his fingers brushing the tip of the branch. The men on shore were yelling something, urging him on. Dowie stretched with every fibre of his being and managed to snatch hold of it. The men started to pull, and with an audible sucking noise Dowie felt himself being pulled free.

Something grabbed his ankle from below the surface of the marsh. The men on the far bank heaved, but the thing in the water was stronger. Dowie tightened his grip on the branch, but it was no use. He let out a moan as he lost his grip. Cold fingers dug into the flesh of his ankle, pulling him down with preternatural strength.

He gave one last cry of despair, and disappeared.

Chapter 17

Within the Pentacle

*H*ow is the patient, Lady Colville?'

Doctor Hunter was reclining on the easy chair by the fire, his fingertips resting at his lips to form a pyramid. He seemed to Lady Colville unnaturally still, his eyes glassy and watchful beneath hooded lids.

'He is sleeping, Doctor.'

'Good.'

Four hundred feet below, Lance Corporal Anthony Fordyce was in the process of igniting a certain cache of gunpowder.

A tremor shook the ground beneath Lady Colville's feet. She grasped the mantelpiece to steady herself, then moved to the window to see what was happening. A group of men, women and children ran past in the direction of the castle, as if in flight from something. Some of the men were shouting, but Lady Colville couldn't make out what they were trying to say. When they reached the castle they pounded on the gates.

'Something is happening outside,' said Lady Colville, turning from the window.

Hunter merely grunted.

Lady Colville edged her way back to the mantelpiece, where she spied Mrs Boswell's treasured hat pin, the little salamander with rubies for eyes. She picked it up and turned it in her hand. 'I fear for Mrs Boswell,' she said. 'Perhaps we could send for her. Her presence alone would be a great comfort to Mr Boswell.'

Hunter seemed irritated. 'Why disturb the woman when she would only worry? Did you not hear Doctor Johnson? We are to remain here until further notice.'

'But I have a terrible feeling that something—' Abruptly Lady Colville's expression changed, and she raised a hand to her temple. 'Oh,' she said faintly. 'Oh, no.'

Hunter glared at Lady Colville. 'What is it now?' he said between gritted teeth.

Lady Colville pulled on her shawl and made a gesture towards the door. 'It is Mrs Boswell. She is in terrible danger. We must warn Mr Boswell! We must—'

A further series of explosions shook the ground beneath her feet.

Hunter was on her before she knew what was happening. His arm shot out like a cobra and he grabbed her wrist, twisting it until the piece of jewellery fell from her grasp. She turned to gaze into the black pools of Hunter's eyes, and in that moment with a terrible clarity saw him for what he was.

Lady Colville knew the expression "*time stood still*" from romance novels, but she never knew it could actually happen until now. The grandfather clock in the hall, always so persistent, stopped dead in its revolution. In that single breathless moment, all past and all future seemed to flow into an ever-present stream of living energy, a perfect circle of light indistinguishable from her essential self.

There had been visions before, of course, but never one so powerful. Her spirit felt as if it had been flipped out of her body and launched into the ether.

She was no longer in the drawing room on High Street. Stars wheeled overhead. Her brain was assailed with a thousand disconnected images… visions of terrible rites held in the darkness of the primordial forest… of drums throbbing deep within the jungles of some lost continent... of an ochre sun setting behind the great monoliths of the Druids... of mighty pyramids raised by unseen hands... and she saw a sea-girt city of glittering crystal, and a creature that was taller than a man upon the ramparts, similar in form, though his body was covered in iridescent scales like those of a snake, and his face was both terrible and indescribably beautiful.

Then she remembered everything.

Her grandmother had told her the tales of a mighty race of warriors who had come from the stars to enslave mankind. The first men worshipped them as gods, building idols in their image and raising temples in their honour. But after an age these Dragon Lords grew greedy and deceitful. Temples ran red with the blood of men, women and children, but still their terrible thirst was unassuaged.

And they lusted for more than blood, and found that they desired the daughters of men in a carnal way, and they mated with them and impregnated them with the seed of the stars.

And the daughters of men gave birth to something that was neither man nor god but *demigod*, imbued with the gift of seeing.

After an age of darkness mankind rose up to overthrow their reptilian masters, banishing them to the depths of the earth. The hybrid offspring of the Dragon Lords, the *sennachi*, were stripped of their honours and possessions to become a wandering tribe, named after the great civilisation they had helped to build. Shunned and disgraced, these Gypsies ventured across the great desert, crossing an ocean of sand on a train of caravans that stretched as far as the eye could see. A great many died before they could reach the more temperate regions of the North. In the land of the Gaul they prospered, but would never again settle or cultivate the land, for they were persecuted and reviled as a race tainted with the blood of the star-beings.

All this Lady Colville knew in the twinkling of an eye, but she pulled a veil over her thoughts, lest Hunter saw her for who she truly was: a child of the *sennachi* tribe, in whose veins flowed the blood of kings.

Hunter twisted Lady Betty's arm behind her back and dragged her to the window. 'Do you see that?' he hissed in her ear, holding her chin and twisting her head until it faced the waning moon. 'It is nearly time.'

'Time for what?' gasped Lady Colville.

All the way down the High Street fires were breaking out. Lady Colville watched a man leap from the highest window of his house rather than burn to death in the flames. The streets below were a confusion of people, some of them still in their bedclothes, their faces Greek masks of tragedy as their homes and livelihoods were consumed in flames.

'The city will be purified by fire,' said Hunter, 'and the dead will rise and walk the earth once more. See! the words of the prophecy are coming to pass! *She* is coming. Can you feel Her breath on your cheek? It is a fiery furnace! Can you hear the beating of Her wings? It is a great wind from the East! All hail Mother of Dragons! Most worshipful Serpent Queen of the Qlipoth!'

'Who's that then?' quipped Lady Betty. 'The mother-in-law?'

Hunter jerked Lady Colville's arm behind her back until she squealed. 'Lilith of old, Queen Lamia, roused from her thousand-year slumber.' With a sigh of anticipation, Hunter caressed Lady Colville's cheek with a long, reptilian tongue that flickered out from between sharp little teeth.

As Lady Colville endured this gross licence, she caught sight of a movement reflected in the window. Boswell had entered the room.

'That doesn't sound too good,' she said, playing for time. 'I'll wager she's not a morning person.'

'Silence!' Hunter cried, then gripping Lady Colville around the neck with his arm, he reached into his pocket with his free hand and took out a glass phial. As he fiddled with the cork stopper, Boswell edged his way towards the fireplace and curled his fingers around the poker.

'What have you done with Mrs Boswell?' said Lady Colville.

The Fall of the House of Thomas Weir

'She will join you in a place of honour,' said Hunter, 'to bear witness to a great transformation. Her offspring has been chosen. By her blood will the doors of *Sitra Ahra* be flung open.'

Boswell had the poker in his grasp. He tip-toed towards the window while Hunter grappled with Lady Colville. Hunter had succeeded in opening the phial and soaking a handkerchief in its contents.

Lady Colville tried to divert his attention. 'I think I'll pass, if it's all the same with you. I am throwing a soirée tonight and have an appointment with my stylist. But all the best with that...'

'Enough, strumpet!' roared Hunter.

Then everything happened at once. As Hunter pressed the handkerchief to Lady Colville's face, Boswell rushed forward with the iron raised, ready to strike. Lady Colville, overcome by the powerful sedative, slumped in Doctor Hunter's grasp. Hunter dropped Lady Colville and spun to face his assailant. Boswell, weakened from his trials, was too slow for Hunter's predatory reflexes. The latter moved to intercept the blow, catching the poker on its downward trajectory and twisting it from Boswell's grasp.

Just at that moment they heard the click of a key being turned in the lock.

*

Lord Chalmers was standing in the ruined forecourt of Roswell Castle, staring sadly at the corpse of his former friend and associate Doctor Hunter. They had released Archie Gunn, leaving him some tobacco and spare coin for his trouble. Now the curtain of night had descended, the five men were themselves eager to get going. 'There is just one thing that troubles me, Doctor,' said the magistrate.

'Yes, Lord Chalmers?'

'Why bother?'

'Why bother with what, Lord Chalmers?'

'What I mean is, these Anunnaki went to the trouble of killing

169

the horses and burning the carriages. They even removed the head from one of their victims. Why leave the other bodies for identification? Why not just toss them down the well, or toss them on the fire and be done with it? That way, nobody would ever know they are not who they say they are.'

'For one simple reason,' said Johnson. 'In order to keep the portal open, the five invocants must remain within the pentagram, even in death. If their murderers disposed of the bodies it would only close the portal, and their means of return. Should anything go wrong the imposters would be trapped in this realm in their reptilian forms, which would be to reveal themselves to the world. They must have deemed this place sufficiently secluded to get away with leaving the scene of their crimes intact.'

An ear-shredding cry, a sound no earthly beast could make, rose from the darkness of the valley below. The men froze and looked at one another, then slowly turned to look over the parapet. The castle stood on a projection of rock that climbed high above the forest. Across the wooded glen, the silhouette of Roswell Chapel loomed large. With its reptilian gargoyles and esoteric carvings, the Sinclairs' ancestral place of worship had a sinister reputation: it was rumoured an underground tunnel ran between the chapel and the castle, and that the surrounding woods were haunted. Whatever made that cry, it came from somewhere out there in the woods. Moments later the call was picked up again, this time from a different location, and closer.

'Something stalks us,' said Queensberry, reaching for his pistol.

'Is it them?' said Lord Chalmers.

'I think not,' said Johnson. 'The Anunnaki have already left this place. But there are older things that lurk in the deep places of this world, things that might have slipped through the portal unattended.' Johnson's eyes darted to and fro as he took measure of his surroundings. 'Put away your weapon, please, You Grace,' he said, observing the Duke's loaded pistol. 'It has no currency here.' He reached into his pocket and produced a stick of chalk. 'This will be our principal weapon against the forces of darkness.'

The Fall of the House of Thomas Weir

The pentagram that covered the courtyard floor had faded until it was barely visible. Johnson went over the outer and inner circles with his chalk, then redrew the five-pointed star, ensuring each point touched the inner circle. 'This pentagram was designed to summon demonic beings from the lower dimensions,' he said. 'To reverse the spell I must repurpose it.' He moved around the circle scribbling words of power, which read like so much gobbledygook to Chalmers and Queensberry. Next Johnson drew esoteric symbols in each of the valleys and mounts of the five-pointed star. 'I could have done with some holy water and a Bible. Nevertheless, if our hearts and our wills are pure, we may yet survive the ordeal.' After he had finished, he took a step back to admire his handiwork.

It was not a moment too soon. The cry from the forest was taken up again, this time answered by a jabbering series of whoops and howls from all around. It was the call of the primordial jungle, and it filled them with an unholy dread.

'We are surrounded!' cried Queensberry.

Johnson gathered everybody around him, issuing orders to each man.

First, they had to get rid of the bodies.

'Are you sure?' the magistrate protested. 'These bodies may be used as evidence!'

'Quite sure, Lord Chalmers. As long as these bodies remain within the pentagram, the spell of invocation is still active, and the portal remains open.'

'But those things in the forest—'

'Won't last long without recourse to their own dimension. Now let us move quickly!'

Each man grabbed an arm and a leg, and they heaved the corpses over the edge of the well, glancing nervously at the surrounding darkness as they worked. The bodies fell silently, without the telltale splash of water one would expect to come from the bottom of a well. After they had dealt with the bodies, Johnson instructed Chalmers and Queensberry to build a fire, while the two dragoons were tasked with retrieving the horses. The Duke, normally averse to taking orders, scurried off to do as he was told. This Doctor Johnson had proven his worth in handling the Deacon Brodie affair, and Queensberry grudgingly admired the man, knowing he could be trusted without question. As for Lord Chalmers, the magistrate already viewed Doctor Johnson as something of a wizard. The two aristocrats gathered fallen branches from under the trees that grew from the battlements. By a stroke of luck they discovered a cache of chopped wood stored against the rain in the ruined watchtower. They stacked the logs near the well, packing it with dried leaves and kindling and surrounding it with blocks of stone, then set the whole thing alight with their flints. Pleased with their work, they stood back to watch as the flames grew higher, casting flickering shadows against the castellated battlements.

As soon as the last horse crossed the line to safety there came a terrific crash that reverberated around the forest. The men all turned to look at once. The line of trees near the chapel seemed to jostle and sway, accompanied by the sound of breaking branches. Something as big as an elephant was coming. The horses reared and whinnied in terror, their dumb eyes registering a stark terror of the unknown.

When the leviathan reached the edge of the wood it stopped. The men waited several agonising moments, before the silence was broken. It was a loud bovine bellowing, yet of an unearthly depth and timbre. The sound contained a haunting quality like the song of a whale or the cry of a wolf, but deeper by far. Johnson was reminded of a contrabassoon, the deepest of the orchestra's wind instruments, played to such solemn effect in Bach's *St. John Passion*, but there was nothing soulful or comforting in this. With a curious snuffling sound the creature made its way around the castle wall then, with a grunt of indifference, the whatever-it-was shuffled round and slouched back the way it came. The men's relief was palpable. But it was not to last.

Moments later the sky above their heads erupted in a fury of black, leathery wings. It might be argued that this new menace winging its way towards them belonged to the corvid family, but these were no ordinary crows. Each was about the size of a man, black as shadow, with vast, eagle-like pinions. Their backs bristled with spines like the quills of a porcupine, and their cries were rasping and shrill as they lunged and swooped around the heads of their prey. The men raised their arms to cover their eyes, desperately trying to fend off this new threat from above.

Chalmers and Queensberry piled more wood onto the fire, while the dragoons fired at the flying demons with their muskets. When the ammunition ran out, they threw stones and anything else that came to hand. Johnson twirled his staff around his head with devastating accuracy, having learned his lessons well on Arthur's Seat. Eventually, after battling the predators for what seemed like eternity, the first rays of dawn crept over the horizon. The tumult died down, and the company found themselves alone once more, exhausted, but alive.

*

Margaret Boswell collapsed against the door, exhausted, her throat raw from screaming. It was hopeless; she would need to have her wits about her to rescue her daughter. She made a conscious effort to calm her breath and took stock of her situation. The attic room was stacked from wall to wall with junk. The window looked onto hard cobblestones ten flights of stairs below. She examined her surroundings. The crates contained moth-eaten clothes, some dog-eared books, and a heap of old bedsheets.

Mrs Boswell lifted out one of the sheets and looked over to the window. Maybe. She tipped the contents of the crate onto the floor. There were perhaps a dozen sheets. She tied a pair together, then tried to pull them apart. It was a good knot, and it held. She added another, and then another, her fingers working rapidly, until fifteen minutes later all twelve sheets were joined together. She moved to the window and looked down. It was a drop of some fifty feet. The sheets would stretch to half of that, give or take. Frantically she began tipping over boxes and found some old scarves and rags, which added to the length of her makeshift rope. It would be enough, provided the rags could bear her weight.

She picked up the chair she used to pound the door, then raised it over her head and threw it hard against the window. It bounced harmlessly against the frame. She picked it up again, and this time put all her strength behind the throw. The glass splintered. A third throw, and the glass shattered outwards. Mrs Boswell wrapped her hand in a rag to clear away any remaining shards of glass or splinters of wood. Then she wedged the chair between the floor and the window frame, wound the end of the sheets around the legs of the chair, and tossed the coiled bundle through the window.

The end dangled maybe ten feet from the ground below. Grasping the improvised rope in both hands, Mrs Boswell stepped onto the windowsill. *What am I doing?* she thought, as it suddenly occurred to her that climbing down the side of a five-storey building might not be the most sensible course of action. *I don't need to do this. Perhaps if I just wait, then everything will turn out alright. Perhaps Jamie will come, or Mother Superior will return, or…or….*

No. There was nobody to help her. She would have to do this herself. She turned to face the room, tested the rope by pulling on it a few times then, saying a prayer both for herself and for her daughter, Margaret Boswell took a step backwards into the unknown.

*

Mrs Irene Miller and Mrs Brenda Cunningham, those two scowling gargoyles of Niddry Street, looked across the aisle at one another and even managed a smile. Their husbands, fidgeting by their sides, could afford a sigh of relief. Today was not about them, and everything about Billy Miller and Nell Cunningham, the young couple who were about to take their vows before God. The fathers had every right to be optimistic. This union would bring about peace between their two wives, who had been at war now for the best part of twenty-five years. Maybe even a lasting peace, especially if the marriage proved fruitful.

The bride and groom stood nervously before the altar with their backs to the guests. Mrs Cunningham stifled a sob at the sight of her daughter in her wedding dress. She had picked out the material herself, sewing for nights on end by candlelight to get it ready.

Mrs Miller was no less proud, but knew in her heart that her Billy was too good for the Cunningham girl. Oh, she was pretty enough. Even sweet, in her way: she could cook, clean, sew, and she had a good heart, which was enough for any other sort of man. But her Billy wasn't just any sort of man. He was refined, sensitive, like a proper gentleman. Not for him a tradesman's life like his father. Her Billy should have been a minister, a gentleman of leisure, perhaps even a Lord or a Duke.

As for Brenda Cunningham, she was convinced her daughter was marrying a brute. She had held such high hopes for her Nell, and to see her settle for such a lout of a man, well it made her heart-sore. The Millers were notorious drunkards; and as for the mother, well, the less said about her the better.

Oblivious, the Reverend Drysdale grinned broadly, opened his arms expansively, and addressed the congregation with his customary preamble: *'Dearly Beloved, we are gathered together here in the sight of God, to join together this man and this woman in holy matrimony...'*

Everything was going rather splendidly, thought Drysdale, until he reached the part which always made him a little apprehensive: *'Therefore if any man can show any just cause why they may not lawfully be joined together, let him now speak, or else hereafter forever hold his peace...'*

No sooner had Drysdale delivered this fateful challenge, than it was met by a peculiar grinding noise coming from the central aisle. The whole congregation leaned over to see what was happening. One of the flagstones on the floor was being moved away, as if pushed from below. Smoke came streaming out of the gap, followed by a lugubrious pair of eyes. Ladies fainted and men stood and gaped, as a pair of hands appeared at the edges of the hole like two great spiders. The thing flopped onto the floor like a huge, ugly fish and lay there panting, before it dragged itself to its feet and grinned stupidly at the congregation.

Somewhere at the back, an old lady screamed.

The congregation looked on, mute with horror and speechless with indignation, as one after another they emerged: ragged, leprous things with festering sores covering every inch of their emaciated frames.

Two burly Glaswegians were guarding the door at the back of the church. As the revenants came shuffling towards them the two men braced themselves. Nobody had invited these cretins. The first steward stepped forward and smashed his assailant across the bridge of its pug nose, using his head as a blunt instrument. The gate crasher reeled, a look of dumb shock registering on its ugly face, then lunged, sinking filed teeth into the steward's broad neck. The second steward didn't hesitate. He took the whisky bottle from his coat pocket and lamped the bastard from behind. This was enough to start the whole congregation, who came hurdling over the pews to have a go at the intruders.

Reverend Drysdale, once he got over the initial shock, pulled the heavy crucifix from the wall and rushed up the aisle and into the fray. He swung the crucifix like a Viking with his axe at the backs of the intruders, yelling the Lord's prayer at the top of his lungs. 'Our Father.' *Thwack!* 'Who art in heaven.' *Thwack!* 'Hallowed be they name…' *Thwack!*

The wooden doors groaned, bulged, then all at once burst open, and the fight spilled out onto the street, where other melees were already in progress.

Nell Cunningham raised her hands to her mouth and stifled a scream. Her wedding was ruined before they even got to the reception.

*

Captain George Grenville of the 2nd Dragoons stood high upon the castle battlements, watching his beloved city burn. Flames leaped from tenement to tenement. Smoke streamed from the windows and closes, and from out of the smoke, a steady stream of ragged half-men vomited up from the diseased belly of the town, blinking like escaped convicts into the half-light of day. They swarmed up the Royal Mile like a plague of rats, gathering strength and multiplying as they progressed, overwhelming all in their path.

'So many...' murmured Grenville.

Everywhere was pandemonium. Outside St. Giles Cathedral two monsters were fighting over the body of a girl, pulling on her arms and legs until they nearly broke her in two. Her screams rent the air. The victor managed to wrestle the doomed girl from his rival's grasp and loped off like a Barbary ape with his prize tucked under his arm.

In the middle of the street a carriage had overturned. A group of revenants were in the process of extracting its traumatised occupants, while others descended on the horses like a pack of hyenas, tearing off and devouring chunks of dripping flesh while the poor beasts were still in their death throes.

Elsewhere men were mustering, running out from their places of business with what weapons were to hand, only to be torn limb from limb by the advancing horde.

The old Dutch steeple of Tron Kirk was engulfed in flames, showering the unfortunate bystanders below with molten lead. It was a piteous sight to see, those poor souls screaming in agony, running blindly into the hands of the revenants.

Grenville slumped back against the wall, undone by his own pride and obstinacy. His name would go down in history as the man who had opened the gates of hell. 'What have I done?' he murmured, and just like that, his mind snapped.

By the time Staff Sergeant Brown puffed up the stairs to report to his superior, an eleven-storey tenement on Parliament Square was ablaze. 'My God,' murmured the orderly, witnessing for the first time the devastation Grenville's orders had unleashed.

Captain Grenville blinked stupidly at his Staff Sergeant, his eyes glassy and unresponsive. 'God?' he roared. 'Yes, yes! It is a valediction from God, do you see? We are being punished for our iniquities.'

'Sir, if you would only just give the order—'

'Bring me my bagpipes!'

'Your... bagpipes... sir?'

'Yes man. Are you soft?' he roared. 'Bring me my bagpipes! They call Edinburgh the Rome of the North, do they not? Then I shall be Nero, and play while she burns.'

Reluctant, stiff with shock, Staff Sergeant John Brown turned to go.

Down on the lower level of the esplanade, the troops were waiting, staring up at the solitary figure of Grenville as he shook his fists and raved at the sky.

'What orders from Captain Grenville?' said a young officer uneasily as Brown approached.

'What?' said Brown, still reeling from the gunpowder explosion.

'Orders man!' cried the officer. 'Can't you see the city is ablaze, and overrun with vermin?'

'Yes, I am perfectly aware of the situation, Lieutenant Steele.'

'Then what is to be done!'

'Done? Nothing, sir. The captain requires his bagpipes.'

'Good God, man. Has he gone insane?'

'I think he probably has,' admitted Brown, then pushed past to carry out his order.

*

'Ah, there you are,' said Grenville, eyeing the bagpipes in Staff Sergeant Brown's hands. 'Give them here.' He placed the pipes under his arm and grinned maniacally at his Staff Sergeant. 'What shall we have? Something poignant, eh? I know!' The crazed old captain squeezed his arm and the great Highland war-bagpipe wheezed into life, sending out its plaintive drone across the Castle

The Fall of the House of Thomas Weir

Esplanade. The men looked up, their emotions stirred by the haunting refrain of *Garb of the Old Gaul*, a slow march associated with the Royal Scots Greys:

In the garb of old Gaul with the fire of old Rome,
From the heath-covered mountains of Scotia we come;
When the Romans endeavoured our country to gain,
Our ancestors fought, and they fought not in vain!

Captain Grenville rolled his eyes to heaven as he played, no longer sensible to the horror unfolding below. He gave it his all, his fingers dancing up and down the chanter like a fluttering white bird. When he had finished, the men below looked up expectantly, eagerly awaiting the order to mount. Instead, Grenville saluted, reached into his holster, and before Staff Sergeant Brown or the men below knew what was happening, cocked the trigger of his pistol and blew his own brains out.

Brown staggered back, his head reeling. Then, wiping blood and gore from his face with his sleeve, he leaned over the parapet and vomited. Tears sprang from his eyes. After he had regained something of his composure, he straightened his tunic and picked up the bagpipes.

The men down below recognised the stirring strains of *Highland Laddie*, and all at once the blood was roused within them. Recognising the silhouette of their loyal Staff Sergeant and his call to arms, a war-like spirit descended. They longed to feel their steeds between their legs and cutlasses in their hands.

'Oh men!' cried Lieutenant Steel. 'Old Grenville has fallen! Now let us away to the stables!'

The men didn't need to be told twice. With a great thirst for vengeance they made their way down to the stables where their faithful greys were tethered.

Artillery clattered, sabres rattled, buckles jingled, drums rattled, horses whinnied, and amidst this great hue-and-cry the men leapt onto the grey horses from which they derived their name and clattered out onto the forecourt. Steele led his spirited steed to the front, then wheeled around and addressed his Dragoons in a clear, ringing voice.

'Gentlemen,' he cried, 'our brave captain has fallen, destroyed by a menace that infests our city and threatens our very existence. Let not his death be in vain! Let us ride out now, and cut these villains down to size. Show no mercy. *Nemo me impune lacessit!*

The crossbar was lifted and the gates flung open, and with the motto of the Scots Greys still ringing in their ears, Lieutenant Steele rode out, disappearing in a blanket of smoke.

Chapter 18

A Feast for Crows

*F*unny, thought Mrs Boswell, *that when things seem at their absolute worst, there is always some new torment waiting in the wings to vex us.*

Here she was, dangling precipitously from the attic window of Canongate Orphanage with nothing to break her fall but hard cobblestones, and nothing to keep her from falling but a moth-eaten bedsheet. Then, as if this weren't enough, a huge explosion shook the Printing House opposite, blasting windows from their frames, showering the poor woman in shards of broken glass. Flames licked the side of the wall above her head, threatening to incinerate her already precarious lifeline. She fed the sheet through her hands in a frantic motion, walking her way down the side of the building, until she found herself twirling from the end of her rope like a demented spider. Randomly, she hoped that nobody could see up her dress, which billowed indecently in the wind.

Finally the bedsheet succumbed to the flames. Mrs Boswell shut her eyes and said a prayer for her daughter as she dropped through empty space.

She landed badly, then clambered to her feet using the wall for support. The fire had spread to the orphanage, leaping in through an open window on the third floor. The same room where Mrs Boswell had left Veronica!

She tested her leg. It was badly sprained, but not broken. Using the wall for support, Mrs Boswell inched her way down the lane and rounded the corner onto High Street. She limped up the short flight of stairs to the main door of the orphanage, then pushed it open to reveal an empty hallway.

She used the banister for support as she climbed the main staircase. When she reached the door to the girls' dormitory, she shook the handle. Her efforts alerted the room's occupants. A shower of tiny fists rained against the door, accompanied by a hysterical outpouring of screams. An older voice rose above the clamour, begging for order.

'Sister Grace, is that you?' said Mrs Boswell, inclining her ear towards the door.

'Oh thank the Lord, it is Mrs Boswell. Please let us out, we have been locked in here, and the drapes are on fire. I tried closing the window to keep the fire out, but it's jammed!'

Mrs Boswell looked down at her feet where smoke was creeping through the gap under the door.

'Where is Veronica? Is she there?' she cried, rattling the doorhandle.

'Oh Mrs Boswell,' sobbed Sister Grace from the other side of the door. 'She is not. The Mother Superior took her: said she had been chosen. I tried to tell them Veronica was not an orphan, but they wouldn't listen. And when I tried to stop her, she… She beat me!'

Mrs Boswell bit her bottom lip to stifle the scream. 'Save your breath. I'm going to get you out of there. Tell me where I can find the keys.'

'Hanging behind the reception desk. Please hurry!'

Mrs Boswell made the torturous descent back down the stairs, then hobbled across the black and white tiled floor to the reception desk. There was an empty space on the wall where the keys should be. *Dammit*, she cursed under her breath. She flung open the desk drawer, hoping to find a spare set. Cursing again, she pulled the drawer free from its runners and emptied the contents on the counter. In her frantic search she hadn't noticed the tall figure of the Mother Superior standing in the doorway.

'Are you looking for these?' she gloated, swinging a set of keys from her fat finger.

Mrs Boswell limped towards the Mother Superior and reached out a hand for the keys, only for them to be snatched away with a smirk that Mrs Boswell found infuriating. Despite the horror of the situation it seemed the Mother Superior wished to engage in some childish and sadistic game, keeping the keys just out of Mrs Boswell's reach.

Mrs Boswell did not wish to give her tormentor the satisfaction. She cast a desperate glance at the smoke billowing down the stairs then, biting down on her bottom lip, she kicked her tormentor hard between the legs. The very act of striking a nun on the private parts horrified Mrs Boswell, yet at the same time it was not an altogether unpleasant experience. The big woman winced and relinquished her hold on the keys. Mrs Boswell caught them as they fell then bolted for the stairs.

But Mother Superior was fast. She launched herself forward, catching Mrs Boswell by the ankle as she reached the first step. Mrs Boswell kicked out furiously with her good leg at the Mother Superior's head and missed. She kicked again, and her foot caught the plinth on which the heavy marble bust of the president rested. The bust wobbled, then toppled, landing with a dull crack on Sister Daphne's head.

Mrs Boswell didn't stop to see if the nun was dead or not, but hobbled up the stairs, plunging through the smoke towards the door. She fumbled with the keys, then inserted the first one in the lock. It didn't fit. She tried another. It was useless. Sister Grace cried out to use the smallest one. Mrs Boswell could scarcely breathe as she rattled the small key in the lock, until finally with a click the door swung open.

The blast of heat hit her like a furnace. The children were lined up ready to go, coughing and spluttering, their heads covered in their blankets. 'Come on!' cried Mrs Boswell. 'Out! All of you. Now!'

Sister Grace led the way, grabbing the first girl by the hand, while the rest followed down the stairs and onto the street.

'Keep running and don't look back!' Mrs Boswell cried after them. Once the last girl had left the building, Mrs Boswell turned to leave, grasping the bannister as she hobbled down the stairs.

As she cleared the last step a hand gripped her ankle. She heard a gloating cackle as the roof beams crashed down around her.

*

The five riders stood on the crest of Pentland Hill, watching plumes of smoke curl and rise from the rooftops of Old Town. From their vantage point, Castle Rock appeared as a steaming dunghill before the distant blue haze of the Firth of Forth.

'Good Lord,' Lord Chalmers cried. 'The city is ablaze.'

'I fear Captain Grenville has exceeded his orders,' murmured Johnson.

The riders descended the hill in single file with a renewed sense of urgency, while the horses zig-zagged their way around rocks and rabbit holes with all the surefooted grace of their royal line.

An undulating landscape of farmhouses and meadows sped past in a blur as the riders drove on towards the Flodden Wall. One hour later they reached the gates of the city at West Port, their steeds bathed in sweat and snorting plumes of steam.

The sentries had long since abandoned their posts, leaving the gate unmanned. To the north the King's Stables Road followed the line of the Flodden Wall, winding its way around the back of Castle Rock. To the east, the tenement flats of Grassmarket remained intact, though up on High Street the fires raged unchecked. The very sky above their heads was ablaze with orange light.

After a brief consultation the men decided they would divide into two parties. Hector Gillies would direct Lord Chalmers and the Duke of Queensberry along the King's Stables Road to the back door of the castle. Doctor Johnson and James Douglas would go to James Court, by way of Grassmarket and West Bow.

Lord Chalmers begged Johnson not to attempt such a hazardous undertaking alone, but Johnson was resolute. 'The Castle must have a chain of command,' he reasoned. 'I will deal with Hunter myself,' and with these words he wheeled his horse and galloped off, leaving his companions in a cloud of dust.

*

Something was going on up there, thought Bill Fernley. He could smell it. He overturned the slops bucket for something to stand on and tried to peek through the grille. He couldn't quite reach it. 'Oy! Charlie!' He beckoned to his cellmate, a small, ferret-faced individual pretending to be asleep on the bottom bunk.

With a sigh, Charlie rolled out of bed, walked up to his cellmate and bent over with his hands on his knees. Bill Fernley leaped nimbly onto the smaller man's back, a routine they had practiced a dozen times before. He peered through the grille onto an empty corridor. It was quiet; too quiet, as the saying goes. Something was clearly amiss. Bill craned his neck and tried to see along the gloomy corridor towards the stairwell. Down here in the dark they were the last to know anything. All the scum of the earth—the murderers, rapists, thieves, pickpockets and vagabonds—were left here to rot. The upper levels were for men convicted of lesser crimes, or those with money. They could get anything they wanted up there. Good grub, extra blankets, smokes, even newspapers, whereas Bill Fernley and the rest? The bloody High Street could have up and moved to China and he'd be the last to know about it.

The guard's chair at the end of the corridor was empty. Young Jim Rankin should have been on his early morning shift by now. So where was he?

Bill sniffed the air, detecting the faint whiff of sulphur. For a smuggler and pirate like Bill Fernley it was a pleasant smell, reminding him of cannon fire and victory. But down here in the dungeon it was… out of place, somehow. Just what the hell was going on?

'*Pssst. Bill.*' It was Jack Darnley, his shipmate from the next cell. 'What the hell's going on out there?'

'Hard to say. Something queer, that's for sure.' Bill looked towards the stairs again. Everything seemed hazy, unclear somehow. Like a mist before his eyes. And that smell again. Gunpowder, and the smell of woodsmoke. He was reminded of melted tar and burning timber from his days as a buccaneer, and a single thought, patiently waiting its turn among other more random thoughts, suddenly clawed its way to the front of his brain: Fire!

After struggling manfully under his burden for several minutes, Charlie's legs finally gave way and the two men fell sprawling to the ground. Bill shot up and began to yell. Smoke was seeping in through his grille now. This didn't look good. All the way down the block, inmates were yelling and kicking up a fuss. Bill Fernley looked ruefully at his cellmate, a diminutive forger with a hunched back. What an ignominious end to an illustrious career. To be the terror of the high seas, captain of his own sloop, only to die trapped and cornered like a bloody animal. He wasn't scared of dying, but he always thought he'd die at sea with a cutlass in his hand and a bellyful of rum. He sat on the edge of the bed and put his head in his hands.

After what seemed like an age the sound of running footsteps echoed through the corridor.

'Jim Rankin. Is that you?' hissed Bill, putting his ear to the door.

'Yes, it's me,' said the prison warder.

'Now you tell me what's happening, boy…'

'The prison's on fire. We… I need to go.'

'Well! And just what were you planning on doing? Would ye leave your old pal Bill here to barbeque in his cell like a dog?' Bill could almost hear the cogs grinding in the younger man's head.

'If I let you go…' said the prison warden, 'you must promise to mend your ways.'

The Fall of the House of Thomas Weir

'If you open that door, I'll go straight to a monastery and take a vow of celibacy.'

'I'm serious!' cried the young man, his voice shrill and insistent. The grin faded from Fernley's face. He placed a hand on his heart. 'I swear it, son. No more buccaneering for Old Bill. I swear it on me mother's grave. Now unlock the door, there's a good lad.'

With a sigh of relief Bill Fernley heard the key turn in the lock, and the heavy iron door swung open. Hunchback Charlie, Bill's erstwhile cellmate, wriggled past the two men and sprang up the stairs with a whoop of delight.

A suffocating smoke now filled the corridor. Screams of rage and confusion rang throughout the block. Rows of grasping fingers poked through grilles, fists slammed against metal doors. The young warden looked at Bill and his courage seemed to fail him. He slapped the keys down into Bill's hand and cried, 'Let this be on *your* conscience!' and with these last words he was off. Bill looked at the keys, perplexed, then started for the stairway after the warden.

The smoke was now so thick he could barely see. Cries of despair from his fellow prisoners followed him up the stairs. Some begging for mercy, some rasping out threats, promising to cut off Bill Fernley's unmentionables if they were to ever get their hands on him, vowing vengeance from beyond the grave.

Leave 'em, said the voice in Bill Fernley's head. *These are bad men. Evil men. Let 'em burn. You'll be doing the world a favour.* The voice in his head was rasping, insistent, familiar. The voice of his father.

Bill Fernley hated his father.

'Sod it,' he said, descending the stairs to where fifty of Edinburgh's most dangerous criminals were incarcerated. 'Best get started then... Who's first?'

*

Doctor Johnson and Sergeant Douglas arrived at Grassmarket only to find the famously bustling marketplace a wasteland. Sacks of grain had been piled high in a barricade that stretched from one end of the square to the other. Crude weapons such as clubs, scythes and pitchforks lay in heaps on either side, some still in the hands of their fallen owners. Nothing stirred, apart from a rusty shop-sign creaking in the wind, or carrion feasting on the dead, or the occasional twitch of a lace curtain from the surrounding tenements. Otherwise Johnson and his companion might very well have been the last two men on earth.

Bowfoot Well, a solid stone drinking fountain in the middle of the square, dripped with gore, as if some poor wretch had been flayed alive against it, but whether revenant or man Johnson had no way of knowing. Nor did he want to know.

They ran into their first group of revenants on West Bow, the latter emerging from a darkened close. They descended on poor Sergeant Douglas like a swarm of ants on a stag beetle, tearing the doomed rider from his mount before he could reach for his pistol. His screams were mercifully brief. Johnson spurred his horse, but the creatures were on him before he could make good his escape. His mount reared up as two revenants grabbed the reins, while a third attacked the horse's flank. The beast fell gurgling to the ground, throwing Johnson to one side.

Meanwhile Bill Fernley and his gang, enjoying their first taste of freedom in five years, stepped out from a broken jeweller's shop window, their pockets dripping with stolen pearls and gold chains. They hesitated at the sight of this fat Sassenach, his sleeves rolled up and his fists raised, as cool as a country squire facing down a gang of poachers.

'What do you think,' said Bill Fernley. 'Should we help him?'

'Nah,' said another. 'It's nane of our business. Let's go.'

But Bill Fernley had already made up his mind. He picked up a rock and launched it into the crowd.

'What the hell are those things?' asked Bill's partner-in-crime, Jack Darnley.

'I dunno,' said Fernley, rolling up his sleeves. 'Let's go find out!' And before anyone could protest, he launched himself into the fray.

'Come on lads,' said another of the looters, following their leader's cue. 'Let's get laid into them!'

Soon men and women of all ages emerged from alleys and doorways, snatching whatever weapons were to hand as they closed in on the enemy. The looters got there first, piling into the revenants with great force. The violence was swift, brutal. No mild-mannered citizens these, but dockside toughs who revelled in violence. The revenants fought with all the savagery of cornered beasts, but the townsfolk fought harder. One lad retrieved a scythe from the frozen fingers of a fallen comrade and swung it in a wide arc, depriving two revenants of their legs in one brutal sweep. Still they came, hopping on the palms of their hands, snapping and snarling like ravenous midgets.

Jack Darnley was pinned against the Bowfoot Well, his attacker's sharply-filed teeth just inches from his neck. Johnson picked up a heavy chunk of masonry and hurled it, striking the revenant hard against the back of its cranium. The creature turned on Johnson and grinned, pleased at the prospect of fresh meat to sink its teeth into. Johnson regarded the creature with something akin to pity. It was so disfigured with leprosy that its head resembled little more than a featureless rock with a gaping hole of ragged teeth. It lunged at Johnson, but Jack Darnley was faster, plunging his dagger into the revenant's back and killing it instantly.

After the dust of battle had settled and the last of the revenants chased off, Johnson turned to thank the men who had come to his aid, but they had already dispersed, slinking off into the shadows with their stolen booty.

'Wait!' cried Johnson, stopping to pick something up. 'You forgot this.' Bill Fernley, the last of the men to leave, turned to look. It was the string of pearls that had fallen from his pocket during the fight. Bill looked from the stolen pearls to Johnson's kindly face, and overwhelmed with emotion he fell to his knees and wept, confessing his crimes and begging forgiveness.

'It is not my place to absolve you, friend,' said Johnson, placing a plump hand on the penitent's shoulder. 'But I owe you my life, and if I can be of assistance, in this life or the next, I am your man!'

Bill Fernley felt his heart swell, and he rose to his feet as if picked up by an invisible hand. With barely a glance at Doctor Johnson, though with a feeling of profound gratitude he turned to leave, but not before the doctor had pressed the pearls into Fernley's hand and said, 'Do some good with this.'

Bill Fernley did not need to be told twice.

*

Once the last of the townsfolk had collected their wounded and limped back indoors, Johnson found the desecrated body of his fallen comrade, and the tears he had been holding in for so long flowed copiously down his fat jowls. He covered the body of Sergeant James Douglas in broken masonry to keep the vermin from further defiling him, then after saying a prayer he continued onto Westbow: friendless, horseless, his eyes full of tears for the senseless waste of life.

The hill was impossibly steep, and Johnson was tempted to crawl on his hands and knees or give up and find another route, but somehow found the strength to keep going.

The house of Thomas Weir stood on a steeply sloping gradient. Due to a peculiarity of town-planning, the west face of the house climbed six storeys above the street, whereas the south face seemed almost twice as high. The whole building with its pentagonal tower seemed curiously twisted to accommodate this sharp angle.

Something was happening inside. A lurid yellow light blazed from each window, while silhouettes drifted from room to room. From the sound of the fiddle, the laughter and the shrieks of ecstasy it would seem someone was having a ball in the derelict house. It presented a curious counterpoint to the surrounding chaos, as if this house belonged to a different place and time altogether. Johnson crossed himself and suppressed a shudder as he rounded the corner onto Upper Bow. There was something uncanny about those flickering lights and sounds, and he was relieved to turn the corner and his back on the house of Thomas Weir.

When he reached the High Street the air was thick with smoke. It billowed up the street like a living thing, choking and devouring as it grew. A stark, isolated scream pierced the brooding silence, punctuating the madness that had the city in its thrall. Johnson covered his head and shoulders with his coat and plunged in.

Faces emerged as in a nightmare, appearing and disappearing behind the veil of smoke: terrified faces with rolling eyes, leering faces, haunted faces, nightmare faces without eyes, faces without lips, faces without noses. Halfway across Johnson was almost bowled over by a solitary, flaming carriage wheel that came bounding down the cobbled street, closely followed by a riderless and terrified horse.

Miraculously, he made it safely across the street and hurried into Boswell's close. He knew something was wrong as soon as he reached the top of the stairs and found the door swinging open on its hinges.

'*Hello?*' His call was answered by a foreign-sounding voice from the drawing room.

Johnson entered to find a semi-conscious Boswell slumped in a chair, while his Bohemian manservant Joseph stitched a nasty-looking gash on the side of his master's head.

'My God,' said Johnson. 'What happened here?'

Joseph explained in his broken English that he was returning from his errands when he met Doctor Hunter in the doorway with Lady Colville in his arms. Hunter had pushed past the bewildered manservant with some muttered excuse about taking Lady Colville to a hospital. Joseph entered the drawing room to find his master lying in a crumpled heap on the floor. Fearing him dead, he was relieved to find the weapon had only glanced off his head. He ran out to accost Hunter, but the Doctor was already halfway into a black carriage that raced off before Joseph could catch them.

Boswell, still woozy from the blow, came round by degrees,

focusing on the concerned eyes around him. 'My friends…' he murmured weakly, then, 'Where the devil have you been, Joseph?'

Joseph looked at him strangely. 'You not remember? Maybe knock on head touch brain. You send me to house of father on errand.'

'Of course,' replied Boswell. 'And my wife and daughter: are they safe?'

Joseph looked confused, then shook his head. 'No. No wife. No daughter. Only father.'

'But… if Margaret is not there then… where…?' Boswell sent Joseph to the mantelpiece where the married couple habitually left formal but affectionate notes for one another. It was tucked in behind the clock just where Boswell said it would be.

He snatched the note from Joseph, tore it open, and quickly scanned the contents. 'Dearest Bosie, Have taken some things to the orphanage on the way to Auchinleck. We will see you in a few days. Your adoring wife, Maggie. P.S. I took all your linen handkerchiefs. Will bring you back some new ones.'

'*Canongate* Orphanage?' said Johnson, trying to control the tremor in his voice.

'Yes that's right,' said Boswell. 'The Reverend Baxter said they were in need of donations. But wait… it's all coming back to me now… Doctor Hunter. He… he was hurting Lady Colville. He said something about my daughter… how her blood would be a sacrament… something about a door…'

'This is bad,' muttered Johnson, wringing his hands. 'We don't have much time. Your wife and your daughter are in terrible danger. Are you fit to move?'

'I… I think so. Still a bit woozy. What is this all about? What is happening?'

'I'll explain as we go. Get your coat. And bring those blasted pistols of yours.'

Boswell left the room, returning moments later with two loaded pistols. He handed one to Johnson. 'Have a care, sir,' he said, demonstrating the mechanism. 'The safety switch is here.'

The Fall of the House of Thomas Weir

The two men's eyes met. Doctor Johnson studied his friend's haunted expression, and the grey streaks of hair above his temples which had not been there before. 'Oh God sir,' cried Johnson, his firm jaw beginning to tremble. 'It was sheer hubris and vanity on my part that brought us to this. But if anything has happened to your dear family...'

Boswell was alarmed at the change that had come over his friend, normally so self-assured. 'There now, Doctor Johnson... Samuel. If any man can bring the city back from the brink of despair, it is you. You have never let us down before.'

Johnson took the handkerchief from his pocket and blew his nose. 'I don't know what I'd do without you, Jamie.'

Boswell placed a hand on his beloved mentor's shoulder, and the two men briefly embraced. Then they opened the door and descended into the maelstrom.

*

Following the disastrous "Lang Siege" of 1571, which saw the castle pounded almost to rubble by English cannon, Edinburgh Castle was rebuilt stronger than ever, with the addition of the distinctive half-moon battery, a semi-circular wall which dominated the southern face of the castle, and the Portcullis Gate, approached from the rear via King's Stables Road.

The three riders thundered along this broad thoroughfare to the stables and dismounted. The early morning sun glinted from cobblestones; steam rose from the warm ground to mingle with the horses' breath, while the pungent smell of hay, horse manure and sweat filled the air, reminding the old men keenly of summer days and carefree youth. A sudden breeze carried with it the scent of burning wood and flesh across the rooftops of the city, and the men were recalled to the urgency of their mission. Lord Chalmers looked up at the watchtower, squinting into the morning sun. Deciding secrecy was the best policy, they approached the Portcullis Gate obliquely, by means of a secret staircase carved into the side of the rock. The men approached the gate and called out. They were answered by a high, quavering voice from within. 'What is the password?'

Lord Chalmers turned to their guide, Hector Gillies, who stepped forward. 'Mons Meg!'

Silence.

'Well?' said Lord Chalmers.

'That is yesterday's password.'

'Come on, man. This is a matter of life and death.'

'Identify yourselves.'

'Sergeant Hector Gillies,' said the diminutive dragoon. 'I am accompanied by the Magistrate Lord Chalmers, and the Duke of Queensberry himself. Let us in, or so help me God, your court martial will be ready by the morning.'

There was another brief pause, then a grinding and clanking of chains against rusty cogs as the portcullis door rose, revealing a fussy-looking little man in highly polished boots.

'So it's you, Staff Sergeant Brown,' said Gillies. 'I should have expected as much. Where is Captain Grenville?'

'Captain Grenville has been relieved of duty, on account of his untimely death. I am acting commander—'

'Grenville? *Dead*?'

'Alas, yes. By his own hand, I might add.'

'Where is Lieutenant Steele?'

'Lieutenant Steele has gone out. Along with the rest of the battalion.'

The men followed Brown up the stairs to the watchtower, where they could observe the whole city. A huge set of gates beyond the empty parade-ground held the populace at bay. The townsfolk were surging forward, desperately trying to get in. The smoke fouling up the High Street was so thick the crown-shaped spire of St. Giles Cathedral was barely visible.

With the enemy driving them on, men, women and children were being crushed against the doors, which groaned with the pressure of a thousand bodies. They were suffocating, pounding their fists and screaming in terror. Many had fallen and were being crushed underfoot.

'Sergeant Brown,' said Lord Chalmers, without taking his eyes from the scene of horror below. 'Give the order to open these gates.'

'I cannot allow these monsters—'

'Don't be a bloody fool, man. Do you want to be responsible for mass murder?'

Before Brown had a chance to respond, the Duke of Queensberry's voice rang clear across the parade ground. '*Open the gates!*'

The two sentries posted at the gates lifted the heavy iron bar, and a mass of townsfolk poured in, dodging and leaping over one another like sheep driven into a pen.

For one terrible moment it seemed as if the revenants were going to enter the castle the same way, when from out of nowhere a loud trumpet blast cut the air.

The cavalry raced in from either side of the High Street, blocking the enemy in a pincer movement before they could gain access.

Steele's battalion had been reduced by about half, but had managed to rally for a last-ditch effort.

*

As Johnson and Boswell stepped out onto the street, they almost collided with a small girl running in the opposite direction. Johnson grabbed her by the shoulders and looked into her fear-filled eyes. 'Be careful, child! Where are your parents?'

'I have none,' said the girl, puffing out her tiny chest. 'I am from the orphanage.'

Johnson knelt down to study her face. Though her scrawny frame gave her the appearance of a ten-year-old, there was a maturity in her eyes beyond her years.

'The orphanage?' cried Boswell, yanking the child by the arm.

'Yes sir,' said the girl, almost terrified out of her wits by the look of intensity on Boswell's face. 'But you must let me go, I am looking for someone.'

'Who? Who are you looking for?' said Boswell, shaking the girl.

'*Oww!* I'm looking for the Boswells' residence, sir!'

'I am Boswell! My family! Have you seen them?'

'No, no,' said Johnson. 'This won't do at all. Look at this poor child. She is terrified out of her wits. It looks like she hasn't eaten in days.' Johnson brushed an absent strand of hair from her eyes. 'Tell me, child, what is your name?'

'Rachel, sir.'

'Rachel,' said Johnson. 'What a lovely name. Come with me, Rachel, and we'll find you something to eat.'

Johnson took the waif in hand and led her back into Boswell's apartment.

Safely indoors, the child sat quite contentedly, her scabby legs swinging from Veronica's highchair as Joseph placed some leftover ham on the table before her.

Johnson pulled up a chair and sat himself down in front of the girl. 'Now listen, Rachel. My friend here needs to find his family. We think they are in terrible danger. His little girl is not much younger than you are. Her name is Veronica. Have you seen them?'

Rachel nodded vigorously, then launched into her story between mouthfuls of food.

'They came to our orphanage with presents for the girls. But then the President came and said they were going to take Veronica away. Sister Grace, that's the nice lady that looks after us, she told the President he wasn't to take Veronica, because *she* already had a mummy and a daddy. It wasn't fair, sirs. It's only the orphans that get chosen. That's how it works. But the President had made up his mind, and when Sister Grace tried to stop him, that's when the Mother Superior hit her, and locked us in! Then… Then there was a big fire, and I thought we were all going to die. But Mrs Boswell, her that was so nice to us, she unlocks the door and lets us out. She told us to run, and not look back. I was the last out. But I lost the others in all the smoke. That's when I saw it...'

'Saw what?' Johnson whispered, leaning forward in his chair. 'What did you see?'

'A big black carriage, sir. It was pulled by black horses with flaming eyes, coming out of the smoke like messengers from h— From *down there*. I saw the Mother Superior drag Mrs Boswell out of the fire and bundle her into the back of the carriage. That's when I climbed underneath and held on for dear life. I wanted to see where they were going.'

Johnson looked amazed. 'You did a very brave thing, Rachel dear. Now tell me: where did that carriage go?'

Rachel's eyes stretched all the wider, and she spoke in a scandalised whisper, as if frightened of being heard. 'The *Wizard's* house, sir.'

Johnson and Boswell exchanged nervous glances. 'The wizard? You mean Thomas Weir? The Warlock of West Bow?'

Rachel nodded solemnly and took a big drink of milk, holding her glass in both hands.

'Of *course*,' murmured Johnson. 'Listen' he said, gathering the two men in a huddle. 'Here's what we must do.'

Chapter 19

The Battle for Old Town

Fire needs fuel to survive, and by noon the inferno had more or less burned itself out, having reduced much of the city to a charred and smoking ruin.

Soon the heavens opened, releasing an all-consuming deluge that smothered the last of the flames. By the time the smoke had cleared the wooden tenements of Old Town had been reduced to a slimy black mush, though many of the more solidly built stone tenements such as Boswell's had survived the devastation.

A bitter stand-off was unfolding on the High Street between the city guard and the revenants. The former had abandoned their mounts and were organising themselves in lines before the castle gates, while the enemy gathered for a final assault.

Compared to the disciplined troops, the invaders were scattered and disorganised. Some lost heart and loped off into the shadows, content with raking around for dead bodies to drag back to whatever hole they had crawled from.

It looked like the battle was won before it had even started, when from out of the smoking ruins of the city stepped the Bone King.

On his head he wore the helm of some long-dead knight,

with a leather cuirass to protect his hoary old torso. His strong fingers gripped the hilt of a murderous mace, forged in a less civilised time when a man would split his neighbour's skull for merely looking at him in the wrong way. The Bone King stood on the main thoroughfare and looked grimly at the numbers arrayed against him.

When the revenants saw their leader they rallied round, jeering and baying in triumph at his belated entry on the field of battle. The Bone King looked appraisingly at his troops, almost paternally, then all of a sudden he cried out in a voice hoarse from decades of silence. 'My sons! Only a paltry rabble stands between us and the taking of the city. Let us desecrate the corpses of our enemy. The heads of the City Fathers we will set on stakes at the Flodden Gates. Fight for me and I promise you, this very night we will feast like kings!'

A little further up the street Lieutenant Steele was rousing the fighting spirits of his troops in his own way.

'Dragoons! This stronghold we now stand before is the heart and soul of the city we love. They used to call her Maiden's Castle, on account of her impregnability. Let us now put that name to the test. We will protect her honour, and the honour of this city, by sending these demons back to the Pit!'

The Bone King, who was within earshot of this defiant speech, emitted a dry, throaty chuckle that sounded like scree sliding down the flanks of a mountain. He raised his mace, and his followers surged forward.

The front row of dragoons dropped to their knees and fired on the advancing horde. A dozen revenants fell before they reached the castle gates. As the first row of dragoons reloaded their weapons the second row fired, and a dozen more of the enemy fell.

The revenants were on them before they had a chance to fire a third time.

Bayonets! cried Lieutenant Steele.

A desperate battle ensued at the very gates to the castle, a close quarter struggle the likes of which had never been seen within the walls of the city before. The revenants were pierced many times by bayonets, but they were relentless, tearing into the soldiers with bare hands, clubs and sickles. The Grey Dragoons stood their ground, valiantly defending the gates, while the townsfolk watched from within with bated breath.

Down came the rain over all, turning the battleground into a sludgy morass; the combatants struggled on, slipping and sliding on the rain-slicked cobblestones, reduced to animals fighting for their lives, hacking and parrying until Queensberry and Chalmers, watching from above, could no longer tell which was man and which revenant.

*

Johnson and Boswell crept stealthily through Old Town, slipping from backstreet to backstreet to avoid being seen, while all around them battle raged. A drooling revenant in rags came loping towards them, heading in the direction of the castle, then carried on past as if Johnson and Boswell didn't exist.

As they walked, Boswell questioned his friend on everything that had happened since his confinement, including the startling discoveries Johnson and his associates had made at Roswell Castle.

'And what of the doors that Doctor Hun— that that *thing* who kidnapped Lady Colville was talking about?'

'The doors of Sitra Ahra,' Johnson confirmed. 'The gateway to Hell itself.'

'And we are to find such a place in the House of Thomas Weir?'

'It was under our noses all along, Boswell. Remember, Old Town is built on top of a volcanic pipeline. All volcanoes have a central vent, called the pipe, with subsidiary vents branching off in all directions. The various wells around the city serve as outlets to these subsidiary vents. But I believe if we locate the basement of Weir House we will find a much deeper well, this one serving as the main conduit, a pipeline leading directly to a magma chamber at the heart of the earth.'

'And this is where we will find my wife and daughter, in the basement of Weir House?'

'Yes,' said Johnson. 'I believe so.'

Boswell had to force himself to ask the next question. 'And what will they do with Veronica?' His voice was little more than a husky whisper.

Johnson seemed equally reluctant to speak. 'The Order mean to sacrifice Veronica, if they can, and by her blood they will open the gates....'

'And what will come out through those gates, Doctor Johnson?'

Johnson heaved a sigh. 'They call her Lamia, Queen of Despair,' he said at last, 'though she has gone by many other names. In the Bible she is Lilith, first wife of Adam, born not of his rib, but independently of him. She is the personification of lust and ruin. Refusing to lay with her husband, Lilith fled to the desert where she began consorting with demons: *Her house sinks down to death, and her course leads to the shades. All who go to her cannot return and find again the paths of life.*'

'What is it that she wants, Doctor?'

'She longs to take possession of a human body once more, and usher in a second Age of Darkness.' Johnson looked soberly at his friend. His face was drawn and haggard, his eyes still badly bruised from the attack in Boswell's apartment. 'Your daughter is to be the vessel, Boswell.'

Boswell clenched his fists and suppressed a shudder. 'How do we stop the bitch?'

Johnson's eyes betrayed not a flicker of emotion. 'There is only one way to save your daughter,' he said, weighing his words carefully. 'According to the prophecy, someone must take her place.'

*

Rainclouds gathered overhead, lit sporadically by flashes of lightning. Darkness seemed to congregate above the roof of Weir House in a great whorling mass, drawing crows from every corner of the town. They came twirling and flapping in huge flocks, cawing into the wind, to settle in the eaves of the building.

Johnson paused with a hand resting on the brass doorhandle, a curious device in the shape of a leering gargoyle. It seemed burning hot and icy cold all at the same time. 'There are those in this house who would unleash a terrible evil on this world,' he said, steeling himself to open the door. 'We must locate the basement. That is where they will be attempting the ritual, and that is where we will find your family. Be careful. The forces of evil are arraigned against us. Unspeakable things have gone on in this house throughout its long history, things which have left an impression, like a stain that cannot be removed and sullies everything that it touches. I believe that evil draws evil unto itself, and that this house acts as a conduit for all things impure and unholy. Trust in the Lord, Mr Boswell. And if all else fails…' Johnson opened his coat to indicate the loaded pistol, 'trust in this.'

Taking deep breaths, the two men stepped inside.

*

The battle for Old Town had been raging back and forth for several hours when the crowds abruptly parted. A hush descended as the Bone King himself entered the fray. He looked around, trying to find a worthy adversary. This came in the form of Lieutenant George Steele, who had thus far been directing the battle from the wings. At the sight of the direful King he drew his sabre, which flashed threateningly in the afternoon sun.

The Bone King grinned at his challenger. 'Step down from thy steed,' he cried, 'and let us meet on the field of battle as equals, thee and I.'

Never one to refuse a challenge, Lieutenant Steele climbed down from his mount, much to the horror of his men.

'Lieutenant,' whispered his valet, who had remained steadfastly by his side for the duration of the battle. 'Do not throw away your life needlessly for these vermin.'

But Steele was deaf to his young squire's pleas.

The Bone King made the first move, swinging his mace with deadly precision. Steele was fast, and dodged out of the way just in time. The mace smashed harmlessly into the ground. As the Bone King raised the mace a second time, Steele struck out with his sabre, piercing the cadaverous King under his arm. It was a lucky strike, being the only part of the King's body his leather cuirass did not protect, leaving the soft parts vulnerable. The Bone King did not blink as the sabre pierced his flesh. He brought the mace whistling down a second time. This time it found its target, shattering Lieutenant Steele's left arm. The men looked on, horrified to see their champion at the mercy of his nemesis. But the downward swing of the mace upset the King's balance. He staggered forward. Steele struck again, this time severing the Bone King's hand, mace and all. The Bone King let out a howl of frustration and Steele pressed his advantage, this time running his enemy through the heart.

The death of their leader sent the revenants into paroxysms of rage. The cry went up that the patriarch of their clan had fallen. Enraged, the enemy came scuttling in from surrounding closes, wynds and vennels like a swarm of cockroaches. Some had abandoned their weapons altogether in their fury. They tore into the troops like foxes let loose in a chicken coop, biting, tearing, gouging with a bloodlust that was something less than human. Soon the proud regiment which had started that day with two hundred men was reduced down to fifty. Like a branch of oak whittled down to a stub by a whirling blade, they defended themselves with increasing impotence. George Steele held his cutlass in his good hand, parrying and swiping for all he was worth, meanwhile desperately trying to defend his young squire, who was under his protection. But even that brave warrior was forced to retreat until his back was against the very doors to the castle.

High upon the battlements, the spectators saw which way the

battle was going and groaned in unison. The civilians on the lower levels looked up and begged their lords to open the gates. But the Duke of Queensberry knew that to open the gates would be to bring disaster down on all of them. He shook his head grimly, though inside his heart was breaking.

Chapter 20

The Warlock of West Bow

Nothing made any sense.

The staircase followed impossible rules of geometry. It was a startling effect, like the popular optical illusion of boxes which at first appear convex, then by some curious shift of perception reveal themselves to have been concave all along. Johnson put his foot on the first step and began to descend the stairs to the basement, only to find that, halfway down, he was actually going up. He wondered if it was a peculiar effect of the geometrical patterns on the wallpaper, or evidence of more sinister forces at play.

He didn't like it one bit.

'I do not like it one bit, Boswell,' he wheezed. 'If I am going up, I like to know I am going up. If I am going down, I like to arrive at a point lower than where I started from. This is neither here nor there. It feels like we are going nowhere at all.'

Boswell plodded on, his mind a million miles away.

They reached a level of the house where all rules of perspective and proportion had fallen by the wayside. Had Euclid paid a visit to the House of Thomas Weir, he may very well have gone back to his desk and burned all his journals, presumably before being carted off to the lunatic asylum. Either the corridors were impossibly long, or else the lines of the walls converged prematurely, terminating in miniature doorways, or disappearing entirely into a point infinitesimally small. Sometimes it seemed that depth was an illusion altogether, and the corridors mere daubings on plasterboard, a stage set reflecting a madman's *idea* of a house, rather than a physical place of bricks and mortar.

Shadows rudely disrupted any sense of symmetry, shadows blacker than night, shadows which bred monsters.

A profound sense of melancholy lurked around every corner, as if the walls themselves wept at the futility of existence. And always the feeling of being watched, the feeling of being trapped inside some intricate Chinese puzzle, a puzzle designed by some malevolent genius who waits and watches, ready to snap jaws shut on the unwary intruder.

And everywhere mirrors: flat, concave or convex, framed or plain, round, square or rectangular, they lined the walls, appeared unexpectedly around corners and furnished every room. Johnson found multiple versions of himself disappearing into infinity: short and squat, impossibly tall and thin, like some carnival hall of mirrors.

As they moved deeper into the house, Boswell's vision began to fail him. The man walking ahead of him was just a blob of grey against the darker colours of the house. Boswell felt himself wading through some liquid-like substance, his limbs straining against it. The distance between the grey blob that was his friend and himself increased, until Boswell realised he was all alone. He tried to cry out but his throat was filled with the same molasses-like substance that slowed his movements. He groped around in a panic, only for his fingers to brush against a door handle. He pushed his way inside.

*

Time, inextricably linked to space, went awry in the house of

The Fall of the House of Thomas Weir

Thomas Weir. Johnson didn't know how long he had been talking, or if he had been talking at all, when he realised that Boswell was no longer by his side. He stopped, overcome with an inexplicable feeling of dread. He wanted to call out for his friend, but didn't dare. Who knows what he might have summoned from the shadows?

It was too late. Something was approaching. Johnson heard the steady *tap tap tap* of a walking stick from around the next corner. Louder and louder it echoed throughout the corridor, until it became a furious pounding in his ears. Frantically, he looked around for somewhere to hide. There was a door just up ahead. If he was fast, he might make it in time before *they* caught him.

He reached for the handle and opened the door.

*

Mrs Boswell was aware of being half-dragged, half-led down a series of steps. There was a strong sense of dislocation from her own body. She knew she was being coerced, her arms held fast in a vice-like grip, but she was powerless to prevent it.

The stairs levelled out and she found herself in a chamber that smelled of old earth and damp stone. A cellar. She was led towards a wall. A strong pair of hands twisted her body and yanked her arms upwards. She could hear the rattle of chains and felt cold iron biting into her wrists. A female voice murmured something in her ear, but no meaning filtered down to Mrs Boswell's disorientated senses. She tried to think of the past few days, and her mind was assaulted with a chaotic jumble of images. Sir William and Mother Superior, the orphanage, the attic, poor Sister Grace and her box of letters... then the image of Veronica blotted out all other thought, searing its way into her brain, and she opened her mouth to scream...

*

The room was simply furnished, consisting of a small bed made up with white sheets, a plain dresser and a tall mirror on a stand.

Johnson crossed the floor tentatively. When he reached the window he wiped away the grime with the sleeve of his coat, making a clean little circle through which he could gaze out onto the world.

What he saw forced him back a step, his jaw hanging slack in stupefaction. With a pounding heart he peered through the hole again, this time with his left eye, in case his right had been deceiving him.

The tenements on the far side of the street had simply… vanished. The house stood alone on a barren hill of rock. Even the castle had gone.

Everything was familiar, and yet unfamiliar.

Across the valley, Arthur's Seat loomed six times as large as the benign humps of grass he had climbed only a few days ago. Now it was a towering cone of basalt, like the shadow of some titan, belching sulphurous fumes into the atmosphere, sending a volcanic cloud of ash to blot out the stars in the sky. Periodically a flash of lighting would illuminate the clouds from below, throwing the volcano into stark contrast against the darkening sky.

Johnson looked on, trembling with fear and awe. It was as if he were witnessing the moment of creation itself, a battle between gods and titans. And yet he also felt elated, filled with a tremendous sense of privilege. He, and he alone was allowed this glimpse onto God's workshop. The house seemed invisible, the very walls and ceiling a mere veil of gauze through which to view this primordial, awe-inspiring vista, as if the house itself were a telescope into the abyss of time.

Was he not the first man—nay, the first sentient being—to gaze upon such wonders? He felt infinitesimally small in the presence of its immensity. The petty concerns for his health, his worries about the future, his financial woes, his vanity for his reputation, all seemed to slip away. He was a gnat in the storm, a plaything of titanic, elemental forces beyond his control, forces in the face of which neither himself, nor the Boswells, nor the besieged city could have any importance.

It would take a further two-hundred-and-fifty million years before the immense, lava spewing volcano would become the familiar spent stub of a hill, an Ice Age before sheep could safely graze upon her tamed and chastened flanks. Johnson wondered if his mere presence out of the loop of time, slight though it was, could alter the chain of events that led to his own creation. Had everything been ordained from the very beginning? A causal chain of unalterable events set in motion by the Cosmic Watchmaker himself? He would need to speak to Hume about it, if he ever survived his current predicament. But then again, the collection of dust and fire of which the sentient being known as David Hume consisted was at this moment swirling in the abyss, and would form and reform innumerable times before it conjoined to make the man.

A slight movement drew Johnson's attention to the mirror beside him. The bed, reflected on its tarnished surface, looked rumpled. He turned his attention away from the maelstrom outside. All of a sudden he was returned to himself. The bed was clearly unoccupied. He looked in the mirror again. Yes, there... pale and sickly, almost translucent, the invalid in the bed looked directly into Johnson's eyes.

'Sam? Is it really you?'

The colour drained from Johnson's face; the mirror showed him how old and haggard he had become. 'Tetti?' he said. 'But how...?'

'I am so cold, Sam,' said Johnson's long-dead wife. 'Come and warm my hands.'

'But of course, dear,' said Johnson, rushing forward to take her hands. They were as cold and white as snow.

'Oh Sam,' she sighed. 'Do you remember those warm evenings we would sit by the fire? Or rather I would sit by the fire, and you would be scribbling away at that dictionary of yours.' Her voice was heavy, laboured, wheezing with the effort of speaking. 'Did you ever finish it, by the way?'

'Yes, Tetty. Oh Tetty!'

'But Sam, why are you crying? Come here you big goose.' And she opened her arms for Johnson to lay his head on her breast. 'There, there,' she soothed, stroking Johnson's cheek with an ice-cold finger.

'Oh Tetty,' cried Johnson. 'Can you forgive me?'

'Forgive you,' murmured the woman on the bed drowsily. 'Whatever for?'

'For being alive. For letting you die. Oh Tetty. I should have taken better care of you. You were always such a fragile thing. I should have spent more time with you. I should have told you how much I loved you... I... I...'

'Well, what's done is done. No point crying over spilt milk, Sam dear. After all, I am much happier, now. It isn't so bad, being dead. And there is no pain. Perhaps you could join me. Would you like that, Sam?'

Johnson pressed his face into his dead wife's nightgown. It smelled musty, with a sickly-sweet undertone. He felt something against his cheek, movement, as if something were alive, squirming under his wife's cold flesh. He looked up at her blue and bloated face through tear-filled eyes. How could she have seemed so alive only moments before? The tongue squirmed in her mouth; her lips protruded slightly, revealing something green inside. To Johnson's horror a fat, sluggish toad emerged from between her turgid lips, followed by another, and then another. Johnson raised his head to scream, then caught sight of himself in the mirror. He was lying on an empty bed.

*

Maggie Boswell felt cold stone against her back. The sack over her head obscured her vision, though she was aware of shadows around the room. She could discern separate voices: deeper male voices at first, followed by a lone female speaking in clipped, imperious tones. Mrs Boswell could only discern snippets of what was said, but one man seemed to be in charge, whereas the female, whom Mrs Boswell thought to be Sister Daphne, was begging some favour, despite the haughtiness of her tone. Various words drifted in and out of Mrs Boswell's consciousness: *'grant what was promised'* ... *'did what you said'* ... *'children'* ... *'risked all'* ... Then a deeper male voice: *'unworthy vessel'* ... *'appetiser'* ... *'disrobe'* ... There was a long pause, a brief scuffle, followed by strange grunting, gurgling noises, a terrible cry of triumph, and then silence.

Mrs Boswell struggled hopelessly against her chains. How had it come to this? Self-pity was a luxury she could ill afford. She relaxed her arms in their bondage and tried to clear her mind, to sharpen her senses. Her sole concern was not for herself, but for Veronica. Oh God, where was she? What had they done with her? And where was her husband? Surely by now he realised she and Veronica were missing, surely he and Doctor Johnson were looking for them?

*

Boswell entered the room and immediately the atmosphere around him changed. He could breathe again. He rubbed his eyes, and gradually his vision was returned to him. The blobs of colour took on familiar details and sharpened edges. From the shape of the eaves and broken window, Boswell recognised the room he had blundered into as the one seen from the street two days, and a lifetime, ago. A rocking chair had been placed by the window, as if its occupant liked to watch the world outside. The empty chair filled Boswell with an inexplicable feeling of dread.

As if in response to his fear it started to move; small arcs at first which gradually widened, until it was swinging violently, threatening to topple at any moment. Despite his dread, Boswell felt himself pulled inexorably into its compass.

The room was filled with the sound of someone softly singing and the *click-clack-click* of knitting needles. He was instantly reminded of his dear, sweet mother, who used to make everything seem all right, an angel of mercy who protected him from his father's stern reproofs, who had soothed him to sleep and sang away all his pain. When she died, a large part of him died too. Boswell took another step towards the rocker, emboldened by the familiar sound of the knitting needles, lulled into submission by the softness of the singing. He took another step, and the smells of home assailed his nostrils, of bannocks on the stove and freshly cut hay wafting in through the window. Suddenly his heart was filled with longing to see his mother again. He murmured her name, and placed a hand firmly on the back of the chair to stop the rocking motion. The mirror by the window, one he hadn't noticed before, had been positioned in such a way that he could see the occupant of the chair from behind.

Who knows how long the dried-out husk of a body had been mouldering at the window, the clothes hanging in tattered rags, the jaw hanging slack, as if proclaiming to the world the thrill of being dead?

Boswell stepped back in horror. Impossibly, the hands on the chair tightened, and the arms strained as the corpse raised itself up. It turned its empty eye-sockets on Boswell, still grinning its slack-jawed grin. His heart in his throat, Boswell staggered back. The corpse took a step towards him, its grey hair seething with grave worms. Boswell staggered back towards the door. It took another step. Boswell yanked and rattled the door handle. It was locked. He shook the door, crying out for help.

Then the corpse did something entirely unexpected.

It raised a withered arm, pointed at Boswell, threw back its head and... laughed.

It was not a kindly laugh, but brittle and unforgiving, quickly joined by others from the shadows, unseen things who shared the cruel joke. Boswell felt crushed under the weight of it.

He was a plump schoolboy again, teased by his classmates for his underdeveloped and hairless body. He was an awkward, gangling teenager, laughed at by the village girls for his shyness and his pimples. He was a student of Law, mocked by his peers, derided for his clumsy poetry and ridiculed for the searing honesty of his journals. Every humiliation he had suffered, the public ridicule he had been exposed to and the indignities of his life were now visited on him all at once; he felt naked, exposed, fraudulent. He fell to his knees and buried his face in his hands, whimpering like an unhappy child.

The laughter stopped as abruptly as it had started. When Boswell looked up, he was no longer in the house of Thomas Weir. He was in the Court of Sessions on Parliament Close, except now it was he who was on trial. Daylight streamed in through the tall windows, alighting on the dock where he stood. The presiding judge was a corpse, absurdly dressed in robes of state with a festering wig perched atop a sunken face. Death itself had come to judge him.

'James Boswell,' it said. 'You stand accused of being a speck of dirt on the face of humanity. A malodorous carbuncle on the backside of existence. You are a talentless hack. A corrupter of public morals. A philanderer. A vain popinjay with not a shred of human decency. You are altogether an absurd, ridiculous, and insignificant little man. How d'ye plead?'

Boswell turned to look at the faces in the public gallery. The front row was reserved for close family: Margaret, Veronica, his dead mother and still-living father. His peers—Goldsmith, Garrick, Gibbon, Burke and the like—were also in attendance, and perhaps the cruellest blow of all: Doctor Johnson, who was shaking his head sadly at the accused. At the back stood all the women he had ever bedded or had tried to bed in his lifetime, and to see them all crowded into the same room with his wife and mother produced an avalanche of shame.

Boswell looked down at himself. He was as naked as the day he was born, his plump white body grotesque in the cruel light of day, his nakedness an affront to those austere and formal halls.

'How d'ye plead?' roared the judge again.

'Guilty!' cried Boswell in a tremulous voice, and a hush settled over the room.

A titter arose from the public gallery, followed by a smattering of polite coughs. Then somebody let rip with a huge raspberry, which started them all off. Within minutes the helpless spectators were rolling in the aisles; Johnson and his father stood arm-in-arm, supporting one another in their mirth, while the women all pointed at Boswell's nakedness, laughing until the tears came streaming down their faces. Even his lovely Veronica was laughing nervously, looking from her father to her mother and back again, not quite sure what else to do.

Boswell was struck with an overwhelming urge to put an end to his absurd and meaningless existence. He felt an aching emptiness inside. As if in response to his deepest and darkest desire, a rope dropped down from above, its knotted loop a challenge and a promise of oblivion. Boswell looked through the noose at the people, who were now in such a paroxysm of mirth that they appeared to Boswell as chattering monkeys, slapping each other's backs and bouncing up and down on the benches. With a sigh of profound resignation he placed his chin over the cradle of rope, a spectacle which his audience found even funnier.

He caught the eye of his daughter in the crowd. She seemed distraught. Afraid. And then the face of his daughter merged with that of the girl with the doll. His little ghost girl. His guardian angel. *This isn't happening*, Boswell told himself. *Somewhere in the real world my wife and daughter are alone in the dark.*

He tried to remove the noose from his neck, but before he could release himself the corpse judge cried, 'Guilty as charged!' and with the fall of his gavel the ground fell away.

The noose around Boswell's neck tightened, choking the life out of him.

Then nothing. Blackness.

The first bullet shattered the mirror into a thousand pieces.

Boswell was sprawled on the floor, hacking and spluttering for breath.

'Don't look into any more mirrors,' said Johnson matter-of-factly. He was standing in the doorway, calmly reloading his weapon. 'It's how they find their way into this world.' And to Boswell's look of utter astonishment he added, 'This house feeds on negative thoughts, such as guilt and shame. Don't give them the satisfaction.'

'But how…? What…?'

'My God, Boswell. You look as though you've seen a ghost. Here. Take hold of my arm.'

Boswell gritted his teeth and allowed himself to be pulled to his feet.

'Come with me,' said Johnson. 'I have found a way out of here.'

Chapter 21

Queen of Despair

*O*n the ramparts of Edinburgh Castle, Lord Chalmers turned away, unable to watch the last stand of the Royal Scots Grey.

'My God,' cried Queensberry, watching as a great host of bodies advanced along the High Street. 'We are finished!'

Staff Sergeant Brown produced a telescope and stretched it out, pointing it down the length of the Royal Mile towards the advancing horde. 'That is not revenants, your Grace.'

Queensberry glanced at the fussy little sergeant and snatched the telescope from him. 'But you are right!' he cried, peering through the telescope. 'But if it is not *them*, then who...?'

*

Bill Fernley marched at the head of fifty escaped convicts. As they progressed along High Street they increased in size; men, women and children emerged from every shaded wynd and close; the wounded, the frightened, those who had lost their homes in the fire or those who had lost loved ones, picking up whatever weapons were to hand and falling in. By the time the company

The Fall of the House of Thomas Weir

reached St. Giles Cathedral they were one-hundred-and-fifty strong, bristling with pitchforks, sickles, staves, antique muskets, rusty claymores, knuckle-dusters, rocks and catapults. Bill Fernley stopped by the doors to the cathedral, ascended the steps, and turned to look at some of the city's most notorious thieves, murderers and vagabonds at the head of a crowd of tradesmen and washerwomen. No longer did they see themselves in terms of good or bad, rich or poor, old or young. Edinburgh may have been a charred and smoking ruin, but to every last man, woman and child it was home, and they would fight for her down to the very last brick, if need be. It was true, some of his fellow convicts had their own reasons for fighting. Some because they loved violence. Because they expected a reward. Because they hoped to receive a pardon. What did it matter? As long as they fought like lions, he would proudly stand alongside them.

Fernley turned back to look up High Street. There she was in all her splendour, Maiden's Castle: so-called because she was considered impregnable by force. And there *they* were, clamouring to get in, making mincemeat out of the valiant few who could still hold a sword. Bill Fernley felt the gorge rise to his throat, an indignation so overwhelming that it almost choked him. He turned to face his followers, who stood in absolute silence, waiting to see what their de facto leader had to say.

'Lads,' cried Bill, addressing the crowd. 'We have fought many battles together, and seen our fair share of glory. But we have never before fought the likes of this rabble. And so if any of you wish to leave the field of battle, go now! There is no shame in it, and I will not hold it against ye, by God.'

'For the love of Christ get on with it, Bill Fernley!' cried a voice in the crowd. 'William Wallace you are not!'

Bill Fernley blushed to the roots of his hair. 'Aye, well, right then. So that is how it is.' And to spare himself any further blushes he raised his cutlass in the air, jumped down the steps, and ran the rest of the way up to the castle. It didn't take his followers long to fall in behind him.

High up on the ramparts Staff Sergeant Brown shed tears of joy to see such gallantry in action. He raised the chanter to his lips and blew his favourite tune, *Blue Bonnets Over the Borders*.

George Steele and his dragoons were down to the last twenty men. Still they put up a ferocious fight at the very gates to the castle. Steele's valet, a fourteen-year-old boy who went by the name of Alaister Carstairs, fought alongside his master with great gallantry, and would have died happily beside him that day. Luckily for his mother, that day was not today.

The Dragoons heard the stirring refrain of the pipes and knew at once that reserves were pouring in. The revenants heard also, and turned to meet a roaring crowd thundering down the High Street.

With a great cry of joy Alastair Carstairs raised the blue saltire from the dust and waved it in the air.

*

Someone padded into the room, and the sack was removed from Maggie Boswell's head. The five walls of a dungeon came sharply into focus.

Though she was alone and terrified, Mrs Boswell had managed to count the time it had taken the carriage she was bundled into to reach its current destination. She deduced she wasn't far from her own home. The shape of her prison seemed very familiar to her, then with a jolt of horror she realised why. She was in the basement of the house of Thomas Weir. The pentagonal tower had always terrified her as a child, and even as an adult she would cross the street rather than pass it on her way to Grassmarket. She methodically took in the details of her surroundings. A jewel the size of a fist was embedded in each of the five walls, crystalline in form and glowing with an unearthly blue light. In Mrs Boswell's disorientated state of mind it was difficult to gauge the true proportions of the chamber. It seemed both impossibly huge, and at the same time stiflingly claustrophobic. The whole place was abuzz with a latent, malignant energy, while a coppery smell burned the lining of her nostrils.

Mrs Boswell caught only a glimpse of the creature that removed her hood before it scurried off into the shadows to conceal itself in an arched alcove. It was a leprous, servile thing swathed in rags, with sightless eyes and teeth filed to sharp points.

While the wretched servant inspired only pity and disgust, the five hooded figures who now entered the chamber filled her with a dread beyond reckoning. Clothed in robes of scarlet and gold, they took their places around an old well in the middle of the chamber, while the most imposing of the five stood behind a stone altar.

As Mrs Boswell's eyes became accustomed to the light more details emerged. The body of the Mother Superior was slumped across the floor in a pool of her own blood, her face a livid white, the imperious expression transformed into a rictus of ecstasy, as if in her final moments she had achieved some kind of victory over death.

The figure behind the altar removed his hood to reveal the face of a man in his mid- to late-sixties. He was well-preserved—handsome, even—with streaks of white in his iron-grey hair, a strong forehead, high cheekbones and an aquiline nose. His cloak seemed to shimmer, and the gold hieroglyphs which decorated it took on a life of their own in the shifting shadows. The more Mrs Boswell focused on the leader's face the more his expression seemed to elude her. It was like a mask, immobile, with just a hint of cruelty about the lips. But there was something else, a glimpse of something *other* bubbling beneath the surface.

Following the leader's example the others lowered their hoods. Mrs Boswell recognised the "three craws" from the orphanage. There was Sir William, looking as smug as ever, the gaunt one with the doctor's bag who had come to examine the children, and the callow youth with the arrogant sneer of a mouth who wore his thinning hair combed forward, a row of spit curls plastered across his forehead. The fifth man Mrs Boswell did not see at first because his back was partially towards her. But when he turned, the shock of recognition was devastating. It was the Reverend Baxter, the family friend who had personally baptised Veronica. It seemed the final cruelty needed to drive Mrs Boswell to the very edge of her sanity.

A sharp intake of breath signalled the presence of someone chained to the wall beside her. She turned her head to meet Lady Colville's gaze, and the latter's expression was one of sadness and compassion. *Don't look*, her eyes seemed to say. *Keep focused on me.*

A stronger urge pulled Mrs Boswell's gaze away, back towards the altar on the other side of the well. The revenant who had removed her blindfold re-emerged from the shadows carrying a white bundle of something in its arms. It was Veronica. The creature placed the body on the altar then scurried back to its recess. Even as Mrs Boswell's mind recoiled from the reality of her daughter in the hands of those monsters, her body was powerless to move. The scream froze in her throat.

The leader produced a dagger from the folds of his robe. Mrs Boswell watched with impotent fury as he took her daughter's hand in his and made an incision along the length of her little arm. The girl stirred and moaned slightly as he caught the blood in a golden chalice, but she did not awaken. Mrs Boswell considered it the smallest of mercies.

As the Master of Ceremonies filled the vessel he chanted in a deep, resonant voice: '*Lilith, Layil, Ardat-Lili, Laylah… Lilith, Layil, Ardat-Lili, Laylah… Lilith, Layil, Ardat-Lili, Laylah…*'

Once the chalice was filled the doctor stepped forward from his place on the pentagram to bind the wound. They would not let the child die. That privilege was reserved for another.

A vibration began from deep within the well which shook the walls of the chamber: a vibration which was both noiseless and deafening.

The High Priest raised the chalice to his lips. His eyes rolled in ecstasy as he drank from the goblet, taking care not to drain it to the bottom. He poured the rest into the mouth of the well, then raised his hands above his head in a sign of power. '*Agios Es, Makoriton,*

The Fall of the House of Thomas Weir

Divum Et Vorsipelle! Ornate Lakarithor Divinitas Ex Acharayim! Veni, Veni, Nakhatal— Divinitas Et Creatrix! Induperator Est Rakorigon Etiam Reshut Ha-Rabbim! Arcesso Praevalidum Agenti Smola— Invito Makoriton! Agios Es, Nakhatal, Divum Et Vorsipelle! Ornate Rakorigon Divinitas Ex Acharayim!

'Numinous Art Thou, Dragon, Spirit and Shapeshifter! I Praise the Void, Deity of the Backwards Tree! Come, Come, Dragon— Goddess and Creator! The Dragon is the Lord of the Kingdom of Manifoldness! I reach for the Great Emissary of the Left Hand— I Call the Void! Numinous Art Thou, Dragon, Spirit and Shapechanger.'

The ground beneath Maggie's feet seemed to ripple and swell, her vision shimmered, and the four acolytes repeated the terrible words of invocation.

The High Priest was shouting now, roaring above the soundless vibration that hurt Maggie's ears, his hands raised in a gesture of invocation: 'Dark Mother who comes at night on the wings of shadow, Ama Lilith! Hear my calling and come to me! Shelter us beneath the hem of your garment from the burning heat of the sun. Protect us from the scorching winds of the desert. Conceal us with your shadow from the blinding light. Come forth, from the caves of the Red Sea and awaken the power of the Dragon.

'The world awakens to life in your embrace. The doors of Sitra Ahra are open to those who dare to walk your path.

'I call you, Ancient One! I invoke you, Mother of Demons, who sits enthroned in the midst of her aborted offspring! All serve you who are created by you and of your own essence.

'Creator and Destroyer, whose face is bright on the right side and black on the left, come forth to us!

'I summon you by the power of your names: Lilith, Layil, Ardat-Lili, Laylah - Mother of Sin, reveal to us your true form, speak truth and answer truly. Grant us the knowledge and wisdom of the Night! I call you in the name of the Dragon:

'Ho Ophis Ho Archaios,
'Ho Drakon Ho Megas!'

Something vast stirred within the bowels of the earth. The floor shook, then lurched, spreading branch-like cracks from the well to the corners of the room. Masonry tumbled from the high arches overhead and smashed to the ground, narrowly missing the participants in that infernal rite.

Abruptly the well broke in two; a broad fissure opened up to reveal a crevasse of molten lava. Maggie's nostrils were filled with the stench of sulphur. The dais and the altar were cleft in two, leaving Veronica just inches from the void. With a massive lurch the two halves of the room moved apart, separating Maggie from Lady Betty. The cloaked ones swayed and almost lost their footing.

'*She* is coming!' cried the leader exultantly. '*She* is here!'

A moment of silence, and then one clawed hand—or was it a foot?—appeared on the edge of the precipice, closely followed by another.

Few can withstand an encounter with Lamia, Serpent Queen of Qliphoth. The mortal mind withers in Her presence like a rag to a flame. She is old; older than the mountains of the earth, crueller than the tempests of the sea. Few who witness Her passing live to tell the tale. Those who do have no frame of reference with which to process what they have seen. Like a mountain viewed in a lightning storm, only the briefest glimpses are revealed, leaving a negative impression on the retina, the vaguest of outlines, while imagination fills in the rest. To see Queen Lamia in all Her terrible glory brings only madness and death, thus the horror-stricken brain, to preserve sanity, allows only a chaotic jumble of images to filter through, the tip of a folded wing here, a clawed talon there, a crown of bony protuberances, an eye the colour of molten lava, a plague of teeth.

The High Priest barked some incomprehensible exclamation of triumph. The gleam in his eye was exultant, demonic. 'Accept the offering of this child!' he cried. 'Descend into the flesh and manifest your divine being through the altar of her immortal soul!'

The others took a step back, overcome with fear and awe.

Queen Lamia contemplated the morsel laid on the altar before her, and the room became utterly still. Drool poured from the corners of Her mouth in a parody of tears, while the eyes remained as cold and as hard as polished marble.

Maggie prayed for the end of sanity, for anything to take away the horror of what was to come. *Don't wake up*, she silently willed her daughter. *Don't wake up.*

Lady Colville, meanwhile, had been watching, unable to speak, unable to move a muscle, except for her heart, which pounded painfully inside her chest cavity. She knew what she had to do.

Mantis-like, Queen Lamia clambered out of the Great Abyss to sway sinuously over the altar, a monstrous cobra ready to strike.

'Jezebel!' cried Lady Colville exultantly. 'Accursed one! Come feast on a woman for a change!' Then, without a thought for herself or her own safety, Lady Elizabeth Colville bit down on her tongue. Hard. The pain was searing, unreal. She bit harder still, and felt her teeth slicing through the warm pink flesh. Harder still, and it was severed. She spit the severed end towards the reptilian queen, and grinned as the blood flooded down her gown.

*

The scent of the hybrid's blood was intoxicating.

It sang, and its song was sweeter than wine, sweeter by far than honey, sweeter than the dates that grew in clusters from the palm trees on the sun-drenched banks of the Nile.

The Order turned as one, enraptured by the siren call of the *sang-royal*. In their bloodlust they discarded their human masks. Queen Lamia swept her bastard offspring aside like a sea serpent parts the waves in her eagerness for the feast.

Her teeth fastened on Lady Colville's neck like a lioness on the neck of a gazelle. Her reptilian eyes closed in bliss as she gorged on the hybrid blood.

*

Johnson and Boswell arrived belatedly on this scene of carnage, emerging through a secret door via a hidden set of stairs. The two men stared in horror and confusion at the monstrous predator in her feeding frenzy, their brains unable to process what was happening.

A carotid artery as thick as rope throbbed sluggishly as the blood surged to the Queen's reptilian brain, filling long dormant joy sensors with flowers of ecstasy.

A blood-curdling scream rose from Maggie, breaking the spell. Johnson and Boswell both reached for the pistols tucked into their belts at the same time and each fired off a shot. One bullet lodged itself harmlessly between the scales of the creature's hide. The other ricocheted around the room before embedding itself in the skull of the revenant, who staggered from his niche in the wall, plunging silently into the well.

The monster who had stolen Weber's face let out an ear-shredding shriek of triumph; he was on them before they had a chance to reload, pinning Johnson hard against the wall of the dungeon.

Boswell took one look at the scene before him: the unconscious body of his daughter, his wife in chains, screaming incomprehensible threats and entreaties, Doctor Johnson grappling with his nemesis, the four hooded acolytes looking on like dogs begging for scraps, as the bloated, mantis-like Queen sucked the life force from Lady Colville. Boswell took one look at all this, then retreated wordlessly back the way he came, slipping through the secret door and closing it firmly behind him.

Johnson's heart sank as he watched his friend retreat.

Weber emitted a rich, gurgling laugh that bubbled up from his chest. 'Your friends desert you, Doctor Johnson. You have no one left. Become one of us. Feed with us!'

Johnson turned his head to look at the abomination feeding on the life force of Lady Colville. Something inexplicable was happening before his eyes. Johnson felt he was witnessing two separately-occurring realities within the same time and place, a kind of interdimensional crossroads where dreams and reality merged. One reality was inhabited by a vast, hulking dragon hunched over the body of Lady Colville. But at the same time, Johnson could see a naked female form, flame red hair flowing down her back, her mouth clamped down in sensual abandon on Lady Colville's neck. Johnson's perceptions flip-flopped feverishly between the two realities until, overcome with the strain, his exhausted senses settled on the woman. It was as if nature, unable to sustain such a paradox, rejected the less palatable of two realities.

The flame-haired beauty broke contact with the withered corpse of Lady Colville and turned to smile at Doctor Johnson, a trickle of blood running from the corner of her mouth. Johnson watched in terror and wonder as the naked doppelganger of Lady Colville walked unsteadily towards him, drunk with hybrid blood. Alluring, deadly, and heart-stoppingly beautiful, she came to within an inch of Johnson, who struggled under Weber's vice-like grip. She raised herself on tiptoes, her naked breasts lightly pressed against him, her fragrant breath warm against his neck. Lady Colville closed her eyes in ecstasy. 'Kiss me,' she said breathlessly.

Johnson glanced towards the broken body of the real Lady Colville chained to the wall, and laughed in the face of the demon standing before him. 'You are an abomination,' he intoned firmly. 'I would sooner kiss a serpent.'

The Colville creature blinked and tilted her head, but with the cold curiosity of the reptile contemplating the mouse before the kill. Queen Lamia's mouth opened. It was not a sensual parting of the lips. A crevice in her face opened from ear to ear; the top of her head swung back as if on hinges, revealing row after row of shark-like teeth that lined the abyss of an endless hunger.

Chapter 22

The Fall of the House of Weir

Joseph had already become hopelessly attached to the little orphan girl Rachel. He wrapped her up in Veronica's scarf and mittens, then grabbed her hand and led her out into the cold Edinburgh night.

He would follow Doctor Johnson's instructions to the letter. The smoke had started to clear, revealing a wasteland. Dead dragoons lay slumped over the bodies of their fallen enemies. The ground before the castle gates was littered with corpses. Joseph placed a big arm around the girl's shoulders, covering her eyes with his hand. 'No look,' he whispered.

The girl managed a smile. She had seen death before. When you had watched your parents being killed before your eyes, what were the corpses of a few soldiers? But she appreciated the gesture all the same.

The doors to the castle groaned open. The townsfolk were huddled inside, tending to their wounded. Little ones wept for their mamas, while parents looked frantically among the refugees for their own. Many had suffered horrific burns. The few nurses did what they could, reserving their meagre supply of laudanum for the worst cases.

The Fall of the House of Thomas Weir

'Who in charge here?' said Joseph to a harassed-looking nurse who was busily bandaging a child's head.

'You will have to wait your turn like the rest of us,' she said without looking up from her work.

'Is urgent government business,' said Joseph, with as much authority as he could muster.

The nurse looked up, then, and shrugged her shoulders. 'Doctor Grant,' she said, nodding towards the far end of the esplanade.

Joseph found Doctor Grant of Corstorphine in his operating theatre, a hastily assembled canvas pavilion in a corner of the parade-ground. He bid Rachel wait outside, then opened the flap and stepped inside. Grant was washing his hands in preparation for an operation, his shirtsleeves rolled to his elbows.

'You there,' he said to Joseph with barely a glance at the tall Bohemian in his bearskin cloak and high boots. 'Hold this man down.'

As Joseph pinned the old man's shoulders to the bed, Rachel appeared at his side. Before Joseph could protest, the little girl retrieved a cloth from a bucket of water, wrung it out in her tiny hands, and began to bathe the old man's fevered brow with all the tender attentiveness of a loving daughter. The old man on the operating table didn't make a sound, even as the doctor sawed through the bone of his arm and carried on through to the other side. He gazed into the gentle eyes of the girl despite the pain, focusing all his attention on her angelic countenance.

After ten minutes of searing agony, that to the poor man on the operating table was more like ten days, the shattered arm was severed. Grant dropped the useless limb into a basket and applied a tourniquet to the ragged stump. The old man slumped into unconsciousness, but his breathing was steady. He would live.

'Thank you,' said Grant, wiping off his hands with a rag.

'I am about urgent business,' explained Joseph.

'Oh? How can I help?'

'I have message from Doctor Johnson for Lord Chalmers and Duke of Queensberry.'

'From Doctor Johnson, eh?' said Grant. 'I believe you will find His Lordships up on the watchtower.'

Gently, almost reverently, Joseph hoisted Rachel onto his shoulders and climbed the stairs to the watchtower. When he found Lord Chalmers and the Duke of Queensberry, explaining his mission was simpler than he at first supposed. Johnson's orders had been explicit. If he had not returned by daybreak, Joseph was to alert the City Guard. They were to fire on Weir House until not a brick was left standing. His life, and the lives of the Boswells, would be as nothing anyway, should the Order of Draco achieve their nefarious purpose.

Lord Chalmers summoned Lieutenant Steele from the mess hall where his dragoons were recovering from their costly victory over the revenants, sharing pints of foaming ale with Bill Fernley and his band of malcontents. The valiant soldier answered the summons immediately, and didn't hesitate when Lord Chalmers explained the nature of their mission. Steele looked grimly over the battlements at his beleaguered city, and murmured two short words.

*

Morag Mor, or "Big Morag", the legendary cannon of Edinburgh Castle, was last fired a hundred years ago. It was a purely ceremonial gesture, to mark the arrival of King James VII to the city. She had since retired, brooding like a racehorse put to pasture outside Foog's Gate, the principal entrance to the Upper Ward.

'She is the largest of her kind in the world,' explained Steele, patting the iron barrel with his good arm. 'Fifteen feet in length with a barrel diameter of twenty inches. She weighs 15,366 pounds and fires three-hundred-and-eighty-six-pound cannonballs for a distance of two miles on a clear day.'

The men who lovingly maintained her could not explain why they referred to her as "she", but it had become a habit, and habits were hard to break.

The Fall of the House of Thomas Weir

It took ten men to lower the cannon onto her wooden carriage on the esplanade. With a great trundle of heavy wheels she was pulled along High Street, drawing a crowd of excited children in her wake. It was only a short distance onto West Bow, but the hill was so steep it took eight men to hold the ropes, and even then they had to strain manfully to prevent her from breaking free and rolling all the way down to Grassmarket.

When she was on a level with Weir House the men heaved to a stop.

With a great sense of occasion they loaded the cannonball and primed the fuse. Most of them had waited all their lives for just such a moment.

Only three men—a duke, a lord, and a manservant—knew the terrible sacrifice that was about to be made. They looked on with bated breath, hoping against hope that their beloved friends would come bursting from the house at the very last minute.

*

Boswell's fingers worked quickly in the dark. On the other side of that door, his wife, his daughter, and his best friend were in deadly peril, and only if his aim were true did they stand a chance. By running off he had deliberately deceived them all, letting them think he was a coward.

His father Lord Auchinleck had taught him how to load a pistol blindfolded when he was ten years old. 'You never know when you might need to defend King George, Jamie,' his father had said, locking him in the cupboard until he learned. How he had resented him for it! Now he could have kissed the old man. Thirty seconds was his record. Of course, now his hands were trembling on that cold staircase, but his family's lives were at stake, and he couldn't afford a misstep. He took the powder horn from his inside coat pocket and poured it down the barrel as he had been shown. Then he dropped in the shot and tamped it down with the rod. Next he primed the fuse. The whole operation took sixty seconds. Not bad, considering the circumstances. With the weapon primed and ready, Boswell raised it to his lips, kissed the barrel, and without wasting anymore time he kicked open the door.

Everything was confusion. His eyes moved from the naked figure confronting Johnson, to the dead body of Lady Colville chained to the wall, and next to that, the still-living body of his wife. He caught the flicker of something in his wife's eyes, and it kindled his heart. He raised his pistol and took careful aim. He did not have a clear shot.

'Doctor!' he cried. Johnson glanced round, and immediately understood what was expected of him. He ducked. Boswell pulled the trigger. There was a loud explosion and a puff of smoke. The side of Queen Lamia's head was obliterated. She staggered backwards, teetering over the edge of the fissure.

As her arms whipped furiously around what was left of a head, the face underwent a dramatic series of transformations. The flesh shifted and reorganised, sliding through manifestation after manifestation in a desperate attempt to rebuild itself: here was the Empress Wu, and the Countess of Bathory, and Isabella of Castile, and Bloody Mary Tudor, all these faces Lamia had assumed over the centuries, now merging into a singular face of unsurpassing cruelty. Even in her death throes, those eyes expressed her indomitable will. Frozen in her Medusa-like glare, Boswell felt his courage fail him. He dropped his weapon. Meanwhile, Lamia's five hooded acolytes came closing in, ready to tear him limb from limb.

*

The brooding precipice of Weir House loomed over West Bow, glowering like a Cyclops. Lieutenant Steele stood on the escarpment, gazing up at a solitary attic window. His single and all-consuming thought was the destruction of that accursed place. He would lay waste to its foundations, until nothing remained but a loathsome memory. And even that would be erased in the fullness of time.

The Fall of the House of Thomas Weir

'*Fire!*' he cried, and the first cannon ball ripped through the pentagonal tower. With a great shuddering crash which could be heard the length and breadth of High Street, a whole segment of the wall collapsed, sending plumes of smoke and debris hundreds of yards into the air.

Lieutenant Steele hesitated, waiting for the smoke to clear.

*

Incredibly, though the entire edifice had fallen away to expose the basement interior, the tower itself did not collapse. Whatever incantations had been woven into the bones of that place, whatever power resided in those glowing blue stones embedded in the walls, the house remained defiantly erect with an impudence that to Lieutenant Steele was positively indecent.

Daylight, long a strange and unwelcome guest to the House of Thomas Weir, came rushing in, evicting shadows, expelling darkness, banishing evil, and strengthening resolve. Emboldened by the light, Boswell acted swiftly. With one great leap that he would never have attempted unless under extreme duress, he flew across the chasm. The soldiers standing on the escarpment, who witnessed the spectacle with eyes agog, all said they had never seen such a leap. It was a feat to equal the famous "Soldier's Leap" at Killiekrankie, when a desperate Redcoat cleared the River Garry to escape the pursuing Jacobites. Boswell, however, took his daughter in his arms and repeated the feat a second time.

'Go!' screamed Maggie from her fixture in the wall. Boswell hesitated in the grip of panic. He placed the body of his daughter in Johnson's arms and ran to his wife. 'Where are the keys?' he cried, pulling uselessly at the chains that shackled her to the wall.

Mrs Boswell moved her lips to speak, but the strength had already left her body and the words wouldn't come. She turned her eyes weakly towards the body of the Mother Superior, who was sprawled near the edge of the precipice. As Boswell ran towards the corpse, another tremor shook the ground and the body slid towards the edge. Boswell dropped to his knees and grabbed the nun's habit. The floor tilted again, and Boswell slid with the corpse. He found the keys tied to her waist. With trembling fingers he tried to untangle the knot. A large chunk of masonry came crashing down, landing too close for comfort to Boswell's head. The keys were tied fast. The floor lurched again, and Boswell and the body slid to the very edge. Then, just as the nun's body tipped over into the fiery pit, Boswell's fingers released the keys.

Dragging himself to safer ground, Boswell clambered over the rubble to his wife, then pulled himself up and inserted the key in her hand brace. With a resounding click the brace fell away and his semi-conscious wife fell into his arms.

'Come on,' said Johnson, offering his hand from the street outside. With his wife under one arm and his other hand in Johnson's firm grip, Boswell allowed himself to be pulled up and out of the sinking building.

The survivors staggered back, and watched in horror as the house began to groan, then with a great, shuddering crunch of splintered wood and a shattering of glass it slowly collapsed in on itself, sinking like a galleon beneath the roiling sea. Witnesses said later the House of Thomas Weir seemed to devour itself, until all that was left was a sorry pile of rubble, and in the centre, a glowing blue rock about the size of a fist, crystalline in form, and smoking like a fallen meteor.

*

At a later inquest into the events of that day, each man who had witnessed the fall of Weir House gave wildly varying testimonies to the Court of Sessions, causing Lord Hailes to throw up his hands in despair.

The main source of contention concerned what they had witnessed falling into that fiery crevice, once the cannon fire had exposed the basement to the cold light of day.

One soldier said it was a vast, snakelike creature, whose tail flicked and whipped as it plunged, taking her terrible brood with her.

Another said it was a tall, willowy female, naked as the day she was born.

Private Symmons of the 2nd Dragoons swore blind it was none other than a wounded Lady Colville herself, closely followed by her five hooded acolytes. 'They fell together,' he said, 'as if joined at the waist by the same length of rope. And I should know,' he added boastfully. 'I met the lady at the Duke's ball.'

Others saw only shadows. Shadows tearing themselves from the light.

Most, though, claimed to have seen nothing, except when the smoke cleared, revealing three badly shaken adults and a sobbing child, blinking and coughing into the harsh light of day.

While the soldiers gave their testimonies an assortment of curious townsfolk piled in, and had to be forcibly removed from the courtroom and the corridors outside.

Lord Hailes's pallor during the course of the proceedings had turned from a ruddy blush to an angry red, then finally a shade of beetroot so dark that observers worried his head might explode.

This change was all the more alarming as Lord Hailes was known for his level-headedness, and shared with his good friend Doctor Johnson a love of order, logic, and simple decency. Lord Hailes had one other quality, however, which set him head and shoulders above the rest of his peers in the legal profession. Like a shark that can smell a single drop of blood in the ocean, or an eagle that can spy a beetle in the grass from a mile away, Lord Hailes could detect the most innocuous fib as soon as it was given utterance, and then would swoop with all the weight of the law behind him, reducing the liar to a quivering puddle of jelly on the stand. He had what one might call a nose for falsehood, and a knack for getting at the truth.

'Perhaps Your Honour might grant me a private audience,' said Doctor Johnson, approaching the bar, 'to clear up some of the contradictory statements we have heard in this courtroom today. I also have some evidence that should enlighten you.'

'Very well,' said Lord Hailes with a sigh, ushering his old friend into his private room. The moment the door was closed Doctor Johnson removed from his bulky pockets a bundle of letters and documents and placed them on the reading desk before the great judge. 'The Order of Draco need no formal introduction here; indeed you are already aware of my historic association them. These papers, however, provide a detailed account of their most recent doings; I believe you will find some alarming developments.'

Lord Hailes picked the first letter from the top of the pile and began to read. As he perused each letter his eyes grew wider and wider. One hour later he put down the letters, and removing his spectacles, rubbed the bridge of his nose between thumb and forefinger. Then he clasped his hands together and looked searchingly at Doctor Johnson. 'I will only ask you this one time, my old friend. These... Anunnaki, as Weber calls them; they are real? Is it true?'

Doctor Johnson returned the judge's stern gaze. 'Every last word.'

Lord Hailes seemed to slump in his chair, and he released his breath through pursed lips. 'So Weber finally paid for his bargain with the devil. Lord Sinclair too, which comes as no surprise. Never liked him. A little too...' Lord Hailes wafted his hand in the air while he searched for the right word, 'Frenchified for my tastes. Too fancy by far. But Baxter and Hunter were once good men. Regular faces around the Speculative Society.' Lord Hailes lit his pipe and stared thoughtfully at a spider's web in a corner of the room. 'And as for this Queen Lamia. Is she really gone?'

'I am willing to stake my reputation on it. Besides,' added Johnson, removing from his pocket the blue stone he found among the ruins of Weir House, and placing it on the table before Lord Hailes. 'There is the matter of this.'

Chapter 23

The Blue Stone of Enkil

James Court,
24ᵗʰ July, 1773

ix whole days have passed since my ordeal at the hands of the revenants, and four days since my ordeal in the house of Thomas Weir. Perhaps I should say my wife's ordeal, for I believe she has suffered the most out of all of us. Oh, it wrings my heart to think of the suffering I have caused my family! Had anything happened to them I should never have forgiven myself. And yet God, in His infinite mercy, has deemed fit to preserve us (though he brought us to the very brink of the abyss) and for that we must give thanks.

Those poor souls who lost their lives in the fire or at the hands of the revenants we buried side by side with our fallen warriors in the Meadows, a broad tract of land to the south of the city.

A memorial service will be held tomorrow at Greyfriars Kirk for Lady Colville, whose body we were unable to recover from the ruins of Weir House. The corpses of the revenants we piled high in the Nor Loch, tossing their *abhorrent sovereign on top, and setting fire to the lot of them. Black smoke from their immolation clogged up the High Street for hours, causing a great deal of grief to those who recently lost loved ones in the Great Fire, but others rejoiced to know the city was safe at last. A mass was said in St Giles Cathedral for their souls. They may have been corrupted with every vice and degradation known to man, but men they once were, unlike their antediluvian masters, and after all, was St. Giles himself not Patron Saint of Lepers?*

Lord Chalmers and the Duke of Queensberry, those true and trusted friends, have been tireless in their efforts to restore order. Even as I write this they are drawing up plans to raise Old Town, Phoenix-like, from the ashes. Their efforts have not gone unnoticed. His Royal Highness the Prince of Wales, in his infinite mercy, has deigned to grace us tomorrow with his Royal presence. He will carry out those duties expected of the Crown in times of need, with visits to the poor, the provision of alms and comfort to the afflicted, and otherwise overseeing the reconstruction of our devastated city.

For my own part I am tolerably well, in light of my recent travails. Doctor Johnson is as bluff and as hearty as ever; infuriatingly so, and I do believe he and my wife have reached a new level of understanding. She is unfailingly courteous to our guest, even affectionate, at times.

The Doctor, despite his good humour, is constantly preoccupied with a stone that he retrieved from that house of horror. It is crystalline in form, opalescent, and gives off a bluish glow. Doctor Johnson seems fascinated by the way it catches the light, and sometimes sits for hours alone in his study just observing it. He tells me that it is a Blue Stone of Enkil, a relic from the Lost City of Atlantis. He claims that the stone glows brighter whenever the enemy is near, though that is something I hope I never see put to the test.

From *the Casebook of Johnson and Boswell*

Mrs Boswell had been strangely calm all day, and yet, as she went about her duties, washing clothes, caring for the girls, baking cakes for the royal visit and so on, she did so almost as an automaton. Johnson and Boswell could not help but cast worried and concerned looks in her direction, her calm demeanour so utterly at odds with the terrible ordeal she had suffered. Veronica slept peacefully. She would overcome any disagreeable memories with a child's resilience. But Doctor Johnson could see that Mrs Boswell would need to come to terms with her trauma, no matter how violently, in order to heal.

At precisely five o'clock, the floodgates opened. Mrs Boswell, standing in the kitchen with her arms plunged in sink-water and staring vacantly into space, suddenly bowed her head and broke down in heart-wrenching sobs.

Johnson and Boswell, startled by such an outpouring of grief, rushed to her side. Boswell was beside himself with worry. He threw himself at his wife's feet and burst into tears while Johnson, for want of something better to do, produced a clean cotton handkerchief and passed it to the stricken lady.

'Thank you,' she managed between sobs. 'I am sorry.'

'Nonsense, woman. Let it all out. It must have been awful for you. How you must have feared for little Veronica. And as for poor Lady Colville—'

'It is a terrible loss,' said Mrs Boswell between sobs, 'but those poor orphans. I can't stop thinking about them. All those children without anyone in the world to love them, to be so cruelly snatched from the only home they knew, and murdered at the hands of those they trusted most. My heart is broken! What has happened to the world, when a man of the cloth, even a nun, can be so easily seduced to evil?'

'Console yourself, madam,' said Johnson, patting her hand. 'Really, there is nothing you could have done… there really is no need… and… and you have Rachel now…' When the doctor saw how little an effect his exhortations were having on Mrs Boswell, he wrapped his big arms around her in a bear hug, squeezing her tightly to his chest as he burst into tears himself.

Boswell, meanwhile, gripped his wife's knees and made a solemn vow never to leave her side again.

'Get off me the pair of you, ridiculous men!' she cried, though she smiled fondly at her husband despite herself. 'I won't hear of it. Do you think I need you moping around the house all day long, when there is work to be done?' Then turning to Johnson she said, 'Doctor Johnson, I have perhaps judged you unfairly in the past, thinking you a bad influence on my husband. But I see now you are as fixed and immovable as Bass Rock.'

Johnson, moved to tears by what he considered a great compliment, threw his arms once more around Mrs Boswell, and there the three of them stood, locked in an embrace until, overcome by a feeling of awkwardness, Johnson pulled away and blushingly returned to his dinner. But he had shown a glimpse of his great heart, and it was found not to be wanting.

Chapter 24

Nemo Me Impune Lacessit

Being an account of that most noble Prince of Hanover's
Royal Visit to Edinburgh, a most shameful report of High
Treason,
And how a nefarious assassination plot was foiled by our very
own Doctor Johnson.

*[Lord Chalmers]: Hints addressed to the Inhabitants of Edinburgh, and
others, in prospect of His Royal Highness's visit. By an Old Codger.*

*Nothing can be more pleasant than to witness the effect which has been
produced among every order of our fellow-citizens, by the announcement of
His Royal Highness's approaching visit to this the ancient capital of the most
ancient of his kingdoms.*

*The agitated state, not of this island only, but of all Europe, has rendered
it well-nigh impossible for our current reigning monarch George III to make
any excursion to so great a distance from the seat of government. In our time
of great need, therefore, it is incumbent upon his son, HRH Prince of Wales,
to set his foot upon our shores; and there can be no doubt that the reception he
is to meet with will be one calculated to gratify all those feelings with which the*

Andrew Neil MacLeod

Heir to the Throne of Great Britain and Ireland and such an outstanding example of masculine chivalry must be filled upon such an occasion.

We used of old to be reckoned a proud race: let us show our honest pride now; and let this pride consist in appearing just as we are. Let our Prince see us as nature and education have made us—an orderly people, whose feelings, however warm, are rarely suffered to outspring the restraint of judgement.

Printed Pamphlet (excerpt), Edinburgh, 1773

Some five thousand citizens lined up along the Royal Mile to catch a glimpse of the Prince of Wales as he rode from his official residence at Holyrood Palace to Edinburgh Castle on top of the hill. Lord Chalmers waited within the walls to present Lieutenant Steele, who would be awarded a medal of valour, and also Bill Fernley, who hoped to receive a royal pardon for himself and some of his brothers-in-arms.

Doctor Johnson and the Boswells found a spot on the street outside James Court to watch the arrival of the Prince. Veronica was hoisted onto Boswell's shoulders, while Rachel—who had been welcomed into the Boswell fold with open arms—sat perched on her favourite Joseph's shoulders. Doctor Johnson stood slightly apart, surveying the crowd with a distracted air, while Mrs Boswell gazed upon all with calm equanimity.

As the Prince of Wales arrived on a handsome open-topped carriage pulled by four magnificent steeds, the crowd roared their approval, waving their little flags for all they were worth. Only Mrs Boswell seemed out of sorts. Her countenance darkened as the carriage drew close, and the blood appeared to drain from her face.

The youth waving regally from the carriage had an arrogant cast to his features, though his face was otherwise as featureless as an egg, unremarkable in every way. Without his regalia and the pomp and splendour of his arrival he might have passed unnoticed on any busy street. He raised his tri-cornered hat in salutation, revealing thinning hair combed forward over his ears, and spit curls arranged just so in a row across his forehead.

Johnson turned to Mrs Boswell just in time to catch her as she fell. The crowd parted as Johnson laid her gently onto the pavement. She was trying to say something; Johnson drew close and placed his ear to her lips, then started at what he heard.

'Boswell, take your family indoors now.' Without pausing to see if his order had been carried out, he strode off into the crowd.

Once Boswell had gently deposited his daughter back on her own two feet he rushed to his wife's side. 'I'm all right,' she groaned, then suddenly her eyes sprang open, and a hand shot out to grab her husband's wrist. 'Go after Doctor Johnson!' she hissed, her eyes shining with an intensity that alarmed Boswell. 'I think he's about to do something very rash, and it is all my fault!'

Without further delay Boswell gestured for Joseph to attend to his family, and dashed off in pursuit.

As Johnson threaded his way through the crowd, Boswell saw him pull something from his pocket that shone like a blue lantern in the dull afternoon light.

The Prince of Wales's carriage arrived at the castle gates and pulled to a stop. The two sentries posted on either side of the gate saluted, and the doors to the castle groaned open. With a wild huzzah from the crowd the prince alighted from the carriage and raised his hat again.

In what seemed like slow motion to Boswell, Johnson stepped forward while reaching into his pocket. In that instant it dawned on Boswell what his friend proposed to do. He saw the pistol and threw himself forward, seizing Johnson by the shoulders and wrenching him round. 'Are you mad?' he cried.

'Let go,' hissed Johnson, releasing his arm from Boswell's grasp. He raised the loaded weapon again and pointed it at the carriage.

'Doctor Johnson, I beg of you. This is neither the time nor the place to lose your mind.'

'I am quite sane, Boswell. What I do now, I do for my country.

Stand back!'

Johnson took aim at the figure stepping down from the carriage. The crowd froze in horror at the sight of this large man with a pistol aimed at their beloved prince.

Boswell saw his future flash before his eyes. What was the penalty for Regicide, he wondered? Hanged, drawn and quartered? Being immersed in a vat of boiling tar? Whatever it was these days, it would be something singularly unpleasant.

At that moment there was a terrible commotion from the crowd on the other side of the street. A man dressed in rags broke through, brandishing something that looked suspiciously like a blade. It was Archie Gunn, servant of the late Lord Sinclair, and he had a crazed look in his eye. 'Imposter!' he cried as he lunged at the prince. The crowd gasped in unison.

One of the prince's footmen acted swiftly, throwing himself in the path of the blade, saving the prince and impaling himself in the process. The City Guard were all over Gunn in a matter of seconds, piling on top of him and toppling him to the ground. Gunn raised his voice and the words he cried were terrible indeed. 'Accursed be the House of Hanover!' he roared. 'It is tainted with the blood of the—' His words were stopped short by the butt of a rifle knocking him unconscious, while the rest of the guard ushered the startled prince to safety.

The sentry standing at the gate nearest to Boswell and Johnson, who had seen everything, marched purposefully towards Doctor Johnson. Boswell shrank in fear. 'I'll take that,' he said, holding out his hand. Johnson lowered his head like a naughty schoolboy, placing his unfired pistol in the sentry's hand.

''Preciate your zeal in protecting the prince, sir, though God knows how you spotted that madman before me. But next time leave the heroics to us, eh? We can't have you stealing ALL the glory from us poor bastards, can we now, sir?'

'Three cheers for Doctor Johnson, saviour of the Crown!' cried a voice, and the crowd huzzahed wildly, despite the fact that Johnson's gun had not been fired at all, and the real saviour, the footman who had fallen on the blade meant for the prince, was now bleeding out on the cobblestones.

But why let truth get in the way of a good story? They surged around Johnson and raised him on their shoulders, though they staggered under his bulk. For the first time in as long as Boswell could remember, Johnson was rendered speechless, his mouth opening and closing like a great catfish.

After the excitement of the morning's events had died down, the Old Town returned to that semi-calm state that usually succeeded a series of dramatic events, though the city would be awash for quite some time with rumours of conspiracies and plots to destroy the House of Hanover. In some quarters there were even whispers of the return of that tragic prince of the doomed Stuart Dynasty, currently in exile in Italy, though the more sensible elements of polite society soon put such nonsensical rumours to bed.

An unprecedented number of mourners turned out for Lady Colville's memorial service that same afternoon, and not just the aristocracy; the working classes clamoured to get inside, filling the aisles and crowding the yard outside, just to pay their respects to the great lady who had touched their lives.

Mrs Irene Miller and Mrs Brenda Cunningham of 5 Niddry Street and 8 Niddry Street respectively were united for the second time that week under God's roof. Though they nursed a simmering resentment for the aristocracy they would make an exception for Lady Betty, who always had a kind word to say, and never made them feel like she was handing out charity whenever she donated her cast-offs to the Kirk.

After the service, which was read with great sensitivity by the Reverend John Erskine, the guests filed out of the Kirk and made their way through the wrought iron gates, the wealthy to their carriages, the poor to a local tavern where they would get drunk and regale each other with tales of Lady Colville's generosity and wit for several days.

Four men remained seated on a pew to the rear of the kirk,

speaking together in hushed voices. These men alone knew the true value of Lady Colville's sacrifice.

'I fear it is much worse than we at first imagined,' said Doctor Johnson. 'Mrs Boswell identified the last of her "three craws", whose first victim we found missing a head at Roswell Castle.'

'You mean to tell us,' said Lord Chalmers, 'that His Royal Highness is now a shape-shifting reptile?'

'Precisely so,' said Johnson.

'But that is patently absurd!' spluttered Queensberry. 'It is treasonous to suggest!'

'Why is it so hard to believe?' said Johnson. 'You yourself saw them revert back to their true forms just before we sent them to hell in the basement of Weir House.'

'Now hold on a minute, Doctor Johnson,' Queensberry protested. 'I saw no such thing. Granted, I saw *some*thing after that cannonball struck, but it must have been a mirage: a figment of my imagination. After all, I was exhausted from the saddle, and we all know what lack of sleep can do to a fellow.'

'Even so,' said Johnson. 'You cannot deny what you saw in the courtyard of Roswell Castle.'

'I saw five dead bodies,' shot back Queensberry. 'Nothing more. Hunter, Baxter, that Weber fellow you keep banging on about, Sinclair, blast his eyes, and… and…'

'The Prince of Wales, was it not?'

'I'm afraid I was unable to identify the fellow, on account of his missing head.'

'And yet it must have been someone important,' said Johnson. 'After all, if you were a shape-shifting reptile bent on world-domination, who better to masquerade as than the heir to the Throne himself?'

'I will need a little more convincing than that, Doctor Johnson.'

'Very well, then let us examine the evidence. Firstly, the timelines match up. We know the Prince of Wales was convalescing on his royal estate near Roswell as recently as one month ago. And as a Masonic Grand Master, the Prince would most surely have been initiated into the secrets of the Ordo Draconis, the same group who performed the ritual at Roswell Castle in the first place. And you saw yourself how Archibald Gunn reacted.'

'But Gunn was a madman, pure and simple!'

'We also have the testimony of my wife,' said Boswell, 'whose sanity I can vouchsafe for.'

'But perhaps she is mistaken?' suggested Queensberry. 'After all, she has been through an awful lot, old chap.'

'Then there is this,' said Johnson, producing something from his pocket and passing it to the Duke. It was a silver cigarette case with three feathers, the emblem of the Prince of Wales, emblazoned on its side. 'I took this from the coat pocket of the headless corpse at Roswell Castle.'

'So... you knew all along?' said Lord Chalmers.

'I had my suspicions,' confirmed Johnson, 'though at first I was sceptical. After all, it is not every day you discover that the next-in-line to the throne is a shapeshifting entity from the lower-fourth dimension.'

'By God it is not!' cried Chalmers passionately.

The minister, who was folding away his vestments in the presbytery, looked up sharply.

'Nevertheless,' Johnson went on in a lowered voice, 'it is true, and we must now take drastic measures to ensure he—or it—never wears that crown.'

'But what you are suggesting,' stammered Queensberry, 'it... It will surely mean our ruin!'

'Indeed,' mused Johnson, 'which is why we must proceed with caution, but a steady resolve.'

The four friends stood up and made their way to the exit. They walked arm-in-arm between the gravestones, each man overwhelmed by the sheer magnitude of the task ahead of them, and weighed down with the responsibility of it all. When they reached the Heights, they stopped to watch a blacksmith welding shut the entrance to the old MacKenzie Crypt. Johnson stuffed his hands deep in his pockets to protect them from the cold.

After some reflection, Lord Chalmers turned to Doctor Johnson and cleared his throat. 'I have an idea,' he said. 'No doubt you will be included on next year's honours list. Let us bide our time until you receive an invitation to St James Palace. That is when we will strike.'

'Yes,' said Johnson. 'That might work.'

'Leave the finer details to Lord Queensberry and me. Meanwhile, go about your business as usual. The enemy can't suspect a thing, or we shan't get past those guards. It may be our only chance.'

'We shall be as those guardians of old,' mused Johnson, 'the sacred Order of the Thistle, established by King James himself, that noble scion of the House of Stuart, sworn to protect the nation.'

'So be it!' said Chalmers. 'Let us now take the pledge.'

As the sun began its descent behind the Flodden Wall, the four men clasped hands.

'By the sacred memory of Lady Colville,' said Johnson, 'we shall, by whatever means necessary, strive to ensure the Pretender calling himself George Augustus Frederick, Prince of Wales, never wears the Crown of this United Kingdom.'

'I swear it,' said Boswell.

'I swear,' said Lord Chalmers.

The Duke of Queensberry looked incredulously from man to man. 'Hang it all!' he cried at last. 'I swear too!'

In the distance the bells of St Giles Cathedral clanged seven o'clock. Tombstone shadows crept across the yard like fingers stretched into a black velvet glove. When the shadows reached the east wall it would be time for night watchman Alexander Boyle to lock the gates for the evening.

The four men turned to leave.

To Be Continued
In The Next Volume

Of

The Casebook of Johnson and
Boswell:

The Stone of Destiny

Did You Enjoy This Book?

If so, you can make a HUGE difference

For any author, the single most important way we have of getting our books noticed is a really simple one—and one which you can help with.

Yes, you.

Us indie authors and publishers don't have the financial muscle of the big guys to take out full-page ads in the newspaper or put posters on the subway.

But we do have something much more powerful and effective than that, and it's something that those big publishers would kill to get their hands on.

A committed and loyal bunch of readers.

Honest reviews of our books help bring them to the attention of other readers.

If you've enjoyed this book I would be really grateful if you could spend just a couple of minutes leaving a review (it can be as short as you like) on this book's page on your favourite store and website.

Acknowledgements

I owe much to editors Pete and Si at Burning Chair: first, for taking a punt on an unpublished author with a raw manuscript that had never seen the light of day, and second, for helping me to knock this semi-formed lump of clay into shape. Si, as developmental editor, helped flesh out some of the secondary characters and their relationships, for which I am hugely grateful. He also helped me to reorganise the chapters into a more coherent whole, and crucially, to finesse the ending.

Pete checked everything for historical accuracy. And I mean everything. Under his exacting eye a 'cheque' became a 'promissory note', a 'burglar' became a 'house breaker', and 'the press' became 'pamphleteers', to name but a few. More importantly, he pointed out my BIG BAD (the Illuminati) would have been in its infancy around the time of my story, and so I had to invent my own secret society, which was all tremendous fun.

When I first read The Lord of the Rings, I was thrown by one bizarre little detail: Bilbo Baggins' aunt Lobelia carries an umbrella. It may seem odd that in a world of talking trees, magic rings, elves, dwarves and goblins I should take umbrage at the existence of an innocent umbrella, but the fact is when I think of umbrellas, I think of top hats, silk gloves, towns, cities, factories, automobiles, and other assorted Edwardian paraphernalia (and I am thinking here of the modern, folding umbrella). Middle Earth may exist in an alternate universe, but its technology is distinctly Medieval. Fortunately, the anachronistic umbrella was one small quibble in an otherwise brilliant adventure, and you will be glad to know it was not a deal-breaker for my pedantic 12-year-old-self. But if a fantasy writer has to be consistent, how much more so does a writer of historical fantasy, whose story is grounded in the real world? As Pete reminded me: get the facts straight, then you can go crazy with the other stuff. And so I tried to make the setting and characters as historically accurate as possible. The geography of 18th century Edinburgh is much as described; the tunnels under the city still exist, though I have perhaps extended and enlarged them for dramatic effect. Main characters share at least a name with their historical counterparts - Deacon Brodie, Thomas Weir, 'Bluidy' George MacKenzie, the Mad Earl of Drumlanrig, the 'witches' of Nor Loch - it's all true.

There are two flagrant abuses of historical accuracy, however, to which I must confess. The Great Fire of Old Town didn't occur until about 50 years later (though there were frequent blazes on a smaller scale throughout history), and the Prince of Wales, one of our main antagonists, was only about 11 years old at the time, so I have had to age him at least 5 years in the story.

Many thanks go to Liz Adams, who works tirelessly behind the scenes to ensure Burning Chair books reach the hands of as many people as possible, our team of beta readers (Andreas Rausch, Ami Agner, and Joyce and David Oxley), and the Burning Chair writers themselves. A final thanks goes to all my family, particularly my dad and Margaret, and my mum and Garry. But most of all to my inspiring wife Amber, for encouraging me to write, and without whom this book would never have happened.

About The Author

Andrew Neil MacLeod is a Scottish writer and musician with a deep and abiding love for British history and Celtic myth and culture. In the noughties, Andrew's band was signed to Warner Brothers, giving Keith Richards a run for his money while he toured the length and breadth of Britain with bands such as The Libertines.

Andrew has since taken up the pen as a means of artistic expression. For the last seven years he lived and worked in places as diverse as Malta, Abu Dhabi, Dubai and best of all, Le Marais, Paris, while he worked on his first two novels. Andrew has recently bought a holiday home on a remote Scottish island, which he will be renovating with his adored wife Amber and little Shi Tzu Alex. He looks forward to long walks on the beach, fish and chips by the pier, and cozy nights in before the log fire with a wee dram, while he works on his third novel. He also makes a great Cullen Skink.

About Burning Chair

Burning Chair is an independent publishing company based in the UK, but covering readers and authors around the globe. We are passionate about both writing and reading books and, at our core, we just want to get great books out to the world.

Our aim is to offer something exciting; something innovative; something that puts the author and their book first. From first class editing to cutting edge marketing and promotion, we provide the care and attention that makes sure every book fulfils its potential.

We are:
- Different
- Passionate
- Nimble and cutting edge
- Invested in our authors' success

If you're an author and would like to know more about our submissions requirements and receive our free guide to book publishing, visit:

www.burningchairpublishing.com

If you're a reader and are interested in hearing more about our books, being the first to hear about our new releases or great offers, or becoming a beta reader for us, again please visit:

www.burningchairpublishing.com

Other Books by Burning Chair Publishing

Point of Contact, by Richard Ayre

The Brodick Cold War Series, by John Fullerton
Spy Game
Spy Dragon

The Curse of Becton Manor, by Patricia Ayling

Near Death, by Richard Wall

Blue Bird, by Trish Finnegan

The Tom Novak series, by Neil Lancaster
Going Dark
Going Rogue
Going Back

10:59, by N R Baker

Love Is Dead(ly), by Gene Kendall

A Life Eternal, by Richard Ayre

Haven Wakes, by Fi Phillips

Beyond, by Georgia Springate

Burning, An Anthology of Short Thrillers, edited by Simon Finnie and Peter Oxley

The Infernal Aether series, by Peter Oxley
The Infernal Aether
A Christmas Aether
The Demon Inside
Beyond the Aether
The Old Lady of the Skies: 1: Plague

The Wedding Speech Manual: The Complete Guide to Preparing, Writing and Performing Your Wedding Speech, by Peter Oxley

www.burningchairpublishing.com

Andrew Neil MacLeod

The Fall of the House of Thomas Weir

Andrew Neil MacLeod

The Fall of the House of Thomas Weir

Andrew Neil MacLeod